Bittersweet
Bliss

Also by Ruth Glover
  A Place Called Bliss
  With Love from Biss
  Journey to Bliss
  Seasons of Bliss

Published by Fleming H. Revell
a division of Baker Book House Company
P.O. Box 6287, Grand Rapids, MI 49516-6287
www.bakerbooks.com

Printed in the United States of America

Library of Congress Cataloging-in-Publication Data
Glover, Ruth.
    Bittersweet Bliss : a novel / Ruth Glover.
        p.   cm. — (The Saskatchewan saga; 5)
    ISBN 0-8007-5828-5
    1. Frontier and pioneer life—Fiction. 2. Scots—Canada—Fiction.
3. Saskatchewan—Fiction. I. Title. II. Series: Glover, Ruth. Saskatchewan
saga ; 5.
PS3557.L678B585 2003
813′.54—dc21   2002012834

Scripture quotations are taken from the King James Version of the Bible.

To Alvin Deetho
(fond childhood name)
beloved brother

C all it a dream; call it a nightmare; it always began the same way . . .

First was the crackling, then the glow. Next was the smoke, making it hard to breathe. And finally came the gasping, the struggling with the bedclothes, the helplessness. The fear.

She knew it was imperative that she raise her head, spring to her feet, flee the room, but her limbs wouldn't move. She needed desperately to call for help, but her mouth opened in a silent scream, and her throat ached with the useless effort.

The sound grew to a roar as the first flickers of flame lit the room, engulfing it in orange sheets, leaping and twisting. The curtains sparked, caught, and blazed, shooting up the rough wall, reaching fiery fingers toward the bed.

Immobile, her screams lost in her throat or in the inferno, she felt the heat of the blast on her cheek, smelled the crisping of her hair, felt the shriveling of her flesh.

When at last a cry was wrung from her and she wrenched herself awake, it was to lie shivering and sweating, trembling and crying. Praying.

O God! Let it stop! Make it stop! Let me forget . . .

"Ellie!" It was the anxious voice of her father.

Ellie tried, but only a croak issued from her taut throat.

"Ellie! Are you all right?"

Ellie could hear, from the adjoining room, the creaking of the bed and the fumbling of her father as he struggled to his feet.

With an effort she answered, "I'm fine, Dad."

But he was at the door to her room, leaning on the doorjamb, peering through the dark. "Is it the nightmare again? Are you all right? Shall I get a light?"

"Yes . . . no. Just give me a moment—"

Brandon Bonney was accustomed to these bad times in the night, though he didn't understand them, never had understood them. If Ellie understood them, she had never said.

The nightmares had begun years ago, about the time Ellie was eleven or twelve. Serena, Ellie's mother, had been alive then and had been the first to hurry to her daughter's bedside, summoned by her cries in the night. Bran, instantly awake and filled with alarm, had followed, padding into his daughter's room in his bare feet, to lean over the bed and note the terror in Ellie's eyes in the light of the lamp held high by her mother.

"Ellie! Ellie!" Serena had said, setting down the lamp and taking the child in her arms. "What's wrong?"

With Ellie crumpled against her, her thin little shoulders shaking with fright and the heavy beating of her heart, Serena asked again, "What's wrong? Was it a dream, love? A bad dream?"

Ellie hadn't cried. But like a frightened mouse she huddled in the tangled bedding, obviously terrified. It was the first of many such times.

That night and for many nights thereafter, Serena slept with her daughter. In the daytime Ellie, once again her lively, seemingly normal self, insisted it was nothing—"just a bad dream"—and that there was no need for her mother to sleep with her. But at night, as the shadows crept from the corners of the house, Ellie grew silent and tense and gave no resistance when, once again, Serena slipped into bed with her.

"What is it, love?" her mother and father often asked, puzzled and alarmed. But Ellie, if she knew, wasn't telling.

"It's nothing," she insisted, or, "I can't remember."

"It has to be *something*," they said, persisting. "Surely you can remember what it is you see . . . or hear."

But if Ellie was to be believed, lamplight or daylight erased the memory, and her parents eventually came to the conclusion that, consciously or unconsciously, she was afraid to face the demons of her dreams. No matter how much her mother and father pressed, coaxed, or persuaded, she shook her dark head and, though her eyes were haunted, gave no explanation.

"It seems strange to me that a child wouldn't just burst out with the reason for such dreadful fear; children are not usually so secretive," Serena often mused. "Well," with a sigh, "perhaps she'll outgrow them."

And so it proved, to a large extent. The nightmares grew less frequent (or Ellie grew adept at hiding them), though they never seemed to lighten in their intensity.

And never, in the twelve or so years since, had she become accustomed to them or learned to accept them with any degree of casualness. Always, always, she was left shaken, creeping through the next day, a shadow of her true self.

With Serena gone to her grave these three years, Bran Bonney took on himself the concern for his daughter during these frightening times. She was the only chick he had; three brothers, not living past babyhood, lay in the Bliss cemetery, where the woman who birthed them had eventually joined them.

Ellie—Elizabeth Grace—coming along rather late in the lives of Brandon and Serena Bonney, was their pride and joy with her bright ways, her creativity, her enjoyment of life. Spontaneous and imaginative, she was the natural leader of the group of four girls who played together, stayed together, grew up together, terming themselves the "gang." Venturesome, she was responsible for many an act of derring-do, many a scrape, many an adventure during their school years.

It hurt Bran to see Ellie's bright winsomeness dimmed even a little. And surely it was the nightmares that were responsible for what seemed a blighting of her life and prospects.

With the moon through the window his only light, once again the concerned father approached his daughter's shuddering form, doing the only thing he knew to do. Placing his hand on the dear head disheveled from sleep and from wrestling with the vivid pictures of the night, he prayed earnestly, fervently, "Lord, give my girl peace. Deliver her from this torment."

Ellie drew a quivering breath, turned her cheek against the palm of her father's hand, finding comfort in the calluses made on her behalf, and murmured, "I'm all right now, Papa. Go back to bed."

Though Ellie never said, her father, judging by her demeanor and countenance the following mornings, always supposed the nightmares kept Ellie awake the remainder of the night. And so he suspicioned again.

Bran was up at the usual time; Ellie was late in rousing but was washed and dressed when he came in from the barn, an apron cinched neatly around her waist, obviously determined to make the day a normal one; it was, after all, the busy time of the year.

Lugging two brimming pails of milk, Bran stepped into the house—a house he had built with his own hands, with trees from his own homestead—to find the table set, coffee ready, toast in the warming oven, and porridge simmering on the stove. Ellie, busily stirring the oatmeal, seemed pale, quiet. Her face, ordinarily animated with lively eyes and a quick smile, was still. Weary. Tense. Her hazel-green eyes were shadowed.

"Good morning, love," he said, setting down the pails. "You all right this morning?"

"Just fine, Dad."

"Was it the old nightmare?"

"Yes, but," she added quickly, "I think they're not as bad as they used to be. In fact, I'm sure of it. Can you recall the last one? Months ago."

And Ellie, that lightly, that skillfully, that falsely, dismissed the night's torment.

Bran's concern was not so easily appeased. With a shake of his head he went about the task of straining the milk into the separator bowl and, while Ellie took the pails and straining cloth away to wash them, turned the crank, always a satisfying experience and no chore. For many years he and Serena had let the day's milk sit in flat pans for the cream to rise, then skimmed it by hand. So many years, in fact, that the simple but amazing distribution of the milk through the "wings" of the separator, producing "the smoothest of cream and the bluest of milk," never failed to be a blessing.

Ellie toyed with her breakfast even though a busy day awaited her, one of the heaviest of the week—ironing day, only a little less wearying than wash day. Even now the heavy garments awaited, having been sprinkled down the evening before, rolled tightly, placed in a basket, and covered. Already Ellie had set two chairs in place, laying across their backs the padded board that was her ironing surface.

———

Bran studied his daughter's face, wondering how he would have made it without her, yet regretting that she hadn't seen fit to marry. Just what he would do in such an instance, Bran had no idea. But he had bached before, and he could bach again.

In all honesty, Bran Bonney didn't believe he was the reason Ellie remained single long after the age most girls married. And it wasn't for lack of a suitor. Tom Teasdale, her childhood friend and as dear to her as a man could be, had waited patiently, was waiting patiently. No, Ellie had remained single against her father's best wishes for her and in spite of Tom's persuasion.

Looking up and catching her father's glance, Ellie smiled and said gently, "Don't look so worried, Papa,"—it was her childhood name for him and never failed to touch his heart—"I'm fine. Fine and ready to get to work. The weather is beginning to warm up, though, and I'll need to get at the ironing as soon as possible. If you're finished, I'll just clear the table—"

Putting action to words, Ellie put the breakfast dishes to soak in a dishpan of hot, soapy water and left them sitting on the back of the kitchen range for a more convenient time. Bran excused himself and, after a hesitant look at his daughter, picked up his old hat and left the house, headed for the fields.

With the slam of the screen door, Ellie placed both hands momentarily to her temples, her eyes closed. Perhaps it was a sigh that lifted from her lips, perhaps a prayer. Years ago Ellie, along with her dear friend Marfa—together in this as in all else—had knelt at the rude "mourner's bench" one Sunday morning and had, with a short prayer and the required (she thought) few tears, accepted Jesus Christ as her Savior. Rather than being the somber experience she had imagined, having watched many a sin-darkened adult go through the same process with considerable regret for a wasted life, it had been a happy time; her heart was lightened with the assurance that she had made her "calling and election sure." Ever since, prayer had been a mainstay.

Strengthened, Ellie turned to the task at hand. First she took a scrap of old toweling and wrapped it around a brick. With this she commenced polishing the top of the range, a precaution against soot or other dirt transferring to the bottom of the irons and staining the clothes. Then, opening the warming oven, she withdrew the set of irons—rightly called "sad" irons, many a woman thought—and set them on the stove to heat. "No. 1 weighs 4 lbs. and has one end rounded for polishing," the catalog unflinchingly informed; "No. 2 weighs $5\frac{1}{8}$ lbs., No. 3 weighs $5\frac{3}{8}$ lbs. The detachable handle is of wood and fits naturally to the hand without straining the arm or wrist." Oh, if that were a guarantee! After a long day of ironing, not only did the arm and wrist ache but the shoulder, the back.

Nearby she had laid out a clean sheet, to be placed on the floor beneath the ironing board when long items were ironed. There was no way a housewife was about to rewash and re-iron an item because of careless dragging on a dusty floor.

Placing the sad iron stand on the end of the ironing board, she was ready for business.

When the bottom of an iron sizzled to a damp touch, the heat was just right. But Ellie found she was often wrong in her judgment, scorching an article before she knew it, having to toss it aside to be treated and returned to the laundry. More than once her father, like other husbands and fathers in the community, wore a shirt with a clear imprint of the iron forever branded on his back.

If pressing was needed, Ellie dipped a white cloth in water, wrung it out, and placed it over the garment when ironing; this resulted in a good, firm crease. If she got it right the first time, she considered herself lucky; more than once—when she was learning the fine art of pressing—Bran wore trousers with a lopsided crease. And said nothing. And no one, to her knowledge, had pointed it out.

Dear Dad! Patient and loving always, he must be concerned over her reluctance to marry. Certainly he didn't understand it when her friends married and children arrived, and she remained single and childless. No doubt he longed for grandchildren. But she couldn't . . . it just wasn't possible.

With the rigid determination she had learned to summon up, Ellie turned her attention to other things. The trouble with ironing—she thought and not for the first time—was that it left the mind free to wander.

Nevertheless, it had to be done. With the iron handle clamped in place on No. 3 (might as well get the heavy things done first), she lifted it, turned it, licked a fingertip and applied it briefly to the hot surface, heard the necessary *zzzzzz*, and turned with determination toward the ironing board and a pair of her father's bib overalls.

Instantly she was back a dozen years and watching her mother iron bib overalls.

"Mum," Ellie said, dropping her books and lunch pail on the table and speaking excitedly, "we've got a new club!"

"Another one?" her mother asked mildly, well aware of the scope and duration of the last one, unrealistically but imaginatively named "Skull and Crossbones." For many weeks Skull and Crossbones (the girls had been going through a pirate/treasure-hunting/sword-wielding phase) had been the topic of conversation as Ellie reported its progress—the making of a pennant to fly over the raft the girls cobbled together out of odds and ends, the contriving of insignias to wear pinned to their clothes, the locating of a small box to serve as a chest for their collection of chicken and beef bones. Then ideas had seemed to shrivel and dry up, even as the spring sloughs dried up and rafting was no more, and Skull and Crossbones began to lose its allure.

"What's the purpose of it?" her mother had asked once when Ellie was fretting about the lack of inspiration for the future of the club. Ellie, not being a bit certain by this time, had taken the subject to the girls.

Marfa, Vonnie, and Flossy had also been at a loss to define its reason for being. Aside from the now defunct pennant and the motley assemblage of bones that they laid out solemnly in crossed position from time to time, it had no connection faintly piratical. Mainly, it seemed, it was a bond to tie the four together and to make them the envy of lesser mortals who could in no way attain to membership—a "gang of four" they were, and a gang of four they would remain, no matter who hinted, even begged, for admittance. And although the girls had clung to the rather pointless Skull and Crossbones long after its uselessness was established, it had eventually died for lack of purpose. "Childish" they called it, and they discarded it and moved on to bigger and better ideas.

"And what's the name of this new one?" Serena asked concerning the proposed club and wrestling the heavy garment into position to iron the bib itself.

"I . . . that is, we haven't decided yet," Ellie said, reaching for the bread and jam and glass of milk her mother had set out for her.

"And the president of this one?"

"Well," Ellie said a little uncomfortably, having been the president of every undertaking thus far, "we haven't picked her yet. In fact, we haven't had our first meeting. Marfa and I did the planning and have written notes to the others; we couldn't talk in front of all the other kids. We're going to meet Sunday afternoon and make the final plans, prob'ly pick the name for the club, prob'ly pick the president."

"I see. Well, Sunday afternoon should be all right."

Ellie finished her snack and went to change her clothes, her mind busily engaged in the possibilities of the new club.

Such an innocent beginning for something that was to change one small girl's life forever.

⌐───────⌐

Twelve years later, bent over the ironing board and her father's bib overalls and recalling that day clearly, Ellie's forehead beaded with perspiration. A perspiration not caused by the heat from the No. 3 iron.

M iss Wharton, seated at her desk in the front of the school-room, glanced behind and up, checking the clock once again. As always, the face of the "Drop Octagonal" stared implacably ahead, unrelentingly ticking away the minutes of the day.

What was wrong with her? Why this tension for the school day to come to an end? Where would she go other than home—the farm home where she boarded? Whom would she see other than those she always saw—Lydia and Herbert Bloom, home-steaders having opened their home and their hearts to her? What would the weekend offer more than any other—washing and ironing on Saturday, church on Sunday? Other than it being springtime rather than the unending winter, with the promise of a walk in the woods and the picking of a few flowers, it would be the usual weekend. Wouldn't it?

With the children quiet and bent studiously over their desks, Birdie Wharton, on an impulse, pulled a scrap of paper toward her and, with a few strokes of a pencil, figured the boundaries and extent of her days as sounded out, tick by tick, by the Drop Octagonal: Sixty ticks per minute amounted to 3,600 ticks per hour. Multiply by twenty-four amounted to 86,400 ticks per day. Multiply by 365, the number of days in a year: 31,536,000! Was it possible! Totting it up in black and white, seeing it so clearly, so baldly, Miss Wharton's head whirled while her spirits plunged. Like sand in an egg timer life was trickling away, minute by minute, sounded out by the resolute tick of a clock. In like fashion, twenty-eight years had trickled and ticked away. In no time at all the century would have dribbled away; the new one loomed without the promise of any more satisfaction than the last.

Snatching up the paper and crumpling it, she turned to fling the grim evidence of the miserable sum total of her life into the face of the clock, only to catch the wide-eyed gazes of eighteen children. Had she gasped to get their attention? Had she groaned?

Before their questioning eyes, she would spare the Drop Octagonal. With a quick decision she diverted her aim and the wad of paper sailed, true and straight, into the kindling box at the side of the stove. Never in her year's time as teacher of the Bliss school had Miss Birdie Wharton displayed such wanton disregard for decorum. The children may be excused for gaping soundlessly.

Birdie turned calmly enough to face the surprised faces of her pupils, biting back the impulse to bark, "Do as I say, not as I do!" But to spout such a thing would confuse them even more than her uncharacteristic paper throw.

Birdie had taught long enough and was experienced enough to realize that without fail, some child, maybe several of them, would attempt the kindling box shot. And how would she deal with that? She bit her lip, conscious of having slipped in her role as a prime example of what was correct and proper.

With a sigh Miss Wharton glanced one more time at the clock. Simultaneously every eye in the room swung to the Drop Octagonal, anticipating, Miss Wharton supposed, its Friday winding.

<hr />

To date—until the shot at the kindling box—Miss Wharton had been predictable. Every Friday, promptly at two o'clock—right after the second-graders (both of them) took their spelling test and before the three third-graders took theirs—Miss Wharton opened a drawer in her desk, withdrew a brass key, rose from her chair, stepped to the clock on the wall behind her, stretched herself, inserted the key, and, with a flourish, wound it. It was a grand climax to the week.

In the beginning Miss Wharton had wound the eight-day clock first thing Monday morning. But amid the hubbub of settling down after the weekend, the children were not as attentive as she might have wished, and what should have been a moment of drama turned out to be anticlimactic, leaving Miss Wharton strangely dissatisfied.

There were lessons to be learned from the clock! And Miss Wharton was alert for every opportunity to implant lofty impressions in the young minds of her pupils. Today she could tell them, with more assurance than ever, that their lives and their opportunities were slowly but surely (oh, so surely!) ticking away. Monday morning had not proved to be conducive to lessons with morals.

And so a switch to the Friday afternoon winding—and the rapt attention of the children—was made.

It was two o'clock; the Drop Octagonal was sounding out the hour, muted *bong* by muted *bong*. This decorous sound had been a selling point when the "Clock Committee" made its selection from among several in the catalog: "Strikes hours and halves on the cathedral gong bell," they read, and it sounded good, almost reverent, to the committee. For the clock served not only the school but the church, which met in the same building every Sunday. With a restrained, genteel sound from the clock, a strident interruption of study and worship would be avoided.

Two o'clock, and every eye in the room waited expectantly for the ritual of the Friday clock-winding. Every pencil was lifted, poised midstroke.

Miss Wharton could almost see the speculation in their eyes. Was it possible that one of them, having done so magnificently at lessons, having behaved in such an exemplary fashion, might have the distinction of winding the Drop Octagonal?

Miss Wharton had never promised outright that this honor would be given to some fortunate achiever, but she had hinted at it. Not really meaning to, she had planted a seed of hope in their hearts. To tell the truth, she was more than a little dismayed at the passion of expectation that resulted. Some day, she supposed, sorry she'd ever brought it up, she'd have to find a reason, a remarkable reason, for someone to wind the clock.

She knew the exact moment when their dreams took root. It was the unhappy occasion when Little Tiny Kruger (so called to distinguish him from Big Tiny, his father, each so named because of their excessive size), had boldly and unexpectedly raised his hand at clock-winding time and asked, "Miss Wharton, can I wind the clock?"

Being first and foremost a teacher, she had answered automatically, "*May* I wind the clock?"

"Yeah," Little Tiny said, eager now, thinking success was in sight. "May I?"

A vast silence had fallen on the schoolroom. Not only had every head in the room swiveled to look at Little Tiny, but all breathing was suspended in surprise at the audacity of the question and in anticipation of the answer. Miss Wharton could read their thoughts: *If only I'd thought of asking!*

Should Little Tiny, as troublesome as he was, be given the privilege of winding the clock, the children could foresee a future bright with possibilities for each of them, who generally were much better behaved. Perhaps, like the water monitor or the eraser monitor, the clock-winding task could be assigned week by week until everyone had taken a turn. Pity the final child—Letty Zimwalt, if the choice was alphabetical—who would have to wait eighteen weeks. But half the fun in anything was the expectation. Shivers of anticipation ran down seventeen bony spines—Little Tiny's well-padded spine being the exception—as Miss Wharton's answer was awaited.

Such a glorious arrangement was not to be. At least not immediately. Miss Wharton had raised her brows in the manner they all knew meant disapproval of childish misbehavior and said in surprised tones, "Wind the clock? Have you done something that should be so rewarded, Nelman?"

Little Tiny—Nelman—was not to be abashed that easily. "I finished my 'rithmetic," he offered.

"And so you should have," Miss Wharton responded properly. "What *special* accomplishment would we be celebrating by your winding the clock?"

Yes, *what?* questioned seventeen pairs of accusing eyes.

Totally unable to come up with a reason, Little Tiny, on that occasion, sighed and gave up, settling back after sticking out his tongue at several of his peers. But the idea had been planted that perfect performance, ideal behavior for a week, might, just might, result in being granted the giddy reward of winding the clock.

Thus far no one had attained that level of perfection.

But they found satisfaction in watching Miss Wharton as she performed the weekly ritual, though they knew it by heart, some having performed it in their dreams. And even the most unimaginative among them could picture standing on a chair beneath the clock and, filled almost to bursting with pride, fitting the key in the keyhole and winding. Wind exactly twelve times (everyone counted, silently, each time Miss Wharton performed the task; never once had she miscounted, though they waited with bated breath, anticipating an eleven or a thirteen), until sweat beaded the upper lip, the fingers cramped, the back of the neck grew tense, and the tongue was almost chewed through from the concentration required. Wind twelve times and turn, flushed with victory, to find the eyes of every child in the room fixed in envy upon the blessed and favored winder of the clock.

But could it be done with the precision, the neatness, the aplomb with which Miss Wharton did it? Could they give a small flick of the wrist as they withdrew the key and closed the door? Would they remember to turn, chin up, shoulders erect, breathe deeply one time, nodding slightly to all those watching? Could they do it all without grinning foolishly and spoiling the solemnity of the moment? Could they deposit the key in the proper drawer at last without dropping it?

Then and only then—with the dropped key's small *plink*—would pencils return to pages of half-rubbed-out sums. Only then were history lessons resumed, perhaps the reading of the account of missionary Father Le Caron when he reported on the mosquitoes, bad in the 1600s and no better in the 1890s: "I confess that this is the worst martyrdom I suffered in this country; hunger, thirst, weariness, and fever are nothing to it. These little beasts not only persecute you all day but at night they get into your eyes and mouth, crawl under your clothes and stick their long stings through them and make such a noise that it distracts your attention and prevents you from saying your prayers."

Recitation time, story time, recess, lunch, all were inextricably bound up in the unrelenting movement of the Drop Octagonal. It ticked off their days like a metronome, unceasing, persistent. It ticked off the long days and, everyone supposed, the lonesome nights, pressing onward through the dark until it ticked in the sunrise and another day.

The Drop Octagonal was unique; no home in the district of Bliss had one like it. In fact, most homes in the Saskatchewan bush were devoid of niceties or items of beauty, even many necessities having been left behind when the trek west was undertaken, and never replaced. The clock, indeed, was matchless and marvelous.

Its name, however, was a puzzle and a never-ending source of discussion. "It's because of that little window below the clock, that little place where you wind it," some child said thoughtfully, and it was the explanation most accepted. From this glassed-in section the keyhole stared, unwinking, tantalizing the fascinated daydreamer to insert the key.

Once and only once had it been attempted.

One lunch hour, when Miss Wharton was out of the room, Little Tiny had succeeded in persuading Ernie Battlesea, small and easily intimidated, to climb upon a chair, take the key that Little Tiny boldly lifted from the drawer, and prod for the keyhole some distance above his head. With every eye in the room fixed on Ernie and every breath suspended, Miss Wharton was in their midst before they knew it.

The circle of children disappeared as quickly as smoke in a high wind; even Little Tiny deserted his post, leaving Ernie, key in hand, eyes as large as two-bit pieces, to face the dragon as in some fairy tale come alive. He knew his doom had come.

But Miss Wharton, lifting him down and removing the key from his hand, had turned her accusing eyes on the others and said, "Now, will the one responsible please step forward?"

Silence. Profound silence, thick silence. The clock's ticking, in no way deterred by the attempted invasion of its inner workings, was somehow accusing in the awful silence.

"Well, then, Ernie will bear the punishment." And Miss Wharton took her ruler from the desk and turned toward the cringing boy.

It was not to be borne! Little Tiny might be naughty, but he was not a coward. As white-faced as the smaller boy, the guilty culprit stepped forward and took the blame and the punishment. Which, in all truth, could have been much more severe than it was. *Slap, slap, slap*—three halfhearted whacks and Miss Wharton, unaccustomedly white-faced herself, tossed the ruler onto the desk and said, "Go back to your desk, Nelman. And all of you—remember that it's from such small rebellions that uprisings of nations have come."

It was a dreadful thought. Little Tiny, somewhat light-headed—from the punishment and the importance attached to his "uprising"—went to his desk with his fist closed around the bright marks of his daring, shivering at the possible consequences of his act and determined to be an upholder of justice all his livelong days.

No one since that moment had dared touch the Drop Octagonal or its key.

⸻

Just now, it was chiming out the two o'clock hour and the time of winding for the week. With one accord the children's eyes lifted from book and scribbler, ready for the important break when the little ritual should be undertaken once again.

Perhaps it was on a whim, but Miss Wharton—so lately having expressed her impatience with protocol by the tossing of a paper wad halfway across the room—stood to her feet and announced, "This afternoon, before the winding of the clock, I'll share with you a legend that has recently come to my attention, which you will all find of interest, I'm sure."

Pencils were laid in the slot provided on the desktop, eyes blinked in surprise, and faces turned toward their teacher while minds scurried to absorb this amazing break from the usual. What in the world had gotten into their Miss Wharton?

Standing before them in her shapeless gown, her hair pinned back with stern discipline, only her eyes lovely in the intensity of the moment, Miss Wharton had the attention of everyone, from little Ernie Battlesea to Harold "Buck" Buckley, who, at fifteen, was too old, too wise, and too disinterested to be in school but would finish out the year.

"We know that King Francis was dreaming of a New World empire that would match that of France's rival, Spain," Miss Wharton began in a conspiratorial tone, much as if she were sharing a thrilling secret, capturing their attention and their imagination at the same time. "We know he sent out an expedition to survey the American coast, to discover treasure, to claim land, and to look for the true Northwest Passage. But do we know who was chosen as leader of this expedition?"

Numerous voices, having been in school longer than others, piped, "Jacques Cartier!"

"Right. Cartier was a hard-bitten Breton."

Miss Wharton, when animated, was a master storyteller. Today, spurred by some inspiration—or aggravation—she was at her best.

"Cartier sailed into the broad Gulf of St. Lawrence and pushed on, beyond where only fishermen had gone before. He reached the Gaspé peninsula at the tip of the present province of Quebec on a July day, no doubt a hot July day. Imagine with me the wild roses blooming all around him in abundance; savor with me the delicious little strawberries."

"Um-m-m-m." Eighteen voices crooned, and eighteen mouths watered. Winter had been long and hard in Bliss, and summer had not yet revealed all her delights.

"There he erected a thirty-foot cross and claimed the land for France." Miss Wharton, in pantomime, *thunked* a cross into the ground at her side.

"But he had accomplished more than that—he had shown that behind the rocks and the fog of the Atlantic coast lay a wonderful land of grassy meadows with flowers rampant and green trees in abundance.

"The next year," she said after a pause, and with altered voice depicting a rising tide of excitement, "he went even farther, entering the mouth of the St. Lawrence. Traveling along its mighty length, he might well have thought he had found the passage to . . . where?"

"India!"

"He stopped to visit the Indian village of . . . what?"

Silence. A couple of coughs, a few scuffed feet, but silence.

"Stadacona. That much we know. But now—"

Flagging interest brightened. Now—what?

"Now comes the legend part. Do you understand what *legend* means?"

A few nodded heads. Uncertainty written on the faces of the smaller children. It wasn't always easy to teach six-year-olds and fifteen-year-olds at the same time.

"A legend is a story from the past," the teacher explained. "It's usually regarded as historical but not verifiable. That is," Miss Wharton searched for simpler words, "it could be history but hasn't been proved as such. Understand?"

Nodded heads.

"Legend has it that Cartier, while with the Indians and trying to talk to them, pointed to the ground and asked them what the place was called. They replied, 'Kanata.'"

"Kanata," they breathed, savoring the new word.

Miss Wharton turned to the blackboard and in large letters spelled out the word: *K a n a t a.*

25

"*Kanata* was their word for *village*, but Cartier didn't understand that. And so he called the new land Canada."

Amazed looks, some pleased grins greeted the completion of the legend.

"I suggest that each of you go home and repeat this legend, perhaps at the supper table when the family is all together. That way you will be a teacher as well as a pupil. And repeating it will help you remember it; exams are coming, you know." And with that warning to offset the unaccustomed storytelling, Miss Wharton completed her assignment, hoping guiltily at the same time that the paper-wad-throwing incident might be forgotten.

"And now, children, we'll call it a day. And a week. See you next Monday."

"But, Miss Wharton, the clock!" Mystified by the upheaval of their schedule, the children inquired concerning the overlooked winding of the Drop Octagonal.

"Don't worry about it."

"But, Miss Wharton, the blackboard, the erasers!" This from the scandalized eraser monitor.

"Don't worry about it. You can come early Monday and clean them."

And with that the children gathered up their books, their lunch pails, whatever wraps they might have brought in this period between cool spring and warming summer, and slipped, one by one, out the door.

Alone, Birdie sat at her desk, her animation gone, her thin face an unreadable mask. But her head was accusing her heart, asking what this was all about. Why the impulsive toss of crumpled paper toward the kindling box? Why the change in schedule, the abrupt decision to delay the winding of the clock? Why the telling of a story, a legend after all and not history, when the children hadn't yet learned the date of the selfsame expedition? Why the casual excusing of their chores?

One reason. One reason only: the letter, the unsigned letter in the drawer of her bedroom chiffonier.

E llie was putting away the ironing board and returning the chairs to the side of the round table that dominated the kitchen end of the room when she heard the jingle of harness and the sound of an approaching rig.

"It's Marfa," she announced, glancing out and addressing herself to Wrinkles, the cat, who was draped in comfortable somnolence on a rug at the side of the range. Wrinkles, the best of listeners and accustomed to such confidences, blinked one eye and returned to his doze.

"I'll just put the kettle on," Ellie murmured, and Wrinkles flipped the end of his tail to indicate his attention.

Ellie pulled the kettle of water toward the front lids of the range, where it would soon boil. Without time to do more, she turned toward the door, her spirits lifted in spite of herself by the variation in her day and the interruption of her memories.

Marfa—Martha, nicknamed Marfa when she was small—and Ellie had been bosom pals for as long as they could remember, meeting first at Sunday school, church dinners, picnics, and sewing circles attended by their mothers. Starting school together, the years had come and gone with Ellie and Marfa as close as, probably closer than, most sisters. Sharing the good times and the bad, laughing together, crying together on occasion, growing up together, sharing each phase of life, they were inseparable. Marfa's older siblings were married and gone, and back then she, like Ellie, was alone; perhaps this accounted for the staunchness of their affection—they needed each other.

Totally unalike, as different in looks as in temperament, they seemed to complement each other. Ellie was dark-haired and hazel-eyed, with a certain glow of life and vitality, slender of build, quick of mind and movement; Marfa, gray-eyed and brown-haired, was short, given to chubbiness, deliberate of movement. Ellie's sudden smile was as quick and brilliant as a passing shaft of sunshine; Marfa's round face wore a perennial pleasant expression.

Where Ellie was fearless, Marfa was inclined to be cautious; when Ellie's vivid imagination conjured up outrageous escapades, Marfa's more level-headed approach aborted many possible problems. It was Ellie's portion to do the thinking, the planning; Marfa's to help carry out her ideas or, as often happened, to reshape them to reasonable proportions.

Along the way two more girls had attached themselves to Ellie and Marfa. Vonnie was slender, willowy, fair of hair and blue of eye, given to prinkings and poutings and inclined to be self-centered, capable of sudden bursts of sweetness and generosity. Flossy was part Indian, dark of face and eye, quiet, restrained, thoughtful. Together they made up the "gang of four."

Though the hamlet and community of Bliss viewed the four of them with some suspicion, having been the target of their shenanigans from time to time, the girls were tolerated, even accepted with indulgence. They were, after all, part and parcel of the Bliss family and, as such, no better and no worse than many others. And life in the bush, apt to be laden with responsibilities, burdens, and deprivations, was lifted out of its weariness occasionally by a grin and a shake of the head at the mischievousness of Bliss's unpredictable four.

The passing of the years had seen many changes as the girls matured, three of them eventually marrying. Flossy's marriage took her to Prince Albert; Vonnie moved up north with her logger husband, only to have him killed in an accident; and Marfa—Marfa was soon to be a mother.

"Come in, come in!" Ellie stepped out onto the small porch, her face lit by a welcoming smile, her hands outstretched. Marfa, having clambered laboriously from the buggy and tying the horse to a hitching post, stepped up awkwardly and was at once embraced warmly and escorted inside.

"What's up?" Ellie asked almost as soon as she had seated her friend. It was unusual for visits to be exchanged in the summer months when life was unendingly busy. And in the winter the weather precluded sociability; life in Bliss was apt to be a lonely affair any time of the year.

"I needed to get out and away from that hot kitchen, that's what's up," Marfa answered with a rueful laugh. "And I couldn't think of a better place to go. If I go to the folks', Mum'll think something's wrong again and fuss over me." Marfa, in the six years she had been married, had lost three babies, not carrying any one of them to term.

"And how are you? Are you all right?" Ellie asked, needing to know yet hesitating to raise the sensitive subject.

"I'm fine! You know, Ellie, I never carried any of the others this long. It's only six weeks or so now. Just think, I'll be up and on my feet before harvest. Right now I just need a little break."

Ellie sighed. It had long been her desire to open a haven, a resting place of sorts, where the ill and weary or troubled could draw aside from life's burdens for a while, taking time out to recuperate. The flame of concern for others had burned in her heart for a long time—since childhood. Though she had often dreamed and sometimes schemed in the old way, wishing desperately to find a way to carry out her heart's desire, circumstances had dictated otherwise.

It had all been tied in, years ago, with the establishing of the new club . . .

"The fateful hour," Ellie said, her hazel-green eyes glinting in the shadows of The Golden Glade, her own fanciful name for the girls' favorite bushy meeting place, though it was more green than golden most of the year, "is upon us."

Ellie, who more often than not had her nose in a book, was always talking like that, using words that annoyed or tantalized her friends.

Polishing off the last of the cookies Flossy had brought and distributed, Ellie, seated on ground springy with last year's leaf mold, drew up her knees, hugging them with her thin arms, looking around expectantly. Vonnie, Flossy, and Marfa were pulling their legs up in the same manner and draping their arms around them, resting their girlish chins on their bony knees. Or, in Marfa's case, her plump knees.

Three pairs of eyes were fixed on Ellie, the acknowledged leader of the group. Three faces were drawn toward Ellie as surely as iron filings to a magnet. There was expectation in the eyes, eagerness on the faces. When Ellie got an idea, life became interesting indeed.

And it was about time for something new. Her last scheme, a candy-making experiment, had fizzled and failed. They had each filched a cup of sugar from home and, one noontime, had attempted to make candy on the school heater. Their goal had been a worthy one: sell candy to the children for a penny or so and buy handkerchiefs for Yanni Nikolai. Their motive was a mixed one—not only to help poor Yanni, who had a perennial problem with his sinuses, but to spare themselves the awful sight of Yanni continually wiping his poor, offending nose on the sleeve of his shirt. Or, in the summer, his bare arm.

But the syrupy mass had frothed and boiled over, running over the heater and scorching, smelling to high heaven, making the fascinated children cough and gag. School was dismissed for the rest of the day while the fire was allowed to burn out and the heater to cool down, and the girls, overseen by a grim teacher, cleaned up the sticky mess.

Their worst punishment was the sorrowful faces of their mothers as they had mourned the extravagant loss of sugar.

"Go ahead, tell what it's all about," Vonnie said now impatiently, waiting for some explanation of Ellie's new idea. Vonnie hadn't liked being out of the preliminary planning as Marfa and Ellie had whispered and schemed secretly for days.

"I hope our mothers won't get mad," Marfa said with some doubt, obviously still stinging from the scolding that had followed the previous experiment. Catching Ellie's injured glance, she added quickly, "I don't think they will—this time."

The Golden Glade was bathed in the fresh green glow of early spring: The graceful limbs of a willow embraced the hiding place on one side, and hazel bushes pressed close on the other, while a poplar spread its boughs over all. Bush children born and raised, the girls accepted the beauty and fragrance as part of their rightful heritage.

Flossy tossed a few cookie crumbs toward a chipmunk frisking nearby, tail at full-mast, beady eyes watchful. Perhaps it was the sound of the chipmunk's scurry that alerted Ellie. "Wait a minute," she said, lowering her voice and looking around suspiciously, "we better scout for spies. To your posts!"

Without any need for further instruction, each girl scrambled to her feet and slipped through the bush to her designated direction: Vonnie east, Flossy south, Marfa west, Ellie north.

When they assembled again—hair askew, arms scratched—and took their places in the circle, it was to report briskly, "All clear on the western . . . southern . . . eastern . . . northern ramparts."

Even so, knowing how others tried to invade the circle, they drew together more closely than ever. Again they looked to Ellie, expectation in their eyes.

"This is it, then," Ellie said, and even though they had established that no interloper was lurking within their hearing, her voice lowered dramatically.

"We're going to form a new club. It won't be Skull and Crossbones anymore." Ellie's tone had a certain disdain for the club just outgrown, the club of their childhood. With the four girls approaching their twelfth birthdays, dignity and prestige were needed. One and all sniffed at the uselessness, the dullness, of former entrancements.

"Well, what then?" Vonnie prodded.

"It will be a club to help people, help the district."

In view of their close-knit seating arrangement, it occurred to Marfa that "circle" might be more fitting. She offered her idea only to have it rebuffed.

"Just like all the old ladies in the missionary society," Vonnie said scathingly, and Marfa subsided. "Club" would do.

"What kind of things will we do?" Vonnie asked with suspicion. "Make beds? Wash dishes?" Vonnie was averse to work.

"No, no," Ellie continued, shaking her head. "Not regular chores. I mean interesting things. And not at home. We'll branch out. We'll find things to do to help people all over Bliss. We'll be a service club."

There was silence as the girls digested this. It had its possibilities.

"You mean—for money?" It was Vonnie again. Vonnie, always thinking of the sharp angle.

"Of course not! We'll do good deeds, like knights of old. Like the missionaries on the foreign field. Except that it'll be here at home."

No one was more honored than missionaries. It was a high calling. A fine challenge.

"But do what?" Flossy asked cautiously; still, her interest was piqued.

"That's where you all come in," Ellie said. "When you go to church, for instance, listen to people as they talk; see if they reveal some problem at home. Look around neighbors' yards, listen to the kids at school, look at what they wear, check on what they need. Maybe we can fix something. Something will turn up, I'm sure. Something we can do. Something noble. Something chivalrous. What do you say?"

It was a radical idea, appealing to the kind heart of Marfa, the fault-finding side of Vonnie, and raising only a small hesitation in the timid Flossy.

"I can think right away of something that someone needs to do, and why not us?" Vonnie said, and the others looked at her eagerly. This was going better than they had expected. "It's the heads of the Nikolai kids," and Vonnie gave a dramatic shudder; "I don't think they've been washed all winter."

The other girls nodded emphatically, having stood behind one or another of the five Nikolai children when they lined up at school, looking down through the thin blond hair at the grimy scalps.

"Good idea! Excellent idea!" pronounced a pleased Ellie. "That's the very kind of thing I mean. Each of us must keep a list of things to do, and we'll share them when we have our meetings. We'll have meetings once a week at lunchtime, of course, as we have been."

"But school's about out," reminded Marfa.

"Well then, we'll meet like this on Sunday afternoons until school starts up again."

"Sounds like a good idea," Flossy offered slowly. "It'll give us a reason to get together all summer long."

"But—" Vonnie's blue eyes sharpened, "who will be president?"

"Ellie should be president," Marfa said quickly. "It's her idea. I don't want to be in charge; that's for sure."

After some discussion it was decided, with some reluctance on Vonnie's part, that Ellie, having put the new club together, was the one to put it into action.

"Only if you're sure," Ellie said, and she accepted the position graciously when a chorus of affirmation was her response.

"If we're not Skull and Crossbones anymore," Vonnie said, recalling her mother's disapproving reaction to that title, "what'll we call ourselves?"

"I thought," said the resourceful Ellie, "that since we'll be a club that helps people and does good deeds, we should have a name to fit. I thought—"

"Yes?" breathed her three companions. Ellie knew how to build anticipation.

"Busy Bees!" she pronounced.

Vonnie frowned, Marfa looked pleased, Flossy undecided. They discussed alternatives, but no other name was satisfactory to all three, though Willing Workers and Happy Helpers were considered. A vote finally decided the matter; Busy Bees they would be.

For the next half hour the girls chattered on and on about the possibilities that would open to the Busy Bees, how they would make a name for themselves in the community, how their assistance would benefit Bliss, and how they would be appreciated.

"Now, remember," Ellie cautioned, "we're not doing it for fame or fortune. And don't forget—no pay. When people try to thank us, we'll say, 'Give thanks to the Grand Panjandrum Bee,' or something like that."

As always happened when Ellie came up with words and ideas that boggled the minds of lesser individuals, the others gazed at her with admiration as they rolled the noble appellation around on their tongues.

Grand Panjandrum. It was a title and an honor not to be regarded lightly.

With a clasping of hands, the meeting was dismissed.

Just that easily, just that thoughtlessly, Skull and Crossbones—ineffectual and harmless as it had proved to be—was discarded, and Busy Bees was inaugurated, setting in motion events that would spell catastrophe.

<hr />

"The kettle's about ready to boil," Ellie said as she chunked another piece of wood into the range. Marfa, heaving a sigh of content, settled herself at the side of the table.

The oilcloth on the table, mainstay of every homestead, clearly wouldn't do for company, faded as it was and showing wear. With a swish Ellie reversed it—a transformation that the visiting Marfa never tired of seeing. "Something new," the catalog had alluringly offered when it came time for Ellie to reorder oilcloth, "with marble face and turkey red damask patterns printed on the back."

"Two cloths in one," Marfa marveled as the turkey red surfaced and the washed-out side disappeared. And that was the principle: If company came and the top side of the oilcloth showed cracks and wear and tear, it could be deftly turned, and voilà—no embarrassment for the hostess.

The everyday crockery wouldn't do, mismatched, chipped, and crazed as it was, and Ellie turned to the buffet, her mother's pride and joy. For too many years Serena had stacked her dishes in rough open cupboards fastened to the log walls. Ellie could recall the moment the huge crate had arrived and the oak creation had been unpacked.

"Handsome" was the word the catalog used; *handsome* was the word Serena Bonney whispered when the sideboard had been set in place. Small shelves on each side of the German bevel plate glass mirror had immediately received the two or three treasures Serena had brought halfway across a continent and hoarded until this moment. In the buffet's drawers she placed her few linens. Here, after a good harvest—behind its scroll-worked, brass-knobbed doors—she had eventually stacked a complete set of dishes: "Grey Delhi" English semiporcelain ware, costing the magnificent sum of $11.50 and delivered to the post office in Bliss without breakage.

"Well, it's an occasion!" Ellie said with a smile as she lifted the dainty cups from the buffet to the table, for Marfa's lips were smiling and her eyes twinkling. Because of her own small home and limited supply of household goods, Marfa appreciated, even relished, the display of possessions the Bonney house, at long last, had acquired. Trust Ellie! Even though the years had come and gone and childhood was far behind, she still knew how to keep one's interest, to arouse one's expectations.

Abruptly, Marfa asked, "Ellie, how are things with Tom?"

Tom. Tom Teasdale, childhood friend and longtime suitor for Ellie's hand in marriage. Tom, who had waited patiently these seven years, perhaps longer, for who knew exactly when friendship had turned to something more? Certainly Tom, by his very willingness to wait, had established forever the depth of his affection for Ellie Bonney.

"Fine, of course," Ellie answered, surprised. "Is there some reason you should ask?"

"No, of course not," Marfa responded quickly.

Ellie poured the boiling water into the warmed teapot, set it aside, and turned to the kitchen cabinet and a plate of sliced fruitcake, covered carefully against the threatened barrage of summer flies.

"Tell me how you are, I mean really are," Ellie invited when at last she was seated, a serviette on her knees, a dainty cup of tea in one hand, a piece of fruitcake before her.

"There are no signs of trouble," Marfa said with composure. "And even if something goes wrong, I'm near enough through the pregnancy so that everything will be all right, I think."

"You know me well enough, Marfa—"

"Would I fool you, Ellie? *Could* I fool you?" And both young women laughed a bit, admitting to the truthfulness of what Marfa had said. Without a doubt they knew each other thoroughly, almost understood each other's thoughts.

Marfa continued. "When the time comes, Ellie, would you be willing to help? Grandma Jurgenson will come, of course, but you are so good at things like that. It would be such a comfort to have you there—"

"Even after . . . I mean, are you sure?" Ellie spoke tersely, tightly.

"Oh, Ellie! Are you harping back to that childish . . . that time so long ago?"

Ellie, who claimed to have no secrets from her friend, bit her lip. "Of course not," she said. "And of course I'd love to come. Just send George, or maybe one of his little brothers—"

"There are plenty of Polcheks around, that's for sure. One of them will be happy to help when the first niece or nephew is about to appear."

"Oh, Marfa, I'm so happy for you! You've waited so long—"

"Not any longer than you have, Ellie," Marfa said abruptly, staring down into her cup. "Tom . . ."

Ellie looked searchingly at her friend. "Marfa, is there something you want to, need to talk about? Something you're not saying, perhaps?"

"Why, no. I've always told you everything, haven't I?"

But it wasn't so, Ellie realized with a little pang. Marfa had never been able to pour out her grief and pain over the loss of her unborn babies; instead, she had exhibited the "stiff upper lip" that so sustained beleaguered homesteaders, always maintaining that "next time" things would go well. Perhaps it was the only way they all made it through times so difficult they would quell weaker spirits.

And she, Ellie? Had she ever bared, even hinted at, the torment that gnawed at her own spirit?

"More tea?" she asked brightly.

Marfa, with relief, held out her Grey Delhi cup.

The clatter of boots across the oiled floor brought Birdie Wharton's head up from the papers she had been correcting. Outside, she could hear the receding ruckus of the afternoon departure of the children, always more exuberant on Friday. It would have come as a surprise to them, but Birdie also had a sense of relief when, for the final time of the week, the children departed, leaving her to herself for a couple of days.

Against the afternoon sun shining in the open door behind him, the unmistakable form of Little Tiny—Nelman—made his trundling way toward her.

No one could mistake the outline of Little Tiny Kruger. Like his father before him he was oversized; like his father he was fair, cherubic of face; like his father he was good-natured. It was no wonder he was called Little Tiny; no other name would have been appropriate. But there was in Little Tiny a streak of impishness. Not wickedness, still it surfaced wickedly from time to time, a surprising glimpse of liveliness of thought, a rare glimpse of something clever that, if handled correctly, could result in a reflective man of originality and imagination. Was he like his father in this also? Birdie didn't know, nor did she have any inclination to find out. Big Tiny was not a man given to celerity; rather, he was, or seemed to be, a man of deliberate action, leisurely pace, relaxed mien.

The possibility of turning up something special, in Little Tiny as in a few others, was the sort of thing that challenged the teacher in Birdie Wharton. It was the same fever, she supposed, that fired prospectors—sent them to the Yukon to burn out or freeze out, to return wealthy or not return at all. Behind it all, there was the possibility of striking gold.

She was grateful for one thing—Little Tiny was good-natured enough so that he held no rancor against her for his recent chastisement. That experience had in no way dimmed his general air of great good humor. Now, awash in geniality, the picture of a blithe spirit if ever she saw one, he stood before Miss Wharton's desk.

"Yes, Nelman?" she asked, her eyes fixed on the envelope the boy clutched. An envelope that closely resembled the unsigned letter in her chiffonier drawer.

"Mr. Nikolai gave me this to give to you, Miss Wharton."

Mr. Nikolai? Birdie's head whirled. *Arvid Nikolai?* Arvid Nikolai, father of a host of children, with another perpetually on the way? Several, grown and gone, had been replaced by a new batch; there were always Nikolai children in the Bliss school, it seemed. Soon, perhaps, with the marrying off of the older ones, there would be Nikolai grandchildren. But even Arvid's children, though better taught than he in the language of their new country, spoke English raggedly, and their writing was even worse; surely the father's was illegible. And the letter, except for one glaringly misspelled word, had been rather well done.

"Mr. Nikolai?" she said now, gropingly.

"He just came from the post office. So since he was stoppin' at the school to pick up Helma and Velma and—"

"I'm well aware of the Nikolai children's names, Nelman," Miss Wharton interrupted, feeling considerable relief.

"Anyway, he thought he'd drop this off for you," Little Tiny continued, "and he asked me to bring it in. Velma and Helma . . . well, all them," he finished hastily, "were busy climbin' into the wagon."

"Thank you, Nelman," she said and gave him a rare smile, so relieved was she over his explanation.

Little Tiny's face, always fixed in cheerful lines, lit even more than was usual. He blushed, he scuffed his feet, he squirmed, he grinned and escaped.

Behind him, Miss Wharton watched him go, her rather stern face softened and her mouth touched with a suspiciously tender look. Little Tiny was motherless, his mother having died a couple of years before in childbirth. Perhaps that knowledge accounted for the teacher's changed countenance.

"And please," Birdie added, calling after him, "if Mr. Nikolai is still out there, thank him for me."

Little Tiny stamped out of the room, and Birdie's attention turned to, riveted on, the item she had received from him. Letters, in the Saskatchewan bush, were few and far between, items of great interest. With no immediate family nearby—her parents dead and her one brother writing only occasionally—it was a moment of supreme interest to Birdie Wharton.

Turning it over in her hand, there was no clue as to the sender. Still, it was enough like the *other* one to give her pause. With chatter going on outside to indicate that the children had not all dispersed as yet, and with the possibility that one of them might come inside—for a book or for a lunch pail—she laid the envelope aside. She would need privacy. . . .

———

Birdie Wharton had mixed feelings about the school year coming to an end in a couple of weeks. On the one hand, it would give her a much-needed rest. Was she ever and always to be giving out, with never anything to feed her hungry heart?

On the other hand, thinking of ten weeks or so with nothing but herself and her pointless existence to fill her days, she dreaded the summer hiatus.

In that unguarded moment, with no one to see or care, Birdie's eyes were achingly empty. Her face, usually without expression, neither smiling nor frowning but cool and "in charge," now collapsed and sagged, revealing a vulnerability that would have astonished those who knew her best. Or most of them. The Blooms, with whom she boarded, suspected, even felt quite sure, that the "iron lady" was really a far different person at heart. With Lydia and Herbert Bloom, Birdie was cautiously opening up a little, giving glimpses of a self no one else in Bliss had ever seen. With the Blooms, Birdie was daring to be herself.

And "herself"—to Herb and Lydia, dear Christian people that they were—was just fine, even lovable. When she went home each day from school to the simple two-story frame house that the Blooms had built when they came as homesteaders to Canada's vast Northwest, it was as a castaway to an island in a wide, dreary sea, and Birdie refuged there.

Reaching the house, shutting the door behind her, laying aside her books and papers, Birdie would turn, almost apprehensively, rather like an abused puppy, to find Lydia waiting with a cup of tea and always, always with an open smile of acceptance. Birdie was beginning to expect it; she was starting to rely on it.

In this snug farm home enveloped in the arms of the bush, Birdie Wharton had found a nest, a resting place, a security that had evaded her all her life and that she had expected never to know. Oh, she thought she knew it, once. . . . That time and that place were snuffed out of her mind as soon as they intruded. But out of her memory? Her heart?

This relationship with the Blooms was the chief reason she had agreed to accept the Bliss school for another year. This relationship and the envelope once again cradled in her hand. This envelope, and the one in her chiffonier drawer. Abruptly, once again, she laid it down.

Was she such a fool, after all, as to imagine that any man would find her desirable?

Last fall, when she arrived, there had been the expected tentative overtures from various males of the community and surrounding districts. The news of an available woman passed quickly from mouth to mouth in this land of bachelors. One man had come from as far away as Nipawin, having heard there was a single woman in Bliss. These single men—bachelors and widowers—had received short shrift from Birdie Wharton, being sent on their way summarily, even brusquely, before they had a chance to look her over, to inflict the wound of rejection.

And why should she, like a horse at auction, be reviewed for possible acceptance or rejection? Independence—it was what kept her at teaching. The independence the small salary made possible, the ability to stand on her own feet, make her own way. In a time when there were few options for women, Birdie knew herself fortunate to be a teacher. And Bliss was as good a place as any to be, better perhaps, because of Herb and Lydia. Because of them and her job, she didn't need to fear the pain of rejection quite so much.

Birdie Wharton didn't need a mirror to tell her she was plain. Not ugly, which might have been an excuse, but plain. Good features, abundant hair, fine skin, all combined to be plain. Even so, there might have been a redeeming beauty if the eyes had come alive, if the lips had smiled, if the hair had loosened. Never did the hair loosen, but occasionally, in Herb's and Lydia's presence, the lips curved sweetly and the eyes lit and warmed. It was worth waiting for. Lydia Bloom had actually caught her breath the first time she saw it happen—when her boarder's gray eyes had filled with laughter as she was caught unawares by the antics of a small kitten in her lap.

"Birdie," she had said before she could stop herself, "Birdie, did you ever . . . I mean, have you ever worn . . . that is, Birdie, why don't you loosen your hair? It's so pretty, so dark and thick. Look—"

And Lydia, taking advantage of their friendship, tugged at the hair so tightly bound back, pulling curling tendrils free around the severe face. Even that small change brought about a transformation, along with a startled, wide-eyed look on the younger woman's face. Lydia studied the effect of the tumbled strands of hair, the flushed face, the widened eyes suddenly seeming softer, strangely appealing—and almost gasped aloud.

It was all there, as it should be—proper-shaped face, eyes, nose, mouth. All there but disguised by stiffness and an inner control that had never been seen to waver. All there, everything a woman needed to be *womanly*. A woman's slim body—draped in shapeless folds of a dress too large, too colorless. Small feet—encased in sturdy, buttoned shoes, shoes not found in the up-to-date goods listed in the catalog from which Birdie had bought them. How she would replace them was a mystery. Her hands were shapely, her ankles neat, her neck slender, the graceful line of her bosom lost in the gown's ill fit. Yes, the equipment was all there. Never seen for what it could be; the possibilities for beauty to the watching Lydia were astonishing.

Birdie had quickly gathered up her loose hair, pinning it back into its accustomed bun, biting her lip, as flustered as Birdie Wharton ever allowed herself to be.

From that moment, Lydia Bloom saw Birdie as though she were disguised in a costume, an actor in a drama, wearing a mask. Sometimes she wondered if the real Birdie Wharton would ever expose her true self. Occasionally she caught glimpses of her.

All in all, Lydia thought sadly, it was like taking a choice porcelain vase, bundling it in newspaper, and setting it out for all to view, even use.

⊶——⊷

Though it wasn't always evident to others, Birdie Wharton had a love for her pupils. Not just a concern, a love. At least for some of them, she thought honestly, and she strove to find something about the most unlovely to appreciate. All of them, she insisted on believing, had some worthiness, like buried treasure, and she worked to unearth it, feeling gratified when a rare flash of beauty or originality shone from some child's heretofore barren personality. Their minds, she was aware constantly, were like blank slates waiting for what she, their teacher, would write upon them.

Birdie understood that the preceding teacher had walked the room, from the opening of the school day until dismissal, with a strap in her hand, quite successfully keeping order. But along with an orderly room, she had all but withered any spontaneity. Her sternness had also engendered a fear, a distrust, that made the children wary, suspicious, hesitant of opening up or speaking up, even when a new teacher had come along.

Slowly yet surely under Birdie Wharton's quiet and firm but approachable demeanor, the atmosphere was changing: Vigor and creativity were springing to life again in the Bliss school. She would rather deal with the rambunctious actions, the daring opinions that surfaced from time to time, than to prod sheeplike little human beings to dare to open their mouths.

Little Tiny, perhaps first of all, showed signs of being liberated when he lifted his hand and made his request to wind the clock. She should have recognized that moment for what it was; she should have found some way to encourage his venture into liberation. But fearing a wave of such requests, she had, without consideration, refused him. Little Tiny, rather than being daunted, had then urged the winding of the clock on first-grader Ernie Battlesea. Recognizing another bid for self-expression, Birdie should have . . . the truth was, she hadn't known what to do. And under the speculative eyes of the other pupils, she had punished—halfheartedly, it's true—the offender.

Little Tiny's sin, if he had committed one, had been, in Miss Wharton's eyes, to urge the daring act on a smaller child; she might have applauded, inwardly, if Little Tiny had shown a spark of gumption and had himself attempted to wind the Drop Octagonal. Still, she regretted her punishment of the miscreant, wondering if it would forever crush any spark of individuality in the boy. But she hadn't reckoned on Little Tiny's ebullient spirit. Thankfully, he seemed none the worse for the correction, stern though it had been.

And Ernie's tendency to allow others do his thinking for him was challenged; Ernie would think twice before he was so easily led into trouble again. Miss Wharton meant for each child to be a thinker, not a mindless follower.

She had come to know them all so well during the year: the Nikolai children from the Old Country, Hungary in this instance—the twins Helma and Velma, Karl, close pal of Little Tiny, Frankie, the smallest; several Nikolais had finished school and were gone, but there were two or three more at home, and Miss Wharton could envision a continuing parade of Nikolais attending school in the years ahead. Then there was Ernie, with the big, innocent eyes and the endearing grin, and Harold Buckley, "Buck," the oldest in the classroom and soon to be gone, given to tormenting and teasing, full of smirks and silliness. If there was one pupil Birdie found hard to love, it was Buck. As large as he was, he was difficult, very difficult indeed, to control. More than once she had faced him down, unrelenting, until he had given in, either obeying or backing down, though always reluctantly.

But then there was Little Tiny. Little Tiny had wiggled his way into Miss Wharton's heart in a way that no child had since—

There were some things that didn't bear thinking about if one were to keep one's equilibrium, one's peace of mind, one's sanity.

Abruptly, Miss Wharton checked her thoughts of the group that claimed her attention all week, Little Tiny in particular, and turned to the letter lying before her on the desk.

Like the one before it, received a week ago, it was simply addressed to Miss Bernadine Wharton, Bliss, Saskachewan (without the *t*) Territory. Like the one before it, it had no return address. Would it, like the one before it, be an astonishing revelation of some stranger's interest in her—not as a teacher but as a woman?

5

Silence at last, inside and out. There was only the everlasting ticking of the Drop Octagonal. After the events of the last hour or so, Birdie was inclined to view the clock balefully: It certainly hadn't proved to brighten her day; rather, it had pointed out as never before, tick by dogged tick, the relentless passing of time.

Every child, every horse, every rig, was gone. Now was the time to read the letter. Hand outstretched, Birdie hesitated.

Should she wait until she got home? She studied the idea for a moment, then reproached herself for her foolishness. Why was she hesitant? Why couldn't she open the envelope, remove the letter, and read its contents? Was her life so empty, so void, as to find some small sense of anticipation and excitement in the waiting missive? In light of the Drop Octagonal's revelation, possibly.

Considering, full of an unaccustomed self-evaluation, she wavered, drumming her fingers on the desk, studying the envelope. Being a teacher and accustomed to looking for errors, she noticed, on this envelope as on the last one, the word *Saskatchewan* had been misspelled—the *t* had been omitted, making it *Saskachewan*. Not an unusual mistake; many folks had trouble not only in writing the word but in saying it without getting their tongue tangled until practice made the word flow more readily, even as the river itself— from which the province took its name—flowed from its sources along the Rocky Mountains, on and on, its deep channel splicing through the land, a sprawling, giant Y.

Birdie, caught up momentarily in musing on the river and its glorious history, rose and turned to the wall and the map case, a new addition to the schoolroom this year, due primarily to her appeal to the school board. Second to the Drop Octagonal in importance in the minds of the children but first in importance in the mind of the teacher, the maps—six of them: Canada, the United States and Mexico, Asia, Africa, South America, and Europe, each "oil colored and backed with heavy cloth"—opened the world to those who were settled, probably forever, in one small, obscure corner of it. Impulsively she pulled down the map of Canada.

"Here, right here." Her finger followed the North Saskatchewan's beginning at the foot of the Saskatchewan Glacier and along its thousand-mile downhill plunge to Lake Winnipeg. She traced the South Saskatchewan as it branched toward the prairies and located Prince Albert and Bliss in the center of the Y where the North and South branches met.

"Kisiskatchewan," the Indians called it—the river that flows rapidly. Up its waters had come the French in their canoes; in her imagination Birdie could hear the cadence of their songs as with a strong, digging rhythm they pulled against the stream. Laden with furs they floated back down, their canoes settled deep in the tawny water. Then and later, always, the river was a high-way, slowly taking men and their supplies up, quickly and easily bringing them downstream, headed east. Pelt by luxurious pelt the wilderness riches were transported to civilization.

Here in this green and flourishing garden, hemmed in by the river, fate had seen fit to transport her, Bernadine Wharton. The parkland, or bush, it was called; and it was beautiful and it was fragrant, in its wild way. But it was deceiving, so deceiving. The

Saskatchewan way was not an easy way, not a soft way, turning out men and women of endurance and strength or breaking them. Axe stroke by axe stroke they literally carved out their kingdoms—sixty acres of land for a filing fee of ten dollars. By the thousands they came, eventually tens of thousands, for some of the best free land remaining in the world, many of them investing their very lives before they were done.

And she, Birdie Wharton, could file for none of it. Penniless, she could buy none of it. Still, she felt it to be her own; she counted herself a pioneer.

As Miss Wharton the teacher, she strove to instill in her pupils an understanding of the size and scope of their new homeland as it stretched from the wilderness of the Island of Vancouver on the west to Newfoundland—called Cradle of the Wave by the Indians—on the east. She reminded them of the freedom it offered all comers; she challenged them to make it the finest place on Earth.

Flushed with her thoughts and the sight of the matchless country stretched out before her, so much of it still unexplored, most of it still unsettled, Birdie snapped the map back into place and turned, cheeks pink, eyes bright, face alive with her enthusiasm. Turned, to find a man of massive proportions standing, hat in hand, on the other side of her desk.

Big Tiny.

Big Tiny—Wilhelm Kruger—was not unknown to Birdie. Church, Sunday dinners, and school functions such as the Christmas "concert" and Field Day had been times of getting acquainted with the parents of her pupils. Big and Little Tiny lived on his homestead alone, wife and mother having met the fate of so many women of the day and place—death in childbirth.

Perhaps it was his size, perhaps it was the twinkle in his eyes, but Big Tiny Kruger tended, for some foolish reason, to intimidate Birdie Wharton. And so when she spoke now, it was sharply.

"Heavens! Don't creep up on a person that way!"

"Creep?" Big Tiny repeated, his cheeks crinkling as laughter touched his eyes. "Me, creep?"

It *was* ludicrous, having been wrung from Birdie in reaction to being found defenseless, relaxed, guard down.

The pacs on the big man's feet—a leftover reminder of colder days—had quite successfully silenced his advance from door to desk.

"You surprised me, that's all," Birdie defended, making an attempt to settle her ruffled feathers.

"I should have knocked," Big Tiny was quick to offer. "I'm sorry."

Knocked, on an open door? And apologizing for not doing so?

Birdie found herself flushing, a most unacceptable reaction. Would a flush—caused by aggravation—look like a blush? Birdie Wharton despised, above all things, blushing, simpering women.

"I was studying the map," she felt impelled to explain. "That's what had my attention."

"Ya, I saw." Big Tiny, a dozen years or so from the Old Country and speaking and reading English very well, still showed strong traces of his roots in his accent and speech. "It has Bliss on it?" he asked, his gaze going over her head to the maps, once again neatly rolled.

"No, Bliss is far too small. But it does have Prince Albert—"

"Ya?" Interest lit the broad face, shone in the blue eyes, eyes that showed an intelligence often overlooked because of the slow speech, the patience, the stolidity of the man. "Would you mind pointing it out to me?"

"Of course not." Actually, it was the delight of her life, and Birdie turned again to the wall, pulled down the map of Canada, and fondly pointed out the meandering line that was the river Saskatchewan, locating Prince Albert and the Y and Bliss's approximate location.

"There are no red men along the Saskatchewan, I've heard it said," the big man said.

"You are right," Birdie said, surprised. "Swarthy, brown, or dusky is what they are. The explorers and fur traders recognized that and stated as much in their journals. That's probably where you learned it. Are you a reader, Mr. Kruger?"

"Only a little, I'm afraid," Big Tiny said quickly. "Books—they are hard to come by. And when I was in school, in the East, we never studied about the Cree in the territories."

Quick to notice an opportunity, Birdie said, "I could see that certain books come your way, if you're interested. Are you, Mr. Kruger?"

"Very much. I'd like that!" Big Tiny said from his great height. "You could send them with Little Tiny—that is, Nelman. I'd take good care of them and see they get back to you safely."

Birdie looked up speculatively at the big man, face shining with good humor and expectation. "Did you know," she said on impulse, "that among the chiefs—Sweet Grass, Poundmaker, Red Pheasant, and the others—Big Child was actually a small man for an Indian?"

Big Tiny, so called because he was large, threw back his head and guffawed delightedly. Apparently there was drollery in Indian camps, as in white.

"Right here," Birdie said, pointing to the map and in spite of herself taking pleasure in the sharing of knowledge, "in 1876—not long ago—on a grassy knoll on the Carlton side of the North Saskatchewan, white man and Indian eventually met; the Indians had finally recognized the need to treat. The Lieutenant Governor stood regally on the required piece of red carpet, red-coated Mounties stood by stiffly, and the Indians, in full regalia, advanced majestically—they love this sort of thing, you know, pomp and display. Soon the pipe stem—"

"The symbol upon which no woman must ever look," Big Tiny interjected. Surprised again, Birdie lost her thought momentarily.

"Why, yes," she admitted. "Though heaven knows why. Did you also know," and Birdie's eyes snapped, "what happened to women when the missionaries began baptizing the Indians?"

"No, not that," Big Tiny said humbly.

"If an Indian man had two wives," Birdie said, "he couldn't be baptized. So what did he do? How did he solve the problem?" Almost grinding her teeth at the injustice of it all, she continued, "One wife was . . . discarded."

"Discarded?" Big Tiny asked cautiously.

"It was the *way* he did it! The Indian *male* took his wife out in the canoe, presumably fishing. When he returned, he was alone. Next day," Birdie's eyes glittered, "he went to receive the drops of holy water."

"Thank Gott," Big Tiny said seriously, "our preacher don't do things that way. We just need to accept Jesus—"

"Yes, yes," Birdie acknowledged. "A much better system. But where were we?"

"The pipe stem—" Big Tiny recalled.

"It was pointed to the east and west, north and south. Then the Indians, satisfied that the proper courtesy had been shown the Cree people, sat down on the grass, prepared to treat."

"Oh, ya." Big Tiny shifted his massive weight, and the slight motion broke the spell in which Birdie had found herself.

"My goodness! How I do run on! You are a good listener, Mr. Kruger. I've completely forgotten the time."

"You're a good teacher, Miss Wharton. It's too bad," he said, brightening, "there aren't classes for us grownups. Maybe night classes for people like me who want to learn more, particularly about our country. Did you ever think of that?"

"Why, Mr. Kruger," Birdie said, pleased in spite of herself, "it seems a wonderful suggestion."

"But of course not in summer," Big Tiny said regretfully. "Maybe in the fall, do you think?"

"It's certainly something to think about. Now," Birdie was all business, "was there something you wanted to see me about?"

"I was just going by on my way home from the store, and I thought Little Tiny—Nelman—might like a ride. But I see he's gone—"

"Yes, they're all gone. I think I let them go a little early." Birdie, recalling her strange mood of earlier in the day and remembering why it had seemed important for the children to clear out, cast a glance toward the letter on her desk.

"Well then," Big Tiny said, twisting his hat a little, looking at her steadily, "would you like a ride? I go right by the Blooms', you know."

So that's what it was all about! Birdie, who had almost been beguiled into some semblance of camaraderie—two pioneers devoted to learning more about their adopted country—stiffened immediately.

"I'm not ready to go home yet," she said tightly, and Big Tiny Kruger turned toward the door. If he were disappointed, it didn't show on his broad, pleasant, sun-browned face.

"But thank you," she added belatedly, and Big Tiny bowed in her direction slightly, put his disreputable hat on his head, and slipped out as silently as he had come.

Staring at the doorway, empty indeed since the large figure of the man disappeared from it, Birdie Wharton's lips tightened. *Why would anyone be interested in a ... creature like that, when* this *awaits?*

Her eyes dropped to the envelope. In spite of herself she felt a tug, if not on her heart, then on her imagination.

I t was Saturday, time to do all the pre-Sunday chores that fell to a homemaker. Ellie lifted a cake from the oven, thrust a broom straw into it, deemed it done, and set it aside to cool for Sunday dinner.

Bliss churchgoers took literally the admonition of Exodus 20:9–10, "Six days shalt thou labour . . . but the seventh day is the sabbath of the LORD thy God." Saturday night would find not only Sunday's clothes sponged, pressed, and ready for donning the next morning and shoes cleaned and polished but the house spic-and-span as well. Sunday's dinner would be ready—pie or cake covered and waiting, fresh buns baked and awaiting reheating, vegetables peeled and set in water overnight.

At least, Ellie always thought, cleaning up the kitchen for the last time Saturday night, perhaps consoling herself for her single estate, there were no children's baths to give, no little heads to wash. Having been a part of the bathing ritual for many years, she was well accustomed to the Saturday night regimen—dragging in the zinc tub, setting it before the stove and filling it with water, climbing in, doubling up, washing from head to toe.

Growing up the youngest member of the Bonney family, she had the privilege of the first bath. After she was off to bed, her parents took turns, first Serena, presumably not as dusty and dirty as her husband, then Bran, scrubbing away the week's grime. Ellie always felt sorry for her father having to bathe in used bathwater, but he laughed at her concern and assured her he didn't mind her "little bit of clean dirt."

Thinking of those days, Ellie couldn't refrain from smiling, almost chuckling aloud, as memory took her back to that day of the Busy Bees' first assignment: the scrubbing of the heads of the Nikolai children—all but the baby who wouldn't be pried away from his mother's arms. The startled parents, probably puzzled at the practices of these new-country people, had submitted with good nature as the girls arrived, soap and towels in hand, to set up basins on old tree stumps in the yard, fill them with water brought from the range's reservoir, and, one by one, bend the matted blond heads of the children and begin soaping. An assembly line of sorts had been devised, with Marfa and Vonnie washing, Flossy rinsing, and Ellie combing. The Busy Bees had left the Nikolai farm that day riding the crest of satisfaction for a good deed well done. Though they would have liked to, they knew themselves to be too young to give the overburdened mother the stern injunction, "These heads should be washed every Saturday night!"

Tucking away the memory—the inauguration of the Busy Bees' pursuits—Ellie returned to her preparations for Sunday.

She had been well taught; Serena had automatically performed duty after duty, week after week, year after year and, as a good mother, had instructed the daughter who was always at her side.

The final task remaining to Ellie this Saturday was to search out a chicken—the unlucky one that didn't scurry squawking away as quickly as the others—chop off its head, scald and pluck it, clean it, and hang it down the well. Sunday morning, before leaving for church, she would put it into a roasting pan and pop it into the oven. With the firebox stoked with wood and the damper adjusted, dinner should be ready and waiting when she and her father got home. It was a good system; all over Bliss it would be in effect. A good system and, they believed, a godly one.

But there was good sense mixed with bush beliefs. Did not Jesus himself say, when he was criticized for healing on the Sabbath, "Doth not each one of you on the sabbath loose his ox or his ass from the stall, and lead him away to watering?" (Luke 13:15).

In the Canadian bush, not only was there the watering of animals but feeding and milking as well. And if a cow should decide to give birth on a Sunday, or if a horse cut itself on barbed wire, had not the "ox fallen into a pit," and did not the Lord make allowance for that? And did not his Word say, "He also that is slothful in his work is brother to him that is a great waster" (Prov. 18:9)? Waste, as far as the bush people were concerned, was a sin of major proportions. Obviously it went hand-in-hand with sloth. Yes, certain chores had to be done on Sunday, as any day. But there were many that could be taken care of beforehand. Saturday was a busy day.

"Let's see . . . ," Ellie said thoughtfully to nobody but Wrinkles. Wrinkles, ensconced regally on a cushion in a chair, viewed the Sunday preparations with tolerance, having seen them before, as had his ancestors, back and back to the first Wrinkles, so named by a small Ellie because his skin fit him so loosely. "I believe I'll just go out to the garden and pull a few radishes and have them ready for tomorrow."

At last—fresh vegetables, after many months of no green thing. A plain lettuce salad, radishes gleaming like rubies in a simple crockery saucer on the table—these were first. First, and as treasured as though they were gems of incomparable worth. They were the forerunners to peas and new potatoes. Could any dish on a king's table surpass a bowl of tender new potatoes and peas, creamed and slathered with sweet butter? Gardens in Bliss received much tender, loving care, rewarding their keepers by prodigious growth, as though they knew the time was short for performing and producing. In actuality, it was the long growing hours of the brief summer days—when the sun came early and stayed late—that caused garden and grain to spring forth as though by some magic. Summers, short and hot, could result in excellent crops, but often lack of rain brought discouraging harvests. Tightening their belts in the lean years, thanking God for the good ones, the people of the bush persisted, endured, and slowly, slowly moved ahead.

Taking a small basket, Ellie proceeded to the garden, followed by Wrinkles, who wound himself around her legs, tail aloft, when she paused at the radish row. She bent to rub his head, only to straighten at the sound of a well-known voice.

"Hey, Ellie!" It was Tom.

Freeing herself from the cloying cat, Ellie turned with glad steps toward the approaching buggy.

"Tom! Whatever are you doing in the middle of the morning on a busy Saturday?"

"I've called it a day, Ellie, as far as field work is concerned. And that's because my plow should be in. I'm on my way to Prince Albert to get it." Tom, usually relaxed, comfortable, casual, revealed his satisfaction in the acquisition of the new plow by the lilt to his voice and the pleased expression on his face. He had not ordered a gang or sulky plow, or even a subsoil lister—all of which were available and often used on the prairie and in the bush. Instead, Tom had ordered and would put to good use the Brush Plow. Having cleared another portion of his land's dense growth, he thought this plow, intended for "new and brushy land, where there are stumps and roots," would be invaluable, saving time and much human effort.

"Good!" Ellie responded. "That didn't take long, did it? Have you got time to come in, maybe have a cup of coffee?"

"I've got to get on my way; I need to make it back for chores. But Ellie—could I persuade you to come with me?"

Ellie's eyes lit; it was what she needed—a break in the work, a lift to her spirits. Nothing could do it like time spent with Tom.

"Why not!" she answered impulsively. "I'll take the opportunity to shop a little, perhaps."

"Why not!" he mimicked, grinning. "Hustle along, then, while I get turned around."

Hastily changing her clothes, straightening her hair, and washing her hands and face, Ellie was soon ready. Hunting a scrap of paper and a pencil, she wrote her father a note and left it propped on the table.

I'm going to P.A. with Tom. Beans should be ready on the back of the stove. The cake is for tomorrow, but there's fruitcake in the bread box! I'll be home in time to fix supper.

Breathless, she ran for the buggy and Tom. He reined the horse steady while she clambered up into the seat beside him, eyes more green than hazel, strands of hair curling in careless abandon around her face, flushed by the sun and the exertion of the last few minutes.

"Sorry I didn't give you any warning," he said, slacking up on the reins and turning the buggy toward the road, admiring her all the while with his eyes. "But as spontaneous as you are, dear Ellie, I knew it'd be no problem."

Tom knew her well. Ellie smiled and settled back, prepared to enjoy the ride to town (Bliss was termed a hamlet), the unexpected break from work, and being with Tom. It had been here, on this road, they had first met . . .

―――――

Her father called good-bye as she left for school, raising a ruckus among the assembled chickens until a great fervor of cackles accompanied her departure. That familiarity and her mother's wave from the stoop sent her off to her day happy and content. Parents might suffer anxiety, discouragement, and despair, but Bliss's children would remember the warmth of the small home, the loving arms, the good friends, and the security they provided.

The current Wrinkles accompanied her to the road, where he disappeared into the bush, hopefully to a day of mousing; mice in the bush were a scourge on a par with gophers and rabbits and crows.

Ellie might have been in a concert hall: From bush and tree and sky, from fence post and meadow, a sweet chorus of bird songs filled the morning air, a tuneful accompaniment lifting her feet in a step as light as the dandelion seeds floating in the fresh-scented breeze.

The most persistent element of Saskatchewan's weather was the wind. Summer days were cooled by it; winter's subzero temperatures were made excruciating by it. Early in the day as it was, Ellie felt the first touch of the breeze on her face and knew it would dry her mother's clothes quickly, would blow through the kitchen's open door, bringing relief, would skirmish through the fields, refreshing both man and beast.

She had barely turned onto the road when she heard the clop-clop of a horse's hooves. Turning, she saw two mounted children, a boy ahead, a small girl behind peering over his shoulder, urging their horse toward her.

Pulling the horse to a walk, the boy looked down at Ellie. Brown hair fell over his forehead in a way that, as long as she knew him, she would think of as charming. His eyes were bright, alert, his mouth mobile and expressive, gentle for a boy. Of the girl, only the top of her head and one eye could be seen.

"Hello," he said. Not bashful, not brash like some boys she knew. Natural. Comfortable. And so she was to find him always.

"I'm Tom. Tom Teasdale," he said. "Your new neighbor."

Tom. Such a simple name to come to mean so much. Tom Teasdale. Even then, something stirred in Ellie's childish heart. This Tom Teasdale—was it possible he would be different from other boys, different from those with pinching hands and taunting ways, teasing ways, show-off ways?

What she said was, "Is that your sister?"

"Yes. Her name's Rose. Got another sister at home named Delphine, like my mother, but we call her Dee. She's three. Rose is seven. I'm twelve. How old are you?"

"Eleven," Ellie said, adding quickly, "going on twelve."

"You got any brothers and sisters?"

"None alive. Three dead, though. All boys."

The horse plodded along. Ellie matched her steps, scuffing the dust of the road, self-conscious under the gaze of the boy above but not looking up to see if he indeed was watching her. She was glad she'd put a ribbon on the end of her braid even though it would be in grave danger from the snatching fingers of some boy.

"What's your name?" he asked.

"Elizabeth Grace Bonney," Ellie said rather primly. After a moment she added, "Ellie. I'm called Ellie."

"Pretty."

What did he mean? Glancing up quickly, it was to find Tom's eyes on her, frank, earnest, steady. And that, as the years came and went, typified Tom Teasdale—frank but kind; earnest but capable of humor; steady but not dull.

At this point, looking upward, she stumbled, and her reading book slipped from her arms into the dust. Quickly the new boy Tom swung a leg over and slid down from the horse to pick up her book, brush it off, and hand it to her.

Ellie was so surprised that her mouth fell open; her word of thanks was stammered. Properly raised children always thanked adults, but the same rules didn't seem to apply to other children. Ellie was not accustomed to thanking children. But she did that day and many times following.

Tom didn't mount again but walked beside her and led the horse. Rose clutched the mane with a touch of anxiety and rode silently.

"Are there boys my age in this school?" Tom asked.

"The Polchek boys—two of them. And a couple of Nikolais."

Ellie was amazed at how the conversation with a stranger—a boy—flourished and flowed. And so it was almost as though she introduced a friend of long standing when at last they met up with Vonnie and Flossy and Marfa, waiting where four roads met. The girls' waves were restrained, having noted the newcomers, and their greetings, when rider and pedestrians joined them, were muted. But strangers were always of interest, and these appeared more interesting than most, if the reactions of three eleven-year-old girls meant anything.

"This is Tom and his sister Rose," Ellie said, and the girls stood silent and transfixed, their gazes settling on Tom after a cursory glance at the little girl.

"This is Marfa," Ellie continued, pointing out the round-faced, good-natured, plump one, "and Flossy," directing Tom's attention to the dark-complexioned, quiet one. "And this—this is Vonnie."

Ellie pointed out the slender, narrow-eyed blond who, instinctively perhaps, tossed her head and flashed a smile.

From that time on, it was Tom Teasdale and the gang of four, a gang that, by official decree, could not open and allow one more person to join.

Had it been possible, that person would surely have been Tom Teasdale.

Later that morning—after Tom had been assigned a seat across the aisle—he raised brown eyes, candid and friendly under his lock of hair, and smiled, and Ellie found herself gazing down blindly at her arithmetic.

Eleven years old, going on twelve, and gazing blindly at her arithmetic.

———

Today, riding beside him in his buggy and remembering, Ellie glanced at the brown face at her side and the lock of hair, now somewhat sun-bleached and falling in attractive disarray over his forehead, and turned her gaze back to her surroundings. Tom was dear, but—in spite of attending church and Sunday school regularly—had never accepted Christ as his Savior, a troubling factor.

Tom, patient Tom—how long would he wait? She had put him off so many times . . .

Perhaps Tom, ever tuned to her thoughts and moods, sensed this one. Holding the reins with one hand he reached the other toward Ellie, covering her hand with his large, warm one.

He said nothing. And his silence was as a drumbeat in her ears.

"Oh, Tom," she began, painfully, "you know—"

"Hush," he said. "We'll not talk of it today. We'll enjoy the ride and just being together."

So good . . . so kind . . . so—so patient.

If Tom recognized that Ellie gripped his hand with a sort of fierceness, even a desperation, he made no comment.

We'll not talk of it, he had said. Not today.

Birdie sat at her desk, still as a stone and as cold. The doorway, when the broad back of Big Tiny Kruger had disappeared, seemed particularly empty. Blank.

And before she knew it and could throw up her defenses, it happened. So guarded against, still it happened.

Perhaps it was that moment during the day when Little Tiny's face had brought another child's face to mind; perhaps it was the act of Big Tiny when, aware of her as a woman, he had made an overture, offering a ride home and conjuring up remembered responses. And then walking out.

Whatever it was, the damage was done. Memories, unwanted and uninvited, crowded from the dark recesses of her heart where, obviously, they lingered and languished, throbbing with happiness and hurt for long periods of time until, demanding attention, they erupted once again.

As always, when they had succeeded in thwarting her best attempts to forget, they would not be denied—those wrenching memories. Times of bliss—all too brief. Times of anguish. Only the anguish remained.

Birdie's usual fixed countenance crumpled and twisted as the door to the past was thrust open, and the faces—two of them—pushed from obscurity into clarity. The man's and the child's, curiously alike, markedly different.

The happiness had been so brief, the hurt so deep, the pain so dreadful. Even now, the ache was so huge that it was like sound filling her ears, consuming her thoughts, roaring out its anguish, threshing through her heart like some wild storm.

Shoulders stiff, face twisted, eyes closed, Birdie Wharton submitted to the lashings of memories too sweet to forget, too bitter to remember.

Eventually she wilted, dropping her head, laying her ravaged face on her crossed arms on the desk; then and only then did the tempest quiet, washed away in a torrent of tears.

Not until the Drop Octagonal—that dogged timepiece by which her life was ticked away minute by minute, day by day, month by month—ruthlessly indicated that another hour of her time had slipped away, did Birdie draw a quivering breath, raise her head, search for a handkerchief, wipe her eyes and nose, pass a hand over her hair, and finally get to her feet. Like a willow whipped by a fierce gale, she was bent, her thin body straightening slowly until once again her shoulders were erect, head up. Her hands, by instinct, began gathering up the papers and books she needed for the weekend. Her feet, from practice, took her to the door, through it, down the steps, and in the direction of home.

Home. Never had it sounded better; never had it promised more. God bless Lydia and Herbert!

Born and raised in a small town in Iowa, Birdie's childhood days had been times of deprivation and loneliness. Her father, injured on his job with the railroad, was an invalid for many years. Her mother, becoming the town washerwoman, abandoned to a great extent her job of mothering. Lacking many things, it was the loss of her mother's attention and time that scarred Birdie the most. Overworked, overburdened, never strong, her mother had hung on only long enough after her husband's death to see her daughter prepared to teach school; then, with a sigh, she had taken to her bed and was soon gone. Birdie, filled with anguish over the loss of something she had never really had—a mother and a father—faced life alone. Really alone.

Her one brother, older by several years, weary of poverty, impatient with illness and dreaming of a better life, had made his escape to the big city. Following their mother's death, his communications became fewer and fewer. When Birdie—fired with a desire to be on the front lines of life—joined the throngs of emigrants to the vast and echoing plains and plateaus of their neighbor to the north, all thought of brother and sister ever seeing each other again was deemed improbable, even impossible.

At first, for Miss Bernadine Wharton, teacher, it had been schools on the Canadian prairie—challenging, fulfilling. Each move took her farther north; the parkland—that verdant strip across the center of the province—tantalized her imagination, and when in an instant of time hope and happiness had shattered, she had literally fled into the arms of the bush. Here she somehow felt she was tucked away, oblivious, a shadow flitting through the thick growth, lost in the miles and miles of poplar, birch, willow, and the tangle of bush that contrived to make itself nearly impenetrable in places. Intimidating to some, the feeling of isolation was welcomed by Birdie Wharton.

And in this fashion, day had followed dreary day until—wonderful moment!—Lydia and Herbert Bloom had opened their home to her, and their hearts. Birdie dared to believe Bliss might live up to its name. If not bliss, then peace. Until, that is, the memories stirred again.

Perhaps her eyes were still swollen, perhaps the assault of the past had left a stamp upon her features, telling the story, giving her away. More likely it was just the kind heart and discerning eyes of Lydia that made the difference. A timely difference.

The kitchen, when Birdie walked in, was fragrant with the smell of fresh-baked gingerbread; Lydia was in the process of pouring boiling water into the big brown teapot that was central to much that went on in the Bloom household. Summer or winter, morning or evening, in health as in sickness, the pot dispensed cheer and warmth. Birdie, who needed its ministration as never before, turned to teapot, gingerbread, and friend as a flower turns toward the sun.

"Come in, come in!" Lydia sang out, looking up momentarily. But long enough and sharply enough to cause her to suggest, "And why not unbutton those shoes? Here." She scurried to fetch a footstool, setting it in front of the ancient oak rocking chair, one of two that were fixtures at the side of the big range.

Of middle age, short, and given to plumpness, Lydia, comfortable and old fashioned, bloomed with high color, bright eyes, and a frank expression. In looks as in manner a person of openness, there were no shadows in Lydia.

Birdie laid aside her armload of books and sank gratefully into the cushioned rocker, laying her head back, her hands hanging, her feet up. Tears, those betraying tears, tears that seemed so ready today, stung her already burning eyelids.

"Come now," she said to Lydia, with an effort producing a small laugh, "I can take off my own shoes." Lydia had begun the job of undoing eight buttons per shoe.

"We'll just have us a little interlude," Lydia proclaimed, relinquishing the shoe buttons and turning toward the tea things. Having attended a play years ago in Ontario and enjoying the "light, farcical interlude"—the short break, or interval, between acts— Lydia had forever after termed teatime an interlude. "It's a break in the day," she explained. "It shouldn't be considered routine, like a meal. Not ever. It's a time for pleasure, for relaxation. For recuperation, perhaps." At other times, depending on her mood and the need, she referred to teatime as "sheer magic," "medicinal," "restorative," even "pure bliss," depending on what it accomplished.

Any time, according to Lydia, was suitable for tea. Tea was perfect in the early hours, setting the tone for the day, opening one's eyes without the *zing* of coffee; it was wonderfully warming after a cold drive or walk, without the cloy of sugared cocoa. A good cup of tea settled worn nerves after a busy day much better than Bromo Vichy, purported to be "A Morning Bracer, A Headache Reliever, A Brain Cleaner, A Nerve Steadier." All this and more a cup of tea would do, in Lydia Bloom's opinion. Perhaps best of all, it bonded friend with friend as conversation blossomed and barricades dissipated.

Pouring the boiling water into the pot, shrewdly noting Birdie's puffed eyes, Lydia depended once again on the magic of teatime.

Teatime called for dainty cups and for serviettes, a sense of the luxurious even in the distant reaches of the Canadian bush. Putting the lid on the pot and setting it to steep, she reached into the cupboard for the bone china cups. Treasures indeed, these items had been escorted across half a continent, held in abeyance through the Blooms' first season in a tent, and finally unpacked and set with pride and satisfaction in the kitchen of a house still smelling of wood shavings—a touch of home, a touch of class.

The tea was piping hot; the gingerbread was warm, the whipped cream rich. Birdie sipped and let the tea work its magic. Lydia, wise Lydia, neither questioned nor pressed for conversation, least of all an explanation.

But Lydia had seen—in the material Birdie had set down on the table—a letter partially exposed between the layers of books. An unopened letter; a letter that strangely resembled one received not more than a week ago, brought home by Herbert on the occasion of his last visit to the post office. That one, like this one, bore no stamp but had obviously been slipped in the Bloom box, bypassing the postmaster. Written, then, by a local.

Lydia saw the very minute Birdie's gaze left off its weary enjoyment of the cake and tea and strayed toward the letter. Saw the flicker of her eyes, heard the drawing of a quick breath.

Birdie laid aside the dainty cup and the serviette Lydia always deemed a necessary part of a decent tea, glanced apologetically toward her friend and landlady, and said, as she got to her feet,

"Thank you, Lydia. This was so special and more important than you may know—"

Not so, Lydia's wise eyes said.

"And now, I think I'll make my way up to my room and change into something cooler perhaps—"

And read your letter, Lydia's silent lips spoke, adding to herself with great sympathy, *Oh, my dear, I hope you're not going to be hurt again!*

The words, had she heard them spoken, would have astonished Birdie. Wrapped into herself as she was, so secretive, so *alone,* who could possibly have suspected that underneath was a secret that she had no intention of revealing, even of fully facing anymore? As far as Birdie was concerned, bygones should be bygones and Bliss a new beginning.

But in finding a home—not a boardinghouse but a home—Birdie had laid herself open to intimacy and to observation. It hadn't taken much, Lydia would have been the first to confess, to realize something . . . someone, had hurt, and hurt desperately, the empty shell that answered to the name of Birdie Wharton.

Shutting the door to her room behind her, Birdie relished once again the comfort the Blooms had provided: white flocked curtains at the window; one straight-backed chair pulled up to a small table for study purposes with a bookshelf above; gracefully scrolled white iron bedstead; bright quilt across the foot of the white tufted coverlet; chiffonier—a dresser with a beveled oval mirror set in a fancy swing frame and decorated with carving. "Of choice oak," Lydia had said, quoting the catalog, "handsomely finished, with swell front and two small and two large drawers fitted with cast brass knobs and handles and having locks and keys."

And though the keys had been handed over promptly to the new roomer, Birdie had found no use for them—until *the letter.* Then, though with a feeling of shame, she found herself locking the small drawer in which it was kept.

Dropping the books on the bed, exposing the envelope, Birdie laid aside the shoes she had been carrying. With deliberation she unhooked the numerous buttons on the black shirtwaist and skirt she was wearing, slipped out of them, dropped the waist in a box at the foot of the bed to be laundered the following day, and hung up the skirt.

Finally, hesitant, she stood in the center of the room, clad in a white muslin chemise (the plainest the catalog had offered, $0.45 or two for $0.86), thin, alone, uncertain. If she had realized how vulnerable she appeared, she would have snatched up a stiffly starched dress and put it on, hiding behind it, a uniform as surely as though it bore medals for bravery in combat.

As it was, half-clad and not caring, barefoot and not noticing, Birdie unlocked the dresser drawer and withdrew the letter hidden there. Shoving the clutter of dropped books aside, she reclaimed the second letter. Sitting on the bed, her legs curled under her, she opened both letters and spread them out before her.

Teacher first and foremost, Birdie couldn't help but study the paper—torn from a scribbler and not real stationery—and the writing itself, which puzzled her, raising questions, revealing nothing.

Picking up the first letter, she read again:

> Dear Miss Wharton,
> Please excuse my boldness, but I must let you know how I feel. I have been admiring you from afar ever since you came to Bliss. I find myself thinking of you night and day. Because I believe my chances are poor, it would be wiser on my part . . .
>
> to remain
> your secret admirer

Even as she berated herself for being a stupid fool for not tearing it up immediately, Birdie was gently folding the letter, inserting it in its envelope. Nor could she stop the increased tempo of her heart's beat as she reached for the new letter and, picking up the single page, began to read:

> Dear Miss Wharton,
> Again I take pencil in hand to let you know I think about you constantly; you fill my thoughts day and night. I cannot hide

myself from you forever. It is time that we meet face-to-face. I hope, Miss Wharton, that you will meet me Monday after school in the Fairy Ring on the school grounds. Please don't disappoint me. I hope I don't disappoint you.

Until then I remain
your secret admirer

W e'll open the service this morning with a hymn of your choice," Parker Jones said, stepping behind the simple pulpit that had been put into place at the front of the schoolroom. His congregation began leafing through the hymnals that had been brought out of storage for Sunday's service, looking for their favorite selections.

A vigorous bunch they were. Having spent a week at hard labor, they were—men and women alike—high colored from the Canadian sun, scrubbed until their work-worn faces shone. Hair, if they were male, was freshly cut so that the napes of necks gleamed white above the tan below; beards and mustaches were freshly trimmed. Women, particularly the older ones—having no time and small inclination to fool with curling irons—gathered their hair back into the ubiquitous bun. If they should be so fortunate as to own a hat in reasonable enough condition to be worn, it perched atop their head humbly.

Clothes, old though they might be and well-worn, were in good repair: shirt collars and cuffs being turned until the last ounce of wear should be had from them; dresses taken in and let out as age and weight demanded; the seats of serge pants shining beneath many a mismatched jacket. The knees of the preacher's trousers had a glisten to them, which the pious among them equated with time spent in prayer. Women's dresses, if their owners had been in the bush for any length of time, were by and large of the home-made variety; their offspring wore the remnants of clothing brought from "back home," cut down and remodeled time and again to fit each child in order. Here and there a newcomer sported something a little more fashionable; here and there someone self-consciously modeled a stiff new garment, probably ordered from the catalog. But for the most part, new garments would await harvest and the sale of the year's crop.

Whatever the costume, plainness was evident, whether from lack of funds, ignorance of the day's fashion, or a solemn adher-ence to the Bible's admonition in 1 Peter 3:3–4 regarding the wear-ing of finery: "Let it not be that outward adorning of plaiting the hair, and of wearing of gold, or of putting on of apparel; but let it be the hidden man of the heart. . . ." There was little money for frills in the bush and no patience with folderols. Life consisted of the bare bones where existence was concerned: food, shelter, clothes to keep one decent and warm.

But then, every once in a while there was an exception to the rule. That exception had often been Yvonne Carew, Vonnie of the gang of four. Growing up an only child and spoiled, Vonnie had treats when other children had none, new clothes when castoffs were the existing mode, gewgaws and fripperies when other girls felt fortunate to have a hair ribbon. Her mother, as simple and plain as a cabbage from her own garden, had fondly given up all self-gratification in favor of her adored child.

Once again Vonnie was the exception and, as such, the object of much attention. After an absence of several years, Vonnie, now Vonnie Whinnery and a widow, was back in Bliss. The outbreak of greetings, the hugs, the chatter, had delayed the beginning of the service. Finally Brother Parker Jones, with a tolerant smile, had called his congregation to order. Everyone had settled down, but latecomers, catching sight of the vision in lavender—their own Vonnie all grown up and returned to them as pretty as ever— were distracted from worship as they flashed greetings her way, smiling and nodding, locating a seat and turning to the business of worship.

"Who has a selection?" Pastor Parker Jones asked as this hodgepodge of people settled into desks too small or backless benches brought in for the service. At the organ, prepared to pump with a vigor to match her enthusiasm, Sister Dinwoody waited, stops pulled, hymnbook in hand, ready to find the hymn of choice.

It was an opportunity little Ernie Battlesea couldn't ignore.

"Her Golden Hair Was Hanging Down Her Back!" he piped in a clear and carrying treble. His mother gasped, went as red as a turkey gobbler, and jerked wee Ernie by the arm until the lock of unruly hair standing up on the back of his head bobbed wildly.

Poor Ernie, more than one child thought sympathetically. This would be the end of his studying the Home Entertainment page of the catalog, with its enticing Graphaphone display and long list of songs available on its tubular records.

Mothers, on the other hand, were sympathetic with Luella, Ernie's mother, imagining their own reaction and embarrassment should their child burst forth in public with such a shocking, *worldly* title.

For a moment silence gripped the congregation as they absorbed Ernie's surprising request, uncertain of the proper reaction. Then, beginning with the young people, there was a titter of laughter. Quickly hushed on this the Lord's day and in His house, it appeared for the moment that Ernie's monkeyshines would pass without further reaction and they would all settle down to a worshipful hour.

But the good people of Bliss, pious though they might be when occasion demanded it, were also earthy. Moreover, some of them hadn't had a good laugh all week, caught up in the serious business of making a living, preparing for the winter ahead.

Parker Jones, though unmarried and childless, saw the humor in the situation and appreciated the problem that faced his people:

to laugh or not to laugh. Smiling, he quoted from the Book of Proverbs into the silence now fractured with a few restrained snickers, "A merry heart doeth good like a medicine."

It was enough to burst the bonds of decorum, and hearty laughter erupted, to Ernie's dismay but eventual pride and his mother's further embarrassment. But even she, after a moment, managed a smile, though rather thin-lipped, and one wondered just what Ernie's fate would be, eventually.

Finally "Stand Up for Jesus" was suggested, and order was restored. It was a good choice, for singers could not remain seated and "lift high the royal banner," marching, in heart and spirit, from "victory unto victory." Amid the general hubbub of getting to their feet and turning to the correct page, the service resumed its usual ritual: songs and prayers and sermon, all sprinkled with numerous amens. For after all, did not the psalmist himself say, "Enter into his gates with thanksgiving, and into his courts with praise"? There were no high altars in the bush.

Parker Jones, neat and trim even with his best suit turning shiny and his white shirt showing wear, was a figure of quiet authority. Well-mannered, educated, handsome in a dark, lean way, he might well have filled the pulpit of a grander, larger church. But he was in Bliss at the call of the Lord and was content. Most folks knew long before his proposal that Bliss's own Molly Morrison was the object of his attention. And certainly she was worth catching. All Bliss watched and waited, but Pastor Jones delayed, hesitating to subject Molly to the sacrifices demanded of a pioneer pastor.

From the beginning—as soon as axe bit into the virgin growth of the bush—the church had played an important role in the early settlement of the Territories. Many churchmen, like Parker Jones, were men of higher education, well-read and musical, men of training, exceptional leaders. Their zeal for the work of the Lord brought them on the heels of the first homesteaders, themselves pioneers in every sense of the word. Their presence brought a degree of dignity and wisdom to the newly opening West and to people who were starving for a touch of culture, desperate to believe that life would not always be so hard for them, relying on the good Lord as never before. There was no doubt about it, and history would record it: Churches contributed to the spiritual and educational life of the community, bringing hope, comfort, even much-needed social contacts.

Parker Jones was highly thought of in the hamlet and surrounding community of Bliss. Brother Jones, as he was customarily called, cared faithfully for the "flock" entrusted to him and saw with humility the assembled congregation on this day, a fine representation. The Lord's day was honored in the bush, and even though work beckoned and winter crouched on the horizon, threatening and blustering, the good people of Bliss gathered together faithfully to honor their God.

Some, of course, had less than exalted reasons: young men more interested in girls than religion; bachelors desperate to find a wife and having no better opportunity to look over the possibilities; children who would rather romp and play but who meekly followed parents setting a good example.

Looking out over the expectant congregation—crowded into desks often too small and too cramped, feet shuffling on the oiled floor, callused hands opening Bibles carted thousands of miles when most costly items had been left behind—Brother Jones announced his text. If he, poor human clay that he was, should say not one word worth hearing, the Word would minister richly, for he had chosen today's text wisely: "He giveth power to the faint; and to them that have no might he increaseth strength. . . . But they that wait upon the LORD shall renew their strength; they shall mount up with wings as eagles; they shall run, and not be weary; and they shall walk, and not faint" (Isa. 40:29, 31).

Refreshing the spirit, resting the body, encouraging the heart, Sunday did for the people of Bliss what it was intended to do. And when, after the benediction, horny hand gripped horny hand—stiffened as though to grasp a plow handle or a cow's teat or a pitchfork—they were bonded in very real ways. Not only as neighbor to neighbor, pledged to help one another make it through an adventure that challenged the best of them, eliminated the weakest, and tested them all, but spiritually, as brother to brother and sister to sister.

Free of the worries and concerns that plagued their parents and eager to see each other after a separation of less than two days, children pushed impatiently past the lingering adults, escaping to the outside and a few moments of play before heading home.

First, of course, following the benediction, even if one was a child, one must pause politely at the doorway to shake hands with Brother Parker Jones. Then, free, leap from the step and join the other children gathered around the swings and seesaws. Here there was some happy squabbling and shoving, with impatient cries of "It's *my* turn!"

Harold Buckley, "Buck," teetering between the last days of childhood and the beckoning of young manhood, pulled a handmade ball from his pocket, and soon several boys were divided on each side of the schoolhouse in a game of Annie-Annie-over. After a few raucous shouts and a few tosses over the school's roof, a scandalized mother or two bustled over to scold and shut down the unrestrained hilarity and exertion on the Lord's day. After all, Sunday was intended as a day of rest, not of fun and games!

❧━━━❧

It was like old times. With the benediction, Ellie and Marfa and Vonnie made a beeline for one another. Laughing and crying, arms around each other, they all spoke at once, to the amusement and sympathy of bystanders.

"It's so good to see you—"

"I didn't know you were back—"

"How long will you—"

"I'm so sorry about Vernon—"

"When can we get together?"

It was finally agreed that they meet sometime that week. With none of them having children to care for, plans were simple—Tuesday, ironing day, was decided upon, but not without a laugh, each of them recognizing the others' dislike of that particular chore and willingness to put it off.

"We haven't changed much, have we?" Marfa smiled.

"More than we care to admit, probably," Vonnie answered, wiping a tear from her eye.

"Not enough, probably," was Ellie's response, and they all laughed again.

It was decided to meet at Marfa's, the birth of her baby being close and her friends deeming it risky for her to be driving a buggy.

And then it was time for Vonnie to greet Tom, his arms going around all three girls with more laughter, more tears, more chatter.

"You'd think I've been gone forever," Vonnie said finally, "rather than four years. Letters are good, but oh, my—"

"We've so much to talk about," Ellie reminded, turning and following Tom to his rig, "but it'll wait."

Vonnie's eyes, as blue as ever under her saucy lavender hat, watched as Tom handed Ellie up into the buggy.

"I thought," Marfa said casually, "that you had already seen Tom since you got back."

Birdie Wharton had blushed that Sunday morning to find herself dressing with extra care.

But what, after all, was there to change, to improve? Her Sunday shoes were newer replicas of her everyday shoes; her skirt, kept for Sunday and special occasions, was not much different than the two she wore, turn and turn about, to school. Cut from the same pattern, made to the same dimensions and fitting the same, it varied only in its color, being gray where the others were black and navy. Her shirtwaist, instead of being black percale, durable and neat, was white pique, its severity relieved by the addition of an Alastor choker collar and with a small but definite puff to its sleeves. In it Birdie felt quite another person, more poised, more important, more dignified.

Birdie's small salary, by the time she paid a modest amount for her board, left little money for necessities, let alone luxuries. Occasionally she invested in a book or magazine, which she doted on and counted her only extravagance. Necessary equipment and supplies were selected thriftily from the Bliss store's limited selection or ordered from the catalog as need demanded: tooth powder, hairpins, yarn and thread, pen nibs and ink, shoe polish, hosiery—for summer "Black Cotton with patent finished seams, 24 gauge. Fast color and stainless, price per pair $0.05."

Winter hosiery was more costly, but it must be paid—warmth was essential: "All Wool Full Seamless Hose, extra length, double heels and toes, elastic ribbed top, black only, $0.19 per pair." Birdie did a lot of darning and mending on her wardrobe, hosiery in particular. Sometimes the darned stockings rubbed her heels raw, calling for further expense: Petroleum Jelly.

Petroleum Jelly was her only concession to health and beauty. "This is another name for Pure Vaseline or Cosmoline and other titles given to it," the catalog explained. "It is one of the most valuable and also the most harmless and simple articles to have at hand in cases of bruises, chaps, roughness of the skin, etc., price, each, $0.06."

Five cents here, five cents there, and one needed to save *something* for a rainy day. Remembering a time when she had been thrust out on her own with little or no money, desperate and alone, Birdie determined it would never happen to her again. And so she pinched and saved, accumulating a nest egg in case—God forbid—another such grim situation arose in her life.

And so what was there to improve about herself or her wardrobe on this particular Sunday? Why did she suddenly regret the absence of certain fripperies—a modest Chatelaine watch, perhaps, to pin on the bosom of her shirtwaist. Or a simple pair of cuff buttons, chosen from among the more than 80 pairs pictured in the catalog, beginning with "Ladies' or boys' onyx settings, ornamented edges, per pair, $0.25," to "Solid gold, very fancy, raised ornamentation, set with two diamonds. Per pair, $5.50," and a great variety in between. Or how about a fan—the weather was warming, and a fan, to snap open and cool one's self casually, certainly would be acceptable; she'd forgo the "New Empire Fan, that all of the most stylish ladies are using at present," and settle for a "Japanese Folding Fan, made of good quality paper, beautifully decorated, handsomely corded. $0.03." Three cents!

Why, oh why hadn't she had the foresight to invest that much in her own comfort, not to mention self-perception?

Watchless, cuff buttonless, fanless. Giving herself a shake, Birdie studied herself in the beveled mirror, frowning at her foolishness in giving a minute's consideration to blatant tommyrot. Frowning because, in spite of doing her best, it was the same Birdie looking back at her, the Birdie who had not been enough . . . before.

The memories threatened . . .

Hastily Birdie picked up her hair, twisting and pulling, forming it into a bun at the back of her neck. Then, on an impulse, she pulled a few strands loose, as Lydia had done, allowing them to curl wispily around her face, remembering other days and other mirrors when her eyes had held a gleam and her hair had frisked free, tempting a man to run a hand through it—

The memories! And why today?

It was the letters, of course. Much as she disdained them, much as she determined to ignore them, she found herself thinking of them over and over. Perhaps it was the emptiness of her life, the dull routine of her days, the very pointlessness of her future, burgeoning the nameless correspondence all out of perspective until she, who was dedicated to common sense and service, should find her heart lifting with expectation.

Suddenly, in a blaze of anger at her foolishness, calling herself addlepated, Birdie snatched open the dresser drawer and withdrew the two envelopes. About to rip them into shreds, she found herself immobile, unable to bring herself to so summarily destroy the one ray of light in her otherwise humdrum existence.

Hesitating, staring down at the misspelled *Saskachewan*, trembling on the brink of a decision, she found herself smoothing out the envelopes, gently replacing them in the drawer. Replacing them and shoving the drawer shut with some small explosion of feeling, though whether of finality, anger, or frustration was not clear, even to her.

"Birdie! Ho, Birdie! Are you ready?" It was Lydia Bloom at the foot of the stairs, hatted, gloved, Bible in hand, ready to take off for church.

"Coming!"

Hastily now Birdie swept back every recalcitrant tendril of hair, fastening them severely. Reaching for her hat, she pinned the neat but well-worn "Leghorn Flat" on top of her head. Bought untrimmed, it was worn untrimmed. Lydia had offered a bunch of silk and velvet violets for decoration, but until today they had been ignored. Now, at the last minute, Birdie snatched the humble violets from the dresser top, set them on the hat brim, and, with a thrust of a hat pin, affixed them. Startled at her own action and with her hands going to her hat ready to remove the nosegay, Birdie heard Lydia's voice again, more urgent this time.

"Birdie! Herbert is waiting, my dear. Are you all right up there?"

"Yes, of course. I'll be right down!"

At the last moment Birdie picked up the "lapidary cut stopper bottle of diamond brilliance" presented to her at Christmastime by Lydia and dabbed a restrained amount of Queen Victoria Lily of the Valley perfume behind one ear.

Picking up her Bible (a mere formality since Birdie, a self-sufficient woman, had long scorned its promise of comfort and strength) and hanging her grosgrain bag over her arm, she was ready, as ready as she would ever be, for Bliss.

Outside, Birdie climbed into the shiny black rig where Herbert sat waiting patiently, the horses not so patiently. With two seats, resembling a surrey and more properly termed a wagon, the rig was called a buggy by the good folk of the bush. To them, a wagon was that clumsy, utilitarian vehicle used for the hauling of large loads. Or large families.

Whatever the means of conveyance, numerous rigs were making their way to church this Sunday morning, churning up the dust of the road until those afoot would have to undergo considerable brushing off before they could enter the house of worship.

House of worship. It was surprising how the small, white frame building, having echoed to the youthful voices of children all week, could, by some miracle, resound to the hearty singing of hymns and the earnest petitions of prayer and become the house of God come Sunday.

It seemed strange to Birdie, come Sunday, to find herself seated at one of the desks rather than standing at the front of the room. After greeting several people and noting the arrival of a smartly clad young woman whom everyone was greeting warmly and calling Vonnie, she settled herself as comfortably as possible and opened the hymnal handed to her, idly turning the leaves. She had no favorite, she realized when the pastor called for one. And she wasn't surprised when Ernie Battlesea—he of the clock-winding effort—trilled forth a most unacceptable selection.

Throughout the singing, which was hearty and spirited, Birdie participated. She was alert to the announcements, particularly the one concerning the annual Sunday school picnic—races for the children, ball games for all feeling young enough, horse shoes ... lots of lemonade and homemade ice cream ... delicious dishes from the best cooks in the world.

Thus the pastor threw out the challenge, with the smug smile of Bliss's women—who would consequently labor diligently over their own particular specialty—being the expected response. Counted on each year were Mrs. Van Pier's oliebollen, Mrs. Nikolai's paprika potatoes, Mrs. Phaugh's cabbage rolls golompki, and Lydia Bloom's shortbread, to mention a few of the choice dishes proudly prepared and happily shared. This would be Birdie's first Bliss picnic, and she looked forward to the occasion and the celebration of the end of the school term. She understood that report cards were traditionally passed out at the Sunday school picnic.

All this Birdie absorbed. But when the Scripture was read and Pastor Jones launched into his sermon, Birdie tuned out completely.

The windows, three on each side of the building, were high to discourage daydreaming on the part of children who, seated at their desks, should be giving attention to their studies. Still, Birdie well knew that outside the middle window on her left, just beyond the clearing, there was a circle of birches—the Fairy Ring, so named by a fanciful Ellie Bonney years ago and called that ever since. Here the unnamed and unknown writer-of-letters had suggested she betake herself, after school was out and the children were gone on the morrow, and meet him face-to-face.

In all probability that person could be sitting within sound of her voice at this very moment. Birdie's hand went tentatively toward the violets blooming in lonely splendor on her hat brim, only to withdraw self-consciously and hastily. What if, indeed, he were watching? Birdie could feel the back of her neck reddening.

And that wasn't good, because as a rule, all unmarried men and boys sat in the back of the room on the benchlike supply cupboards running down the sides of that portion of the building, the cloak-room. Her mind, in spite of her best judgment, ran over the list: five or six young men, striplings only, too boyish to be interested in a woman pushing thirty; Herkimer Pinkard, he of the lumber-ing walk and the perceptively apropos comments—*Oh, no, not Herkimer Pinkard!;* Jed and Jake West, brothers and homesteading together, supposedly awaiting the arrival of brides from back home; the widower D. Dunn—*Oh, no, she could never abide being called B. Dunn!* . . . Birdie was running out of names. There was, of course—sitting up front where he had sat with his wife until her death a couple of years ago—Wilhelm "Big Tiny" Kruger.

For the life of her Birdie couldn't come up with any suitable suspect. Anyway, she told herself firmly, it's a lot of foolishness. She was not about to meet some strange, quirky male in a place called, of all things, the Fairy Ring! Heaven forbid!

And so, with an effort, she turned her attention to the preacher and his concluding remarks, a quote, he said, from the ninth chap-ter of Romans, verse twenty-five. "I will call them my people, which were not my people; and her beloved, which was not beloved."

And the lonely, hurting heart of Birdie Wharton, wrenched from daydreaming too late, wished desperately that it had heard more.

10

"Miss Wharton, my scribbler is full. I need a new one."

"Miss Wharton, my pencil is gone from my desk. It looks just like that one Buck is using, with the eraser sorta bit off."

"Miss Wharton . . . Miss Wharton . . ."

Birdie stood at the front of the room, waiting for the children to settle down. They seemed noisier than usual this morning, restless, high-spirited. No doubt it was the beautiful day beckoning through the high windows, the gentle wafting of the bush's enticement through the open door; they were half-wild with longing to be out in it. And no wonder. Winter had been long and dark and bitterly cold.

Settling down, getting order, had been even more difficult in winter. Before school could open each morning, coats had to be removed, wet mittens laid under the stove to dry, overshoes unbuckled and set in a straight line below the hanging coats and caps and scarves. Then, shivering children, icy through and through, had needed a few moments at the side of the heater to hold cold hands out to its warmth, cheeks blazing red, first from the cold and then from the heat. Finally, reluctantly, they took their seats, gripping pencils with stiff fingers, giving attention, often lackadaisically, to their books. Not even the accounts of the *coureurs de bois*, those legendary runners of the woods, could bring history books alive in winter.

It was one thing for a boy to dream in summer of wild rivers calling and far horizons beckoning, and an entirely different matter in winter. Winter was a time for shut doors, hot fires, warm meals.

But there had been those who challenged winter: those intrepid, indomitable *coureurs de bois*.

Montreal, so far to the east of them, at one time was considered to be the gateway to the West; beyond it stretched almost endless forest, the empire of the trader and the missionary. The lure of this vast green area was irresistible to young men, and hundreds of them in the nation's early days made their way into its dark shadows. Gaily painted canoes carried them along, shouting their challenge to the wide skies, rowing with might and main up the sunlit waters and over swirling rapids; portages were accompanied by rollicking singing; campfires were bright with laughter and an endless fund of stories.

The voyageur looked the part, flamboyant in a combination of Indian and French dress: bright woolen or coonskin cap on his longhaired head, gaudy sash around his stalwart middle, moccasins on his feet, bearskin coat covering his muscular frame.

From trading post to trading post he went, with legendary feats of courage, daring the elements and beasts, and always with the good humor for which he was remembered. A special breed, the *coureurs de bois*. A special time in history, touched with a romance that had never been seen before or since.

Eastern settlements could ill afford to lose so many youth from their farms, and the government tried to intervene, making it hard, or impossible, for them to go. At times the young men were threatened with severe penalties if they persisted in going off into the woods. At one time they were required to have licenses. Needless to say, where young, hotheaded men were concerned, neither plan worked very well. The fascination of the woods and the life of a *coureur de bois* were stronger pulls than any orders from the government. And because of the demand for furs and the pelts they supplied, these audacious runners of the woods were appreciated, their efforts applauded.

All too soon—with the passing of the beaver—the *coureurs de bois* became part of Canada's colorful past.

Many a Bliss boy, wading spring runoff in his rubber boots, flashed swiftly along a foaming river in a canoe—in dreams. Many a lad set out a trap, catching a measly rabbit and counting it a glossy beaver. Caps of rabbit fur, cobbled together and worn jauntily on young heads, were coonskin in imagination.

But in winter—that time of deep freeze, heaped snowbanks, solid rivers and streams, when even the proud *coureurs de bois* had been near starvation—Bliss boys bowed their flannel-clad shoulders over scarred desks, flexed stiffened fingers or reached to rub chilblained heels, and narrowed their dreams to firesides and cups of hot cocoa.

Just now, with summer not yet fully upon them but with spring gloriously rampant, they were restless with an urgency to be free, to hunt crows' nests, to trap gophers, to search moist meadows for that flame-red flower, the lily that was to be chosen Saskatchewan's emblem, carrying it home as a gift to mother. They longed to leap, Indian-guide style, from grassy tussock to grassy tussock in the low places where the melting snow was draining, to put a handkerchief on a pole and sail a rickety raft over a small slough.

Already winter's long underwear was a thing of the past, and mothers were laundering the fleece-lined, baggy garments, mending them, folding them, putting them away for a few short months. Soon now, shoes would be discarded, and feet, tender from a winter of woolen socks, heavy shoes, and thick overshoes, would ease gingerly—bare at last—into summer and revel in it.

Miss Wharton, not knowing she broke into numerous daydreams, rapped sharply on the edge of her desk and slowly brought order out of the chaos of eighteen children settling themselves to a morning of history and arithmetic, geography and spelling.

One small arm was raised, and one small hand urgently poked the air with three fingers. Ernie Battlesea. Miss Wharton's system to reduce confusion was a simple one: Raise one finger to use the pencil sharpener; two for a drink; three to be excused for the toilet. A nod of the head by Miss Wharton and the supplicator went about filling his or her request with a minimum of disturbance.

Would Ernie never learn that certain needs should be taken care of before school? But being forgetful of rules, and having walked a mile or more after downing a large glass of milk, Ernie was desperate, this morning as every morning.

Having refused him once and having suffered the consequences, Miss Wharton, admitting defeat, sighed and nodded permission.

Much easier—the trip out back of the barn—in summer than in winter. Then, poor Ernie, suffering the same urgency, donned the coat and overshoes, cap and mittens that he had so recently removed, and though it meant plowing through snowstorm and sweeping winds, made his necessary journey.

Permission granted, Ernie made his relieved escape, and Birdie Wharton gave her attention to other things.

Busy as her days were, they usually sped by swiftly. But today the hours dragged. Today the children droned at reading, stumbled at recitation, faltered at arithmetic, dawdled at the blackboard. Birdie found herself turning her gaze toward the Drop Octagonal time and again, to realize finally that several children turned puzzled eyes on the clock each time she did.

Restless, she took a pencil that definitely did not need sharpening and made her way to the pencil sharpener on the sill of the window facing the Fairy Ring. The "Columbus Lead Pencil Sharpener," purchased through the catalog for eighteen cents, reigned in lonesome majesty on the sill in sight of all, a small box for shavings at its side. Picking it up and inserting her pencil, Birdie turned it automatically, grinding away while she studied the woods until, startled, she realized she had only a stub of pencil remaining.

Foolish, foolish! she berated herself, hastily gathering up a handful of shavings.

It had been settled almost as soon as it had been received—the invitation to slip into the birch ring following school today to meet some unknown male, a writer of surreptitious letters. *Never! Not today, not tomorrow, not ever!*

Why then did the day go by so slowly? Why did she have this urge to listen for the approach of a rig or horse? Why did her feet take her to the north side of the room so often, and why did her eyes turn to the bush there and the path into its depths? Why did she note the white gleam of the birch trees, why did her eyes note the emptiness of the ring?

Why did she speak sharply, slashing through Victoria Dinwoody's report on early transportation?

"'Anthony Henday and his Indians,'" she read, Victoria at her shoulder, "'had traveled hundreds of miles across the bush when they came upon a big river, the south branch of the Saskatchewan. He called it the Wakesew, or Red Deer. But they had no boats in which to cross, having left their canoes on the banks of the Carrot River. With willow from the riverbanks the Indians soon made b—boats, covering the frames with cured moose skins. When they were across, they abandoned the b—boats . . .'"

"For heaven's sake!" Birdie, already keyed up, exploded.

"What?" a startled Victoria asked.

"Why can't you call them what they are? Bumboats."

Victoria, twelve years old and wise, clapped a hand over her mouth.

"Victoria?"

"I can't! I can't say . . . that word."

"You can't even write it?" Birdie asked, realizing her annoyance was showing and all unfairly, knowing full well why the proper Victoria couldn't bring herself to use a word that, to her, referred to a rather private part of the anatomy—the, er, nether quarters.

Now see, Birdie thought crossly, *she's got me doing it.*

"I don't think my mum would like me to say . . . it," Victoria stubbornly insisted.

Birdie closed her eyes momentarily and breathed deeply.

"Victoria," she said tightly, determined to be patient, "take the word *darn*. It has two meanings. We use it to describe mending a stocking, and we use it as a euphemism for *damn*."

"Euphem—" Victoria repeated.

"A good way, rather than a bad way, to say something."

"Darn a sock is good . . . ," Victoria said gropingly, her eyes blinking with her concentration.

"But if you were angry and said, 'Darn sock!' you'd mean something entirely different, wouldn't you?"

Victoria blanched at the very thought. Such words were absent from the vocabulary of well-brought-up children. Especially the children of Sister Dinwoody, to whom had been entrusted the sacred duty of playing the organ for worship, and who strove at all times to be worthy of such a trust.

"What I'm saying, Victoria, is that you don't stop saying you darn socks just because other people use *darn* in place of a swear word, do you? It obviously has two meanings." Birdie spoke reasonably.

Victoria looked unconvinced.

"Now take this back to your desk and do it over. Use the proper word for the boat the Indians built and which was much used in the West in those days."

Clever (and stubborn) Victoria solved her problem by deciding to change Anthony Henday and his unmentionable mode of transportation to one that would not challenge her code of ethics. With a sigh she thumbed through her history book. Maybe if she switched to Peter Pond, "a typical, enterprising Yankee. . . . He was one of the men who literally put the Saskatchewan on the map."

With considerable hope that Peter Pond, though experiencing "enough thrills to fill a dozen westerns," would prove to be a man of acceptable character, Victoria settled down to her reading.

And Birdie, having satisfactorily handled that small problem, turned restless once again.

Lunchtime was no better. With resolution she stayed away from the north windows, and when she stepped outside to check on the children and to walk around a little, she stayed strictly on the south side of the building. Realizing what she was doing, and why, brought a rush of blood to her cheeks and a feeling of despair that she should be so affected by a simple, unsigned letter.

With the children settled down to work again, Birdie turned to a stack of magazines and papers, thumbing through them, looking not only for something to read to the children but to direct her own wonderings and wanderings into safer channels.

Picking up an outdated copy of *The Youth's Companion,* her attention was caught by a short account of a peddler of flypaper. Happy for the diversion, she read:

"I have here some of the most wonderful flypaper you ever saw," the salesman said, standing at the door, unrolling his wares for a lady's inspection. "Every inch of it is warranted to attract as many flies as can stand upon a square inch, reckoned to be, madam, in the neighborhood of thirty-two, without uncomfortable crowding."

Who would care if a fly were crowded, Birdie thought disgustedly, *especially if you were in the act of killing it?* Still, she read on, intrigued by the persistent flypaper salesman's tactics:

"That would make," the man continued smoothly, "on a sheet of this size, which contains five hundred squares, sixteen thousand flies. Think of that, ma'am! And at the ridiculous price of a nickel."

Birdie, ever a teacher, began to see possibilities of making this account into an arithmetic problem for the children. Flies being an everlasting nuisance, the problem might challenge her sixth graders:

"Now here, ma'am," the man continued, unrolling a larger sample of his wares, "is a sheet containing fifteen hundred squares. That means forty-eight thousand flies saved from falling into the soup or the butter, madam—"

Abandoning her plan with a shudder, Birdie turned the page. She was soon caught up in the paper's report of the remarkable horseless carriage:

> Advocates of carriages driven by motor-engines assert that they are certain to become popular because they will save money. In England it is estimated that the cost of fodder for a horse traveling twenty miles a day is twopence per mile, while a motor-wagon of two and a half horse-power can be driven the same distance at the expense of half a penny per mile. Another argument used in behalf of the horseless carriage is that two-thirds of the present wear and tear of roads is caused by horses.

The Drop Octagonal, ever timely, never hurried, never late, sounded out three o'clock. Rejecting the accounts she had just read, interesting though they were and with certain mathematical possibilities, she settled on a story found on the children's page—"Eunice's Sampler." It would elicit a few groans from the boys, but with a promise of "Kenny and His Sled Dog" to follow, they would settle down.

The children knew the routine; books were being closed, desk lids opened, and lesson material stuffed inside. A few fingers were raised, resulting in several children making a trip to the water pail, but finally everyone was seated, properly attentive, and story time began.

Birdie never knew that lips could speak certain words while the mind, like a thing set apart, could be thinking of matters entirely separate and distinct. Finally, after struggling through the two stories, she gave one last desperate glance at the clock and, though it was lacking ten minutes to closing time, announced, "Now you may gather up the things you will be taking home. We'll dismiss school a few minutes early today."

When every straggler was gone, when the door was shut and the room silent except for the ticking of the clock, Birdie sat at her desk, listening to time tick away and wondering why she had been so desperate for the day to come to an end.

Finally, abruptly, she rose. Once on her feet she hesitated, then moved slowly toward the north windows. Standing in the shadows of the room she turned her gaze toward the birch circle. The late afternoon sun pierced the bush and lit the small gathering place, a favorite with the children.

Nothing. As she had suspected, nothing. No one.

But wait. There was a movement, someone creeping . . . yes, creeping through the bush, stealthily approaching the birches from the side, pausing just before reaching them, crouching, peering, studying the ring, finding it empty. Finding it empty and standing erect, parting the bushes, making certain. Then turning, sending a searching gaze toward the schoolhouse, frowning, clearly chagrined at her failure to appear.

The face peering from the bush was flushed. It was nervous. It was guilty. It was Buck.

I'm going over to Marfa's this afternoon, Dad," Ellie reminded her father as he made ready to go out to his afternoon's work.

"Shall I hitch up for you?" he asked.

"No need. I'll walk."

Farms in the Saskatchewan bush were, ordinarily, not large, seldom exceeding the quarter-section originally homesteaded. And though homes were isolated because of the bush and the weather, they were not far apart, and Marfa and her husband George Polchek were only two miles away, not an unreasonable distance to walk.

The Polcheks were among those "stalwart peasants" referred to by Sifton, the minister of the interior whose zeal netted tens of thousands of poor, persecuted Europeans seeking free land and an opportunity to pioneer in peace. The Polcheks came in the first wave, and George, being over eighteen, joyfully claimed one of the last homesteads available in the community of Bliss while his brothers and father went farther afield.

George was a pioneer in the true sense of the word, with acreage to clear, ground to break, buildings to erect. Somewhere along the line he had met Marfa and they had fallen in love, and Marfa gladly and willingly joined herself to the enterprise of making a home and a farm out of the raw materials on George's land.

Nevertheless, it was a mighty crude operation that was spread out before Ellie as she made her way from the road up the lane to the cabin on the raw patch of ground so recently wrenched from the bush's resisting grip: a small barn with a sod roof, a garden, a well, a cabin of two rooms, filled with love and happiness in spite of having known tears of disappointment over the loss of several previously expected babies.

The screen door was open, Marfa was watching, and her welcome was warm.

"Come in, come in!" she exclaimed, her small, round figure almost vibrating with pleasure and satisfaction.

"Vonnie isn't here yet, I take it," Ellie said as she stepped up onto the stoop, seeing no rig and knowing Vonnie would drive, having three miles or so to come.

"I think she's turning in now," Marfa said, and the two young women paused on the step, watching and waiting.

Now, as ever across the years, it was Ellie and Marfa together—the one slim and trim and vibrant, dusky skinned and dark-haired, with hazel-green eyes as full of lively interest as in days of childhood; the other, Marfa, shorter, more rotund of figure than usual, with the stamp of kindness and goodness shining from her round face.

And as ever, though Vonnie had grown up as one of the accepted "gang of four," she was a step or two outside the magic circle that united Ellie and Marfa. Outside the circle and, by some inner knowing aware of it, often resenting it, sometimes challenging it, but never able to invade it.

What Vonnie's thoughts were as she pulled up to the cabin to see Ellie and Marfa together as so often before was her own secret. But she did say, as she pulled the horse to a stop and looked at her friends, "Well. And so there you are. Again." And added gaily, "A gang of two."

"Three, actually," Marfa said as she stepped forward, patting her burgeoning middle. "And now that you're here—four."

"It doesn't seem right without Flossy, of course," Ellie added, holding out her hand to Vonnie and helping her down.

At the head of the horse, Marfa looked expectantly toward the barn, and sure enough, a sturdy overall-clad form appeared in the doorway. With a wave, George strode toward them.

George's greeting, spoken in his broken English, was warm. "You girls haf a goot time, now," he concluded, adding as he turned back toward the barn, horse in tow, "and leaf some of dem tarts for me."

"Oh, George!" Marfa laughed, adding fondly, "You'd think I starved him, to hear him talk. Come on in, girls, and we'll see what he's talking about."

With a smile and a courtly dip of his head, George led the horse away, and the three friends went inside the cabin.

It was the first time Vonnie had been back to Bliss since her marriage, and she looked Marfa's home over frankly.

"You're very comfortable, I see." Vonnie was removing her gloves and lifting her hat from her head.

Give her a few more days in Bliss, both Marfa and Ellie were thinking, *and Vonnie will discard her fineries and be back in harness, helping with the milking, hoeing in the garden, putting up jams and jellies with the rest of us.*

"Most everything you see," Marfa explained in response to Vonnie's comment, "was given to us when we married. I don't know what we'd have done without them." And she went around the room pointing out various items—doilies, pictures, cushions, rag rugs, tablecloth, tea towels, pieces of china—all adding to the utility and comfort and even beauty of the small domicile.

"It looks like you, Marfa," Vonnie commented. "Homey, comfortable. And probably happy."

"You're right about that last part," Marfa admitted, smiling, and Ellie and Vonnie knew that if it had been otherwise, if Marfa had been miserable, it would have shown. Marfa was as open as a sunflower.

On the table in the center of the room were a plate of tarts, three cups and saucers, and three snowy serviettes embroidered by Marfa in the long and sometimes lonely winter hours of her confinements.

Marfa made tea and served it; the girls complimented her on the flakiness of her pastry and the daintiness of her linens and talked about old times, those memories that bound them together. The intervening years had erased the squabbles, disappointments, hurts, and jealousies, and only the rosy glow of childhood remained.

"I miss Flossy," they said more than once and shared what news they had of this missing fourth person. Flossy had married a half Indian man and moved—first to Prince Albert and then north to the timber.

"Her husband is in logging, I understand," Marfa said and paused suddenly, remembering, looking at Vonnie with stricken eyes. A logging accident had taken the life of Vonnie's husband.

"Never mind," Vonnie said. "I was going to tell you about it anyway."

Ellie and Marfa listened sympathetically to the account of the accident, Vonnie's shock and sorrow, and her eventual decision to come home.

"There was no reason to stay there," she explained. "I couldn't support myself away out there. You think you're a pioneer, Marfa? You should have seen Chance; it's as raw as they come. I had no idea, of course, when I went."

Vonnie had met Vernon Whinnery on a trip to Prince Albert. He had made it a point, following that occasion, to come to Bliss twice. The third time was for the wedding. But that's the way romances often were, in the bush and on the prairies. Often they were not romances but conveniences, a mate having died and the bereaved husband—especially if he were a father—desperate for help, company, and consolation.

And so Vonnie, not knowing much about Vernon Whinnery except that he was single, handsome, and a good dancer, had willingly taken her chances and moved to Chance.

"It's well named," she said now. "Somebody knew what they were doing when they chose it. But I didn't know. Though I miss Vernon terribly, I have to admit it almost feels like coming back to civilization to come home to Bliss."

Bliss—civilization? Ellie and Marfa, true children of the frontier, might have smiled, if humor wouldn't have been so inappropriate at the moment.

Vonnie's parents were among Bliss's first settlers, and their toughest years were behind them. Here Vonnie had a room of her own, with her familiar things around her and the loving care of parents who idolized her.

"I'd like to stay," Vonnie said simply. "I'd like very much just to stay in Bliss."

The other two murmured encouraging words.

"You've lost your mother since I've been gone," Vonnie said, turning to Ellie. "Of course my mum wrote me about it. I'm very sorry."

Ellie gripped Vonnie's extended hand for a moment. "It's all right," she said. "Dad has needed me—"

"You and Tom," Vonnie said, "I thought you'd marry, of course. So many years, Ellie. How come . . ." Vonnie's voice trailed away.

"It just hasn't been right," Ellie said a trifle uncomfortably. Marfa, knowing that something was seriously wrong, keeping Ellie and Tom from marriage, changed the subject.

"Ellie's become quite the doctor hereabouts. Grandma Jurgenson can't keep on forever, and she often takes Ellie along when she's called to a birthing or an injury."

"It's what's been on your heart for a long time, of course," Vonnie said reminiscently. "You always wanted to do things for people, remember?"

"I remember," Ellie said.

"Remember the Nikolai head-washing experience?"

All three girls laughed, perhaps a bit ruefully, recalling that first experiment in granting their services to Bliss . . . forcing their services upon Bliss, they admitted now.

"Remember the insignia you made, Ellie?" Marfa asked. "That's what it was, though we generally referred to it as a badge—The Badge of the Busy Bees. You made it, Ellie, with your usual creativity. You always came up with the best ideas! That badge was particularly clever; I remember that we all took turns wearing it with such pride. Whatever happened to it?"

"No one seems to remember that," Vonnie said, reaching for the teapot and a fresh cup of tea. "Do you remember, Ellie?"

"I don't remember," Ellie said.

"Perhaps Flossy ended up with it," Vonnie continued. "Of course, we all lost interest in it after . . . after the tragedy. Do you remember—"

Ellie's unseeing gaze was turned on the bottom of her cup . . .

⌾━━━⌾

Hoeing was a job that left a lot of time for thinking, even for a twelve-year-old. Ellie paused, wiping the perspiration from her brow, leaning on the hoe, resting her back. And thinking. And though she was alone except for Wrinkles the Third who was chasing a butterfly nearby, she exclaimed aloud, "Yes, good idea!"

At double speed now she finished the row and turned toward the house. Laying the hoe aside, she opened the door, calling as she stepped in, "Mum!"

"Here, Ellie. I'm right here."

Of course. Ellie was always so eager, sometimes impatient, when she had an idea or a plan.

"I've got an idea!"

Serena looked up from her sewing, smiling faintly. Ellie had taken another flight of fancy.

"Now what?" she asked, snipping a thread.

"Mum, could we have salmon for supper?"

"Salmon?" her mother questioned. "Salmon for supper? That's your grand idea? I have potatoes in the oven—"

"Salmon would be good with baked potatoes. How about it, Mum?"

Serena sighed. "Suppose you tell me why this sudden interest in salmon?"

"I want the can. Can I have the can, Mum?"

"There are cans in the trash behind the barn—"

"Rusty. Old. Bent. I want a fresh, new one."

"Well, I suppose we can have salmon." Fondly Serena laid aside her sewing, went to the cabinet, and checked among several cans stored there.

"Does it have to be salmon?"

"I guess not," Ellie said at her mother's elbow. "Marrowfat peas would be all right, I guess. Any can that size. But I like salmon better than marrowfat peas. So it might as well be salmon, right, Mum?"

"That settles that," Serena murmured and set about opening the can.

"Careful," Ellie warned, hovering at her side. "I want you to take the end off all the way. It's the end I want, not the can."

"Ellie," Serena warned, pausing, "the edges are awfully sharp. You could cut yourself."

"I won't, Mum!" Ellie declared scornfully. "What do you think I am—a baby? I promise I won't cut myself!"

With some reservation Serena cut the end of the can completely off and rather reluctantly turned it over to her daughter.

"Thank you!" And Ellie was out the door and away.

"You should wash it," Serena called after her, but it was too late; the screen door banged.

Holding the round tin object to her small nose, Ellie sniffed and made a face. Swiping it on the skirt of her dress, she continued her way to the end of a nearby shed, her father's workshop.

Once there, she looked around, locating the items she needed—a hammer and a nail. That was enough to transform the can lid into the object of her planning—an insignia for the Busy Bee club.

Laying the round tin piece on the worktable, Ellie carefully positioned the nail, lifted the hammer, and gave it a whack. A hole appeared in the tin. Perfect! Another whack, another hole, and on and on. Positioning, whacking, positioning, whacking.

Finally, with a gust of satisfaction, she picked it up. Punctured with small nail holes, it showed a close-to-perfect BB. Holding it up to the light, Ellie breathed her pleasure in her success. Laying it down again, she gave one final whack to the top edge of the disk, making a hole for a piece of string or an old shoe lace to be inserted, which would tie the insignia in place around the wearer's neck.

The nail holes were rough. Turning it over and laying it down, Ellie hammered until the jagged holes were beaten down and comparatively smooth.

Holding it carefully, turning it, studying it, thinking some more, she looked around, locating her father's vise. She opened the vise a little, then slipped the metal disk into it and tightened it down. Taking pliers, she gripped the edge of the disk and twisted the pliers until the metal kinked in that spot. After loosening the vise, she repositioned the disk, then tightened the vise and crimped in a new place. She moved the circle of tin again and again, continuing to grip and twist until the edge was scalloped all the way around.

Now she held it up with satisfaction: Shiny, crimped of edge, and bearing the initials of the club, it was a badge to be prized.

Prized and shared. Because once Ellie had worn it to a club meeting, shining in its glory on the barely rounded bosom of her dress, and the girls saw and admired her handiwork, they clamored to have a turn at wearing it. "After all," they pointed out, "we're all Busy Bees. One of us is secretary, one is treasurer [a treasury with four cents and not much hope of more], and one is sergeant at arms [whose duty it was to keep unworthy individuals at bay]."

The precious Badge of the Busy Bees would be worn with pride first by one, then another. Until . . . until the club collapsed, the badge was lost, discarded, or stolen, and life, as Elizabeth Grace Bonney knew it, disappeared in a burst of flame and a puff of smoke.

The slanting rays of the afternoon sun illuminated the scene outside the schoolhouse window—the edge of the clearing, the bush beyond, the stark white of the birches. It emphasized the emptiness of the ring within the circling trunks; it touched the lone figure . . .

Birdie stepped farther back into the shadows of the room, watching, numb of feeling for the moment, while Buck—partially concealed, clearly discernible—hesitated uncertainly. Finally, with a shrug of his shoulders, he turned, crashed through the bush, careless of being seen or heard, and took himself off toward the barn. Within moments she heard the pounding of a horse's hooves as Buck flashed past the schoolhouse, heading for the road and escape.

Swiftly now, acting on impulse, Birdie went to her desk, opened a drawer, and lifted out a stack of papers, lessons that she had not yet taken time to correct. Perhaps what she needed would be among them.

Laying the papers on the desk, she began sorting through them, setting them aside grade by grade, child by child. In spite of the dreadful calm of her countenance, her fingers betrayed her and trembled pitifully, riffling through the pages unsteadily. Laying aside the final page, she had failed to turn up what she was looking for.

Taking a deep breath she began again, more slowly, methodically, checking each page, each name. Nothing.

For a moment Birdie stood in the silent room, mesmerized by the clock's *tick-tock, tick-tock*. It had to be here somewhere, the proof she needed. His desk!

Walking rapidly, her heels clicking on the oiled floor already soiled after the weekend's cleaning, Birdie reached the largest desk in the room. In spite of rules and regulations and close supervision, the desktop, like others, was badly scarred with scratches, ink blotches, even initials. Freshly carved: HB. Harold Buckley. Buck, it seemed, was not going to end his school days without a permanent reminder of his presence.

Neither paying attention to the initials nor caring about the desecration of school property, Birdie lifted the desk lid. Inside was a hodgepodge of Buck's leavings: grimy handkerchief, broken pencil (the eraser chewed off), Victoria Dinwoody's hair ribbon, crumpled paper, shriveled saskatoons. A scribbler . . .

Lifting it out, Birdie closed the lid, laid the tablet on the desktop, and opened it, bending close in the dimming light: spelling words, half-completed arithmetic problems. Essays, essays begun and not completed, the most recent being a report on early beaver trade.

Birdie's breath quickened. Lifting the tablet, she scanned it, impatient until she might locate the proof she needed: "A beaver lodge held animals of diffrunt ages. Sometimes, in those days, there were as many as fifty beavers in a squar mile. The Indians capchured them for food as well as for clothing. Machure beavers weighed as much as fifty pounds and although the meat is fat, the Indians didn't mind."

Ignoring the spelling errors, typical of Buck and proving that the tablet was indeed his, Birdie's gaze slid over the report, watching for one word, one particular word, one word with its telltale missing letter *t*. Surely it would show up in this lesson. But not yet. Reading on—"We must never forget that it was the flat-tailed, industrious beaver of the north [Buck was obviously quoting now], with its superior pelt and rich long guard hairs and very fine down, that opened up the Saskachewan. . . ."

If she had doubted it when she saw him skulking around the birch ring, if she had been inclined to hold on to any hope whatsoever, she wondered no longer. For long moments she stared, dry-eyed, while the pieces of the puzzle fell into place. Fell into place and shattered her silly speculations once and for all.

Saskachewan.

Wilhelm "Tiny" Kruger climbed into his rig, the buggy tipping alarmingly as he did so, picked up the reins, and chirruped to his horse. With one final glance back, he waggled a hand toward the store and a couple of men standing there. Their acknowledgment of his good-bye warmed his heart. Although he had been in Canada twelve years and in Bliss only three, he felt a part of the country and the community. He had friends; he *was* a friend.

The hamlet itself was small, built around the store/post office and the single grain elevator. When and if the railroad track came through Bliss, that elevator would be joined by others, for the land was fast being taken up for miles around and becoming productive. And with the clearing of bush and the planting of crops, each year saw an increase in the grain sold and shipped. Contending with catastrophes of drought and weather and short growing seasons, still there would come a time when it was said the Canadian West "produced more wheat gold than all the gold mined in the world." Such riches!—though they dribbled down to a few wagonloads per homestead per year.

The world wanted Canadian wheat, the good milling wheat, the hard wheat—Red Fife first, then Marquis, perfect for Canadian prairie and bush.

Tiny Kruger well remembered the sense of satisfaction his first crop had brought. The wrenching farewell to the Old Country was a thing of the past, the years spent in the east merely a stopgap, the hard adjustment to the new land was fast becoming a memory—a land that was huge and rich, young and eager, welcoming and promising. And productive.

The toil and trauma of establishing his homestead in the territories had been endured, four or five acres had been cleared, stumps had been pulled, and finally—on newly plowed ground just freed from the grasp of the bush—seed had been scattered in the same manner as had been done centuries before when Jesus was a boy.

Every morning he had watched for the little green shoots that meant life and sustenance for him, Isolde, and Little Tiny. Eventually his watchful care and prayer had been rewarded, and stalks—full and heavy—dotted his field. And then had come the harvest, the first golden grain pelting from the threshing machine and trickling through his fingers.

Remembering, Big Tiny Kruger's heart—a heart as big as his big body would allow—swelled with gratitude, satisfaction, and perhaps some pride.

But the house he built—first a cabin, eventually enlarged to a comfortable abode of reasonable size and efficiency—was empty of the love and grace of a wife and mother. Along the way, another of the lost babies—in its struggle to live and to die—had taken Isolde with it.

Remembering, Big Tiny's bulk heaved with the magnitude of his sigh.

Memories sad and happy were interrupted by the pounding of hooves, and a horse and rider flashed past without greeting or glance, a most unusual occurrence in Bliss. But Big Tiny knew horse and rider: Mortimer Buckley's roan with his son Buck astride. Bent low over the mane, digging booted heels into the horse's flanks, the overgrown youth was undoubtedly coming from school. But why in such an almighty rush?

Big Tiny resumed his earlier train of thought: Next best to the golden grain was the golden straw that had sustained it, that had separated from it for another purpose, an important purpose. Piled in heaps called a stack, it meant life or death to a herd. It was extra feed, of course, hay being the most important; though it was not the most nourishing, cattle still seemed to do well on it. Clear a path to the straw stack and the cattle did the rest until, come spring, the stack was nothing but a memory of scattered straws, and the cattle—still alive, though thin—were nosing over the lush green of new growth in the meadows and clearings.

Big Tiny passed the schoolhouse, obviously shut up for the day, the children, like Buck, scattered out across the hamlet and the community to their homes. Somewhere ahead, unless the children had been released early, Little Tiny would be ambling homeward and would be glad of a lift. Home, where the two of them made out well enough. . . .

Enough reminiscing, enough dreaming! Big Tiny waggled the reins and urged the horse to a faster clip. Soon, ahead, he saw the unmistakable form of Miss Wharton, Bliss's teacher.

Big Tiny's thinking might be slow, but it was thorough. His glance narrowed as he studied the slight figure that even he could see was far from erect and confident; no doubt Miss Wharton had endured a long, hard day. Then, with a slight frown, he turned to cast a look backward—the boy/man on the galloping horse had disappeared from sight. Buck—had he been kept in after school? Big as he was, if there had been a problem, Miss Wharton would not flinch from her duty; but would it have been enough to bow her shoulders dispiritedly and to send Buck off in a tear? Thankfully, Big Tiny thought now, there were just a couple of weeks remaining, and Buck would be done with school. What he would turn his clumsy hands and his mischievous mind to was a question his father had pondered aloud a time or two in Big Tiny's presence. "Send him to work in the woods with his uncle for the summer," seemed to be Mortimer's tentative decision. "Give him a chance to grow up. It worked with his brother, and it might work with him."

Miss Wharton, obviously lost in thought and not hearing the approaching rig until it was almost upon her, cast a glance back and stepped quickly from the road to the grass. But she had been surprised, and her start had tumbled a couple of books. With her arms already encumbered, she was at a loss for the moment. It seemed clear that she would need to set down the items she carried, pick up the fallen books, and incorporate them into the load, picking them all up together.

But for the moment, she hesitated, studying the fallen books, halfway reaching for them with one hand, pulling it back as those in her arms threatened to fall, deciding what to do.

No man could leave her in such a pickle, let alone Big Tiny Kruger of the kind heart. Pulling the horse to a stop, he spoke: "Good afternoon, Miss Wharton. Can I—"

"You crept up on me," Birdie muttered. "Again."

Fortunately her gaze was turned elsewhere; she was looking rather helplessly at the dropped books. Big Tiny's small grin would not have helped the situation.

But his voice, when he spoke, was serious enough. "I must say, Miss Wharton, I am truly sorry. Again."

In normal circumstances even Birdie Wharton would have recognized the humor in the situation and might have allowed herself a smile. As it was, his words went almost unnoticed, and Big Tiny, watching, was instantly sober.

"Hold, Dolly," he said soothingly to the horse who, whether she understood or not, was agreeable to a rest.

Quickly for so large a man, Big Tiny was out of the rig, bending over the fallen books and gathering them up. But instead of tucking them into Birdie's arms, on an impulse he turned and put them in the buggy.

"Might as well let the buggy carry them," he said lightly, "and you as well."

The proof of her disturbance over something was clear when, without demur, she allowed him to take her load from her arms and, with his free hand, help her up into the rig.

Settling herself, receiving her material from his hand, Birdie managed to murmur her thanks. "Kind of you."

"Not at all," Big Tiny assured her. "I'm going your way, and I have an empty rig."

It wasn't quite true. When Big Tiny stepped up, the buggy, now filled to three-quarter capacity, tipped alarmingly. Birdie, startled from her distraction, made a grab for the iron armrest and held on until Big Tiny was settled and the buggy had righted itself. But wide as he was, the "emptiness" of his rig was in question; Big Tiny left very little room for Miss Wharton and her books. If she'd been otherwise than a wisp of a woman, the fit would have been impossible. As it was, they rubbed along thigh to thigh, but even that, the man noticed, failed to arouse so much as a flush on his companion's face, sure evidence of her absorption with . . . something.

They jogged along in silence for a while. "You'll be happy to see the school year come to an end, ya?" he asked finally.

"Oh . . . yes. Yes, of course." It was as if Birdie Wharton's thoughts had been wrenched back from some distant and strange place.

"And you'll be losing some pupils."

Birdie looked at him, eyes blinking thoughtfully, perhaps with relief.

"Why, you're right. I believe just . . . one."

"Buck."

"Yes. Yes, of course. Buck." And it seemed that the thought took hold, until Birdie's bosom heaved with what might have been a sigh of relief, and the taut expression on her face seemed to relax.

"Two weeks . . . even less," Big Tiny said, flicking the reins until Dolly quickened her pace, trotting a little.

"Two weeks," Birdie repeated. "Two weeks."

"And then, if I've understood his pa, he'll go to the woods, at least for the summer. That seems like a good thing for a growing boy, wouldn't you say—a summer, maybe longer, in the north woods?"

You'd have thought he had thrown her a lifeline. "Two weeks," she breathed, half desperate, half hopeful. If Birdie Wharton had been a praying person, one almost would have believed it was a prayer.

There's no need to drive in," Birdie protested when they reached the Bloom gate. "I can walk the rest of the way."

"It's no problem," Big Tiny said mildly as he turned the buggy from the road to the Bloom driveway. "Do you always bring home such a lot of . . . stuff?"

"No, usually I don't, except on a weekend." Birdie didn't feel called upon to explain the blindness with which she had scrambled items together—most of them unnecessary—and, clasping them as if her sanity depended on it, had stumbled from the school to the road, along its dusty trail, her numb mind only then beginning to think, to sort things out.

She had in her arms the revealing paper with its significant giveaway clue—the misspelled *Saskachewan*. Once home, she would compare the writing of the essay to that of the two letters. But she had no doubt concerning the writer; it had been Buck, perhaps with help from his older brother who was, by all accounts, as much a rascal as Buck himself. The very thought of their planning, snickering, contriving, made Birdie sick.

The pathetic part, the part that crushed and twisted and pained, was that she had taken the foolishness seriously, that she had given a minute's consideration to such tommyrot. Thank heavens she had retained enough good sense to stay away from the suggested rendezvous! Her humiliation would have been complete, particularly if she had caught sight of the sniggering, peeking Buck.

All this and more she had brooded on as she trudged homeward, arms overloaded, steps slow, self-perception dragging as surely as her feet.

Perhaps it was because her resistance was at such a low ebb that she accepted the ride offered when Big Tiny Kruger pulled up alongside. More likely it was just plain good sense, for she was in danger of scattering papers to the breeze.

She noted, with some surprise, that aside from a cursory sentence or two, Big Tiny said very little. And yet the silence was not uncomfortable; she felt under no pressure to make light talk, and for this she was grateful. And apparently Big Tiny felt no such compulsion either, and so they jogged along in what might be termed a companionable silence.

And it was helpful—the ride. Birdie clutched her books and papers, lunch pail and handbag, stretched her buttoned shoes out toward the dashboard, closed her eyes, and breathed deeply.

If Big Tiny, more finely tuned than one would imagine, cast a keen glance at her from time to time, no one would ever know. But anyone knowing him well might have suspected that he was doing some earnest thinking, perhaps making decisions, laying plans, solving what he saw as a problem; anyone knowing him well might have had a small feeling of sympathy for young Harold Buckley.

Reaching the Bloom homestead, there was no way Big Tiny Kruger was about to let Miss Birdie Wharton out at the gate, to walk the distance to the house by herself, burdened—he suspected—in more ways than one.

"Whoa, Dolly!" he said eventually, and he was out of the buggy and around to Birdie's side as quickly as anyone ten years younger and fifty pounds lighter might have done.

"Here, give me those," he said. "Let me carry them for you." And Birdie meekly handed them over.

If only it were that easy! But of course it wasn't. Nevertheless, Birdie stepped from the buggy with a lighter heart than when she had entered it. And she was able to say with sincerity, "Thank you so much for the ride, Mr. Kruger. It was more help than you know."

But was it? Big Tiny turned his buggy around and headed for the road and home, his nostrils pinched and his mouth stern.

Big Tiny had his standards, and intimidating teachers was not one of them.

Upstairs in her room, Birdie dumped her load on the bed. She had managed the meeting with Lydia very well, due mainly to the rationality that had returned to her thinking on the ride home. Thank heavens for a man who knew how and when to keep his mouth shut! Birdie had a small generous thought for Big Tiny, to her own brief surprise.

"I need to get rid of these," she had said, and she hurried on through the kitchen, to the stairs, and up to her room.

Lydia's fond smile had followed her. "Come down when you're ready," she said, "and we'll have a cuppa."

The first thing Birdie did—proving, perhaps, her recovery and her self-control—was to sit down, remove her dusty shoes, reach under the bed for her comfortable soft-soled slippers, and put them on.

Next, she stepped to the chiffonier, deliberately delaying the moment she reached for the letters, as though they didn't matter, taking time to straighten her hair, rearrange the collar to her waist, drum her fingers, breathing, just breathing.

Coolly she unlocked and opened the drawer and removed the two letters; casually she turned to the bed. Searching out Buck's account of Canada's early beaver trade, she laid it side by side with the letters from the envelopes. There was no doubt about it—they were written by the same hand, though the letters were done with more care and without erasures.

She picked up the letters and calmly returned them to their envelopes. With steadfast step she turned toward the door, heading for the kitchen and the stove. She took a first step—and faltered.

Gasping, falling on the bed in a passion of tears, for one weak moment Birdie cried out her humiliation and hurt.

Rising, wiping her eyes, straightening her shoulders, Birdie marched down the stairs to the kitchen stove, lifted a lid, and, in spite of Lydia's wide-eyed gaze, thrust the letters inside. Turning, dusting her hands in a manner that spoke as loudly as words, she said, "A good cup of tea would go well about now, Lydia."

Wise Lydia; her teapot poured out love and compassion as well as tea. That, along with the subtle strength received in the buggy sitting beside the big man on the way home, ministered very well to the bruised heart and stinging ego of Birdie Wharton.

I don't think I'll go today," Brandon Bonney said at the breakfast table.

"Not go?" Astonishment raised Ellie's voice a notch or two and her eyebrows as well.

Not go to the picnic? The event of the year? On a par with the Christmas concert, the sweetest celebration of the year, and the Fall Frisk, a celebration of harvest completed and crops garnered—and to be deliberately missed?

"I just don't feel like myself," Bran said mildly enough. Even so, Ellie, immediately alarmed, rose to her feet, rounded the table, and pressed a hand to her father's forehead.

"You don't seem to have a fever," she said. "What is it, Dad? What's wrong?"

"Nothing much," Bran said, shrugging, wishing he hadn't mentioned it. "As I said, I don't feel quite myself, that's all."

"You do seem a little pale," Ellie said, stepping back and looking at her father critically. "Does your head ache? What about your stomach—you haven't eaten your breakfast!" There was reproach in her voice.

"I'm not hungry. As I said, I don't feel well. A day at home will fix me up just fine."

"Well, I'm not going, either." And Ellie, her mind made up, settled the question.

"Of course you'll go!" Bran said firmly. "The lunch is all ready—I saw how you baked yesterday; I see all the things laid out, ready to be packed. Tom'll be by to get you. Of course you'll go."

"No, indeed," Ellie said.

"Ellie, please—"

"No, Dad. I know you. You'd never admit to feeling poorly if you didn't. And you'd never miss the picnic unless you had to. I wouldn't have a moment's peace if I left you here, alone and feeling bad."

Nothing he could say changed her mind. She began methodically fixing a pan of hot suds, preparing to wash and dry the breakfast dishes.

"Then I'll go," Bran said. "Get on your picnic duds and pack up the box."

Ellie whirled from the dishpan. "Do you think I'd drag you off to the picnic just so I can have a few hours of fun? Nothing doing! There will be plenty more picnics."

Bran sighed. What a stubborn daughter! Just as stubborn, perhaps more so, than he was. Look at the way she refused to consider marriage. And all because of some dim and distant tragedy that was not her fault. The Mounties had determined that. What if some members of the community—thoughtless, irrational people—blamed her, an innocent child? What if, a few times, the word *murderer* had been whispered where she could hear it, even written on the blackboard at school, sent through the mail a time or two. All this had hurt, apparently maimed, his daughter in a deep, psychological way, so that her life seemed to be warped, her expectations shattered.

Bran sighed, watching the sweet shell that was his daughter and knowing it to be empty of hope and perhaps happiness.

But all that—that bad time—was over and gone, buried in the Bliss cemetery. The years, as they came and went and as Ellie grew and matured, should have dimmed every memory. Perhaps they had.

For everyone except Ellie . . .

———

"And where are you off to this afternoon?" Serena asked, watching her daughter collect certain items for her basket, her Busy Bee basket: jar of soup; pencil and tablet (Ellie wrote letters for her "patients"); needle and thread in case mending was needed; small tin of Camphor Cold Cream—"salve of remarkable healing properties, it cannot be excelled as a soothing and healing application to burns, and a dressing for abrasions of the skin, pimples, boils, etc."; camphorated oil—"excellent for rubbing on chests and throats in case of croup, difficulty in breathing, sore throat, coughs"; olive oil . . .

Simple remedies all, items her mother had approved and which might bring ease to a sufferer, and in any case, would do no harm.

"Is it Aunt Tilda again today?" Serena asked, and Ellie flashed her mother a quick smile.

Such satisfaction for one so young! Surely her "calling" was to care for the sick, the needy, the lonely. Barely twelve years old, and already expending herself for others. And her friends right along with her. Flossy, Vonnie, and Marfa, faithful in this as in all else, were active participants in the Busy Bee motto: "Let us bee about our Father's business."

"Yes, it's Aunt Tilda," Ellie said now. "We went last week, you know, and she just loved having us there."

"Are you sure, Ellie? She can be cantankerous, I've heard."

"She gets a little cross with us," Ellie said, chuckling a bit in recollection of the elderly woman's crotchety ways. "But she can't do much about it; she can't chase us off. And she can only take a swipe at us with her cane if we do something that upsets her."

"I hope you don't do that, Ellie," her mother said. "Remember, you promised me the purpose of the club is to help. You're big enough now to be a real help, if you go about it in the right way."

"Bee-ee-ee helpful, that's me," Ellie sang out. "Aunt Tilda really needs help, Mum."

"I know that," Serena admitted, regretting that her strength these days was too limited to allow her to do more than care for her own family. "It was so sad when Mr. Beam died; at least they managed until then. I hope some family member will come forward with an offer of help before winter; she'll never make it through that alone. Apparently she has no wood up for winter; as for food—no one has taken care of her garden since her collapse—"

"She says she had a brain spasm."

"Brain spasm? I've heard of heart spasms . . ."

"Anyway, whatever happened, she can't get around anymore. And it's hard to understand her when she talks. People bring meals to her, leaving the food close by the bed so she can get it. But she spills something awful. You should see her bedding, Mum. Ugh!"

"You can't wash bedding, Ellie! Don't even try. Maybe the missionary society ladies will come in before long and do that and whatever else needs to be done. In the meantime," Serena finished fondly, "I'm sure she appreciates what you girls do to make her comfortable. I'll talk to the minister and see if he knows what plans are being made for her. He's been writing relatives, I believe."

"Well, I gotta go, Mum." Ellie picked up her basket and turned toward the door, happy as a Saskatchewan lark, doing the thing she enjoyed most—caring for someone sick or afflicted or weak, needy in some way.

"Your badge, Ellie. I haven't seen you wearing it for a while. After all that effort to make it—"

"I have to share it with the girls, so we take turns. Vonnie has it now and she doesn't want to give it up. Ta ta, Mum!"

The Beam homestead was about three miles away, if one went by the road. But people made paths across their property; there were paths going in all directions, paths cutting down the distance and the length of time it took to get to a neighbor, either to get help or to give it. Ellie cut through the woods and across corners of homesteads, traveling well-marked trails, making the distance less than a mile. Vonnie and the other girls did the same, converging on the small cabin and ready to make the life of old Aunt Tilda Beam a little more bearable: chop wood or fill the wood box, wash the elderly woman's wrinkled face or read to her, fill the lamps, sweep the floor—whatever needed doing, they would do, working as true busy bees should do. (There were no drones in this hive, Ellie often reminded them.)

Trotting into the Beam yard, the few remaining chickens—those that hadn't died or disappeared into the bush for lack of care—scattered at her approach, going off somewhere to scrabble a living for themselves. Before she went into the house, Ellie threw out some grain for them and filled their water pail.

There was no greeting from a friendly dog; the old Beam dog was long gone, perhaps along with the Beam son, Clayton. He had filed on the homestead, stayed a few seasons, established his aged parents, and taken off. Everyone assumed he'd be back, come spring and time for field work, but he hadn't been seen or heard from in two years or more. The old father had died, and Tilda, called "Aunt" in the habit of the bush, had slowly grown more feeble, more senile, less capable of caring for herself. The pastor of the small church, alert to the problem, was attempting to organize the ladies of the church so that Tilda was never alone too long and so that there was a supply of food and water, wood and kerosene at all times.

The Busy Bees, ever on the alert for something constructive to do, came as often as time and mothers allowed. Ellie, with her mother's help and the aid of the catalog, had gathered together a few simple remedies to take with her on her "rounds," and she usually found herself rubbing the old woman's back, or feet, or temples with one of her salves or potions. Whether or not they did any good, both Aunt Tilda and Ellie felt the better for her efforts, Aunt Tilda moaning with pain and pleasure, Ellie swelling with a sense of satisfaction known at no other time.

A half-wild cat scooted from the house as soon as Ellie opened the door, and she held her nose. Obviously the last person to leave had failed to put the animal out, and it had been inside too long. Grimacing, Ellie knew immediately there would be cleanup, a task she hated above all.

"Hello, Aunt Tilda! It's me, Ellie Bonney," she called into the shadows of the small room. Shadowed because there were only two windows, and they were small.

In response to her greeting there came a grunt and a rustle of bedclothes. Ellie wisely left the door ajar, both to give light and to alleviate the noxious cat odor.

Although there were two rooms to the log house, one had been abandoned when it came to looking after the elderly woman. Her bed and belongings had been brought into the room where the living was done and where the stove was located, the table, and all the kitchen items; here it was much easier to care for her. And here—while she was still able to get up—she had managed to do a few things for herself.

Ellie laid aside her basket and approached the bed. It too was odorous, and Ellie's nostrils flared again. Staunchly, like a true Bee, she stood her ground.

"How are you today, Aunt Tilda?" she asked loudly, and a claw-like hand appeared at the edge of a quilt, followed by a sticklike arm, pushing aside the bedding until Aunt Tilda's shrunken face appeared.

Today, Ellie realized, was one of Aunt Tilda's bad days. Her eyes didn't focus, her toothless jaws worked as though she were masticating something toothsome, and the words she uttered were meaningless jabber.

Aunt Tilda's arms flailed, and Ellie helped pull her up from the tangle of bedclothes, fluffing the pillow and leaning the emaciated form against it.

The fire was out, of course, and there was no warm water. Ellie knew how to light a fire and soon had paper and kindling flickering, adding pieces of wood as needed. It was then smoke had begun billowing into the room, puffing from the stove in great gusts, rising in waves to the already blackened ceiling. No wonder it had been allowed to go out! Coughing, she fought her way through the smoke to the stovepipe and the damper; to her surprise, it was open.

Ellie was enough acquainted with stoves to conclude almost immediately that there was some blockage in the stovepipe. But what to do about it? She went outside and looked up; sure enough, very little smoke lifted from the pipe; perhaps a bird had built a nest in it. Helplessly she watched, knowing she had neither the ability nor the tools to clean it out, even if she were able to locate a ladder and climb the roof.

There was nothing to do but wait it out. Slowly the fire burned down, died away, went out. During that time and while the stove top was somewhat warm, she put the soup she had brought into a pan and attempted to warm it a little. Then, when the air was clearing, she tucked a towel under Aunt Tilda's chin and spooned the soup into her flaccid mouth.

"Swallow, Aunt Tilda," she said cheerfully time and again, murmuring encouragingly and wiping the chin when necessary, skillfully avoiding the mindlessly waving hands.

When the fire was out and the room cleared of smoke, Ellie set about washing the old lady, brushing her hair, rubbing olive oil into her dry and skinny arms and legs, crooning to her, talking to her even though no understandable answer was forthcoming. Finally it was time to locate the cat's mess and, loathing every minute of it, clean it up and scrub down the floor in that spot. When that was accomplished, inspired, she poured a few drops of her precious Peppermint Oil on the spot, breathing in its fragrance gladly.

At the last, in answer to a plaintive cry for "light," she lit the lamp and set it by the bed. Aunt Tilda could blow it out later.

"There, Aunt Tilda," she shouted, and she was rewarded by a toothless grin and a watering of the rheumy eyes.

"Here's fresh water if you want a drink. Is there anything else you would like me to do before I leave?"

Just a mumble and a restless picking of the quilt.

Patting the frail shoulder and giving the quilt one last tug into place, Ellie turned to go. But first she reached into the basket, removed the pencil and tablet, and wrote a message in large letters:

DO NOT LIGHT A FIRE IN THE STOVE! THE STOVEPIPE IS PLUGGED UP! ELIZABETH BONNEY.

Propping the paper in plain sight on the table, Ellie proceeded to pick up her basket and back out of the cabin, calling, "I have to go now, Aunt Tilda. I'll see you soon. Sweet dreams!"

Lest the miserable cat be tempted to sneak in once again, Ellie pulled the door tightly shut behind her, glad, in some ways, to escape the sickness and smells but having a happy sense of accomplishment.

Home again, weary but happy, Ellie put the basket away, set the empty mason jar aside to be washed with the supper dishes, and reported on her day to her mother.

"Aunt Tilda didn't even know me, Mum. It's awfully sad. I hope I don't end up that way!"

"No one wants to, Ellie. Hopefully you'll always be where family and loved ones are around to care what happens to you. Now, rest for a moment, then wash your hands and help me prepare the vegetables."

The family was at supper when a horse pounded up the drive-way. The rider, a neighbor, leaped from its back, knocked once loudly, thrust his head in the door, and hollered, "Fire! There's a fire somewhere over yonder, Bran! I'm on my way; thought maybe you might be able to come help."

Even as the face disappeared, Brandon Bonney was getting to his feet, turning to the door.

"I'll ride, I guess, but I won't take time to saddle."

Ellie and Serena followed Bran out onto the stoop to see in the distance a black cloud of smoke rising over the bush and shot through from time to time with flickers of flame.

"Oh, my gracious! My gracious!" Serena put her hands over her mouth in dismay, her eyes large in her thin face.

"I'm going, Mum!"

"No! No, Ellie—"

But Ellie was off and running. Running the same path she had taken earlier. Running, straight as an arrow, toward the Beam cabin and the fire.

Gasping, almost staggering, she joined the silent, grim-faced men and women gathered in the Beam yard. No chickens now, no cat.

No cabin.

The fire had not been discovered until it had all but consumed the small structure. Built of the same wood folks burned in their heaters and stoves, and well-aged, it had been a tinder box. Even as the onlookers watched, the blaze slowed, having done its worst. The roof was long gone; soon the entire structure was nothing but a heap of blackened beams with a bent stovepipe protruding at a rakish angle from the rubble. And starkly outlined against the setting sun—the iron bed frame that had held the helpless form of the old woman. On the bed—a heap of ashes.

Men were wandering around the shell of a building, raking, clearing the ground from any possible spread of the dying embers, helpless to do more.

"Who got here first?" someone asked.

"One of the Nikolai boys," someone answered.

"It was in flames when I got here," the boy stuttered, white-faced. "I couldn't get anywhere near it. The flames were shooting out the windows even then."

"Did you hear any calls for help?"

"Nothing. It was silent as the . . . as the tomb," he finished lamely.

Finally—very soon, it seemed, when one realized an entire life's accumulation of goods had just disappeared—someone began drawing water from the well while others dashed it on the smoldering heap until all danger of the flames springing to life again had disappeared. Soon only a few thin wisps of smoke lifted from the ashes.

Still the neighbors lingered, unable to grasp the totality of the destruction, the rapidity with which it had happened, the finality of the life snuffed out—Aunt Tilda's, not of much importance to anybody, but certainly not deserving of this.

"Who," someone asked, voice loud in the silence, "who was here last? Who was the last one to see her?"

Face looked at face, heads shook, eyebrows raised.

"Ellie."

Vonnie, half hidden by the form of her mother, said again, "Ellie Bonney. Ellie was here. . . . She was the last one here."

Ellie. A dozen and more pairs of eyes swung to peer down at her.

Stung into responding, Ellie blurted, "It was out; the fire was out when I left!" And with a sob, "I'm sure it was out!"

The crowd shifted uneasily; there were a few murmurs, a few indrawn breaths, a muted "Ellie Bonney! Ellie . . . responsible."

Standing beside her father in the evening's shadows, Ellie looked—for the first time but not the last—into a ring of shocked faces.

And heard—for the first time but not the last—the whisper, *The child . . . a murderer.*

The Mounties arrived in due time. Questioning various people, walking around the burned-out cabin, they did their best to bring some conclusion to the matter and to determine how and why Mrs. Beam had perished. The Mounties, after all, were the law of the land. They had brought order and sanity to the territories when it seemed chaos would surely prevail; they did a superior job of keeping the peace. Folks rested in their beds more easily because they were on the job.

No matter where the Mounties went, fascinated people stopped what they were doing and turned their eyes to the Red Coats as they rode by, admiring and honoring them, hearts swelling with pride in such a police force.

When two of these men, resplendent in their distinctive uniforms, entered the Bonney residence to question the last person to see the deceased woman alive, Ellie thought her heart would burst with feelings of favor. For hadn't she, along with the rest of the school's children, rushed to the windows or to the fence whenever a Mountie rode by?

Sitting down after introductions and explanations, turning their attention to the child before them, the men invited, "Tell us about your visit with Mrs. Beam, Elizabeth. Why you went."

Ellie explained about the Busy Bees and their devotion to serving others, Mrs. Beam among them.

"And what did you do for Mrs. Beam the day of the fire?" one Mountie asked kindly.

"Well—" Ellie's eyes sought her mother's. Serena nodded encouragement, her thin face wanner than usual.

"I cleaned up . . . the cat's mess," Ellie confided faintly.

Surely that was a flicker of humor on the square-jawed face. At any rate, Ellie took heart and continued.

"I washed Aunt Tilda—"

"Mrs. Beam, she means," her father interjected.

"And then I rubbed her with olive oil, and combed her hair, and fed her some soup . . ."

"Tell us about the stove, Elizabeth. The fire. Was there a fire in the stove?"

As best she could, Ellie explained that she had lit the fire to heat the soup she had brought from home. She described the smoke, the plugged chimney, and how she had let the fire go out.

"It was out before I left," she whispered. "I know it was out."

"Tell us," the Mounties said, "did you light a candle? Or the lamp? Did you leave a light burning when you left?"

"The lamp," Ellie said. "The room was so dark, and Aunt Tilda kept fussing for light, so I lit it and set it on the table beside her where she could blow it out when she wanted to. Then I filled a glass of water for her, and . . . that's all."

A few more questions, and the Mounties thanked Ellie and the family for their help and took their leave.

Ellie, both proud and anxious, stood beside her father and mother as the Mounties rode out of the yard to make their rounds of the community, gather what information they could, and compile a report.

"They'll get to the bottom of it," her father reassured. "I'm sure they'll find some reason, locate someone other than you who was there, someone who was careless with fire, perhaps . . ." Bran's voice died away uncertainly.

Looking up into her father's face, Ellie's eyes, for the first time, filled with that haunted look that her parents came to recognize and to dread. "Papa, did I do it? Am I a murderer?"

Bran and Serena dropped to their knees in the yard, putting their arms around their child, assuring her, both angrily and pathetically, that she was, indeed, no murderer. "Never think it!" they said.

"The Mounties," Bran said more than once, "will find the truth. You'll see."

Even then, they had a reputation for "getting their man." Would it, in this case, be a girl? Serena and Bran pushed away the panic that threatened and put their faith in the law, relieved because the Mounties were on the job. It hadn't always been so.

❧

Early days in the West had been fraught with wildness and wickedness. It had been a wide-open, free-booting, brigand-plagued time in the history of the territories. There was no law, and there certainly was no order.

Before immigrants were wooed and won to homesteading by the government, and while the Northwest was still considered empty, the Indians and the Métis became the victims of Montana-based traders, men without consciences, who crossed the unmarked international border to barter "firewater" for buffalo hides.

Firewater—the heart and soul of the whiskey trade—was a rotgut mixture of watered-down whiskey, India ink, tobacco juice, tabasco, and even vitriol. This diabolic drink rapidly demoralized the natives and disintegrated their culture; the order of the day was arson, rape, and murder—lawless abandon.

Word went rapidly from the frontier to the Canadian Parliament that the American "wolfers" had perpetrated a massacre of Canadian Indians. Although few episodes in the past have had so lurid a history with so little established fact as the "Cypress Hills Massacre," still it was the catalyst that prompted the organizing of some sort of police protection.

When it seemed the Indians would certainly seek their own justice, the government hurried into action, resulting in the establishment of a mounted police force for the Northwest. Aside from the fact that they would be under civil control, they would function like cavalry. Their uniform would be scarlet—a happy choice, reminiscent of the British uniform already recognized by the Indians as representing the Great Queen, and commanding respect.

These men, soon to be called Mounties—discreet, resolute, persuasive—managed without too much trouble or time to impose law with a minimum of disruption and, simultaneously, gain the confidence of the Indians. Before long they would preside over the change that made a wilderness into an agricultural community. Eventually, of course, they made a name for themselves across the country and around the world, with a reputation for patient diplomacy and firm action.

In their red uniforms and on their handsome steeds, the Mounties represented law and order wherever they went. The Northwest—white and Indian alike—learned to trust them, to depend on them.

<hr/>

Brandon and Serena Bonney had full confidence that after the investigation a report would be forthcoming that would clear their child of all culpability in the sad Beam affair.

The report, when it finally filtered down to Bliss and the Bonneys: "Accidental death."

"It's not good enough!" a disappointed Serena said to her husband. "They should have explained how it happened. They should have cleared Ellie of all suspicion. I know people! They'll say Tilda Beam certainly wasn't responsible for the accident, and so somebody else was. And I'm afraid that somebody will always be thought of as Ellie."

"She's just a child, Serena," Bran said gently. "People will be kind—"

Some were. Some were not. Some meant to be. Well-meaning people gave consolation that was condemnation: "After all," they said kindly, "no one thinks that Ellie did anything on purpose. Heavens, no! We all know what a helpful, caring child she is. Good as gold, really."

Or, "Fires happen! And no one, especially a little girl, can be held responsible for a fire."

Perhaps missing the mark most: "Ellie will get over it. She'll forget it. Give her time, and life will go on as though it never happened. You'll see."

But glances that were too sympathetic, pats of consolation, cheery words when none were called for, a few gibes by spiteful children, all kept the tragedy, and the uncertainty, alive for Ellie.

Those, and the dreams . . .

Ellie was making potato salad—the eggs and potatoes had been boiled and the dressing made, and there was no use letting them go to waste. She and her father would have a picnic meal all by themselves.

But there was Tom.

She had gone to the picnic with Tom ever since she finished school at fifteen and considered herself a woman; certainly lots of girls were no older when they married, even began raising a family.

And Tom had offered marriage, right away.

At first her answer had been a light, "I'm too young, Tom! And so are you!"

Tom, grudgingly, had accepted that. By the time she was eighteen, he was more urgent. "I need you; I want you," he had whispered enticingly, snuggling in the buggy or under a willow tree in the evening's shadows.

And though her lips and her heart responded, her mind, her guilt-ridden mind, had put excuses in her mouth. "Not yet, Tom. We're both young—"

"Not *too* young," he said insistently, pressing to overcome her reluctance with the only means he knew—the pulsing need of their healthy young bodies, the approval of their parents, the passing of time, his need of a partner in the great adventure of setting up his own place.

When Ellie turned twenty-one, her mother died. Tom, called upon to be patient once again, accepted the new excuse: "I can't . . . I just can't leave Dad right now, Tom."

Accepted it for a time. Finally even Tom—good, patient Tom—grew impatient with the delay, began prodding into the situation and Ellie's continual objections, thinking, struggling to come to some conclusion.

"It's because you don't love me," he accused, to be met by a fury of denials.

"How can you say that! I've loved you for years, ever since that day when you first came to school—"

"Well, then, what's the problem? Ellie," Tom studied his fingernails, "are you . . . afraid? Afraid of marriage? Afraid of me, perhaps?"

This Ellie strongly denied. And surely she had all the earmarks of a normal, loving, eager young woman. Until marriage was mentioned.

Two Christmases ago, riding home together in the cutter after the Christmas Concert, when it seemed the joyousness of the season was filling all hearts, Tom's hopes rose once more. And once more Ellie—her face rosy with the cold, and the moon making mysterious shadows around her eyes—turned his proposal aside. No longer able to say they were too young, she treated the idea lightly. "Oh, Tom—we have such fun, you and I. It's special whenever we get together. Can't we be happy this way for the time being?"

Tom was not to be cajoled; Tom was not about to settle for friendship. Tom said, his brow furrowed and his tone more serious than at any time before, "Ellie, does your refusal to consider marriage have anything to do with that fire? The death, over a dozen years ago, of that old woman?"

"Why would you say such a thing?" Ellie asked tightly, almost angrily.

"Because I've thought of every other reason, and nothing else makes sense; I keep coming back to the fire. As I think about it, about you, Ellie, you've been different since that time. At first I believed it was natural, considering the shock of that experience, and that it would pass. But I see now that it hasn't; it's become a way of life with you. It's that, isn't it?"

The cutter's runners squeaked over the packed snow; the harness jingled rhythmically; the moon kept pace with them, laying a shiny, silvery path across the snow as they moved along. A night for love and romance.

Ellie's voice was low when she said, "You don't want to be married to a murderer, Tom. Think of trying to explain to your children that their mother—"

"Hey! What's this foolishness!" Tom pulled the horse to a halt and there, in the middle of the road and bundled as they were, took her in his arms, shaking her, rocking her, holding her.

"Never let me hear such rot again!" he demanded. "Anyway, that's all in your head, Ellie, not mine!"

Ellie wept a little—from the force of her feelings. And from the force of his.

"Hey!" Tom said again, watching the tears shine in the moonglow, "None of that! Those'll freeze, you know. And I don't want any frozen ice maiden!"

Even though Ellie managed a weak laugh and Tom wiped away the tears, her heart, deep down inside, remained cold, cold, cold. And his not much better, for nothing had been settled.

Two more years passed; several more proposals and as many refusals.

At times Ellie's heart quailed. How long would Tom—a perfectly healthy, normal young man—agree to wait? She knew it wasn't fair; she knew she was being desperately, terribly, unexplainably unfair to Tom.

◦────◦

When he came bounding to the door, dressed casually for the picnic, ready for a full day of fun and frolic and good food, cheerful and expectant, his eyes full of determination—and ten years older than when he first asked her to marry him—Ellie knew what she had to do. Somehow, in her heart of hearts, she knew.

God help me! she breathed.

"Tom," she said, backing away from his reaching arms. "I'm not going to the picnic."

"Not going?" he repeated blankly. To miss the picnic was to miss half the year's fun, it seemed.

"Dad's not feeling well, and I won't leave him."

"That's a shame—" Tom began sympathetically.

"I need to talk to you, Tom," Ellie said, and her tone was serious enough for Tom's eyes to widen. Bran—was he seriously ill?

"It's not Dad," Ellie said, avoiding Tom's eyes. "Please stop by on your way home. And we can . . . talk."

"We'll talk now," Tom said, and in view of their past association and his uncertainties, who could blame him if he spoke roughly? Was he too feeling what she was? And was he prepared? Ellie hoped so; she hoped so desperately.

And looking at those steely eyes, that firm mouth, Ellie thought it might be so; Tom other than sweet and loving and kind, she had never known. Had God, in His loving kindness and great wisdom, planted a seed of doubt about their future in Tom's heart, too?

Ellie washed her hands and wiped them, took off her apron, and stepped toward the door, Tom, silent now, on her heels.

Automatically Ellie turned toward the bush and a favorite hideaway, Tom following. Pushing aside the limbs and branches, they reached a small bushy enclosure filled with objects that had been of interest to a child in years past. Glancing around and finding no place to sit that was not leaf-littered, Ellie remained on her feet, turning to face Tom.

"Tom," she said steadily, without preamble, "I'm giving you your freedom."

Shocked silence, stunned silence. "What do you mean?" Tom asked slowly, his eyes searching hers.

Turning, pacing the small embrasure, Ellie talked rapidly. "I'm not free to love, to marry. Yes, it's the fire, as you asked me once.

Something, something inside me burned up that day. That's the only way I know how to explain it. I . . . I feel like a murderer—"

"How would you know how a murderer feels? How could you possibly know? There was no such thought in your heart—ever!"

"I mean, I feel like a destroyer. I feel guilty, unworthy."

Tom made a rude noise.

"I don't expect you to understand," Ellie said, and she stopped her pacing and faced him, her face pale, her eyes darkly earnest. "I only know it seems right, hard as it is, to tell you not to wait."

Tom clapped both hands to his head, shaking it as though to fend off something unbelievable.

"Maybe it would help," Ellie went on, bravely, "if I told you about the nightmares.

"They consume me, Tom. Like a message from the pit they take me into the very bowels of that fire. *I* am the one in the bed; *I* am the one helpless, terrified. *I* am the one catching fire, burning, shriveling, screaming . . ."

"Ellie—it doesn't matter. Together we can—"

"No, Tom. It hasn't gotten any better, though I've waited and hoped. I'm so helpless against it. I don't understand it! And through all of it, I can't make myself believe we should marry; I just have this inner hesitation. You mustn't spend any more time waiting for me. Would it help, Tom, if I tell you I think this is best—for you as it is for me?"

And though Tom pleaded, earnestly at first, then heatedly, finally arguing bitterly, Ellie had made up her mind. Across days and months and years she had made up her mind; she saw that now. White-faced she stood her ground: She could not marry him; Tom should not wait.

With the truth finally reaching him that she meant to stand firm, Tom whirled and strode away through the encircling bush. But not before he gritted out roughly, astonishing Ellie and, in the long run, assuaging some of the misery she felt: "If you think I'm going to spend any more time mooning around—you couldn't be more mistaken!"

16

Careless, careless . . . couldn't care less.

Standing in front of the mirror, getting herself ready to go to the picnic, Birdie saw herself far differently than she had that morning two weeks before when she had prepared herself for church and the possibility of confronting an unknown admirer. There had been an air of adventure, a rare lifting of the spirits on that morning. Even so, she recalled bitterly now, her head had warned caution. But her heart—her foolish heart—had demanded anticipation. Her eyes, in spite of herself, had reflected a certain sparkle, her cheeks a rare flush; her mouth had been softer, as though lingering on the edge of a smile. She had loosened her hair, if only for a moment, as an experiment; she had decorated her hat and dressed with care.

Today she was careless—careless of her hair, careless of her attire. And certainly there was no sparkle.

With a shrug she turned from the mirror and the day's hair-pinning operation. Carelessly she chose and slipped into a "wrapper," for which she had paid $0.69, and which, with a sniff, she recognized as an ordinary dress in spite of the catalog's caption: "The best cheap wrapper ever made up. Well made throughout, and comes in steel gray mixtures, half mourning and blue with small white figures and dots."

Though she would never confess to being in "mourning," she felt the dress was appropriate for a picnic and suited her precisely. For not only was it simply made but it was muted in color, restrained as to its puff-top sleeve—an unremarkable garment in all ways.

In spite of its maker's commendation and the assurance that the garment was "fast color genuine Simpson print," its first wash had significantly drained the color from its figures and dots, and in it Birdie felt as pale and washed-out as before she put it on. But what matter? School was out, and aside from handing out the report cards, her need to be exemplary was over for the year.

The last two weeks of school had gone by without further incident insofar as Harold "Buck" Buckley was concerned. In fact, to her surprise, he seemed unusually subdued. He hadn't misbehaved; he had worked diligently at his final exams; he had been polite. Almost, Birdie thought, it was as though he had been caught in his dastardly scheme, chastised, and warned. And though her anger—or was it shame?—burned when she dealt with him in any way, she restrained herself, did what needed to be done, cool and efficient in all, and heaved a sigh of relief when, for the last time, he walked out the school door.

She was not proud of it, but she had been unable to refrain from making one small backlash. Returning to Buck his essay on Canada's early beaver trade, she had circled, far more heavily than necessary, the misspelled Saskatchewan, adding this reprimand in the margin: "Any fifteen-year-old should be able to spell the name of his homeland!" From Buck's surprising beaten demeanor, it seemed he might have put two and two together. For one thing, he refused to look his teacher in the eye. He kept his head down, and he worked, or pretended to work, diligently. Certainly he would never misspell Saskatchewan again.

In spite of arthritic hands, Lydia had managed to prepare a sumptuous feast to be taken to the picnic. Not only had she produced her famous Scotch shortbread in abundance but fresh buns, Prince Edward cake, deviled eggs, and a smoked ham baked and sliced, ready for serving. A separate box held a tablecloth for the long trestle tables that would be set up, the dishes the family would use, a sweater in case the day turned chilly, a blanket for sitting on, goose grease in case of sunburn. Herbert was placing a couple of straight-backed chairs in the wagon. Though Birdie would be expected to sit comfortably on the grass, he and Lydia, with their stiffened bodies and aching joints, would enjoy the picnic from chairs in the shade, spending their time comfortably talking, watching the festivities unfold around them, eating.

With Birdie and Herbert seated on the wagon's spring seat and Lydia ensconced on one of the chairs in back, they made their way, after chores were done, to the lakeside and the picnic spot. Whereas most lakes were sloughlike, this one was larger, clear and sparkling, with a sandy bottom. Although the water was still icily cold and it was considered too early in the year to swim, there were always a few hardy folk who dared it, to emerge, blue and goose-pimpled, proud of their accomplishment while their weaker peers settled for wading.

Since the picnic was sponsored by the Bliss Sunday school, Parker Jones had the responsibility of organizing the day's proceedings. But, wise man, he had delegated the work to committees:

Sister Dinwoody—tables and food arrangement
Herkimer Pinkard—ice-cream freezers cranked from time to time, fresh ice added as needed
Molly Morrison—drinks (lemonade and coffee)
Robbie Dunbar—organize ball game
George Polchek—children's races and games

As the families of Bliss and surrounding districts arrived, Birdie was prepared to hand out report cards to children or parents, to be met with sighs of relief, a couple of groans, a few cries of anguish. There was no arguing with report cards; once the year's grade was recorded, neither heaven nor earth could change a child's fate—going on to the next grade or taking the year over. No wonder report cards were awaited with anxiety by pupil and parent alike.

The Nikolai wagon appeared and disgorged its load—a dozen and more children scattering to the far corners of the meadow to play games, tussle, race, and, in general, have a marvelous time. Arvid Nikolai took a box to the table area, but his family would consume far more than they brought. With so many mouths to feed and supplies limited, the Nikolai children always approached the picnic tables as though they contained a king's feast. And for them they did.

Katrin, overwhelmed mother of this tribe, sank to the grass among the women of the district, one babe at her breast, another pulling at her skirts. Watching, Birdie was assured of a good supply of pupils for years to come.

Neither Arvid nor Katrin read much English, and they spoke brokenly, so Birdie spread out their children's report cards and explained each one. Finally, it boiled down to whether or not they had passed. They had, though Birdie cautioned the parents that Frankie, he of the runny nose and perpetual sniff, needed help. The ailment seemed to run in the family, and Katrin listened with longsuffering as yet another teacher did her best to help.

Birdie, extremely frustrated, could only try to describe the remedial effects of a couple of items she had located in the pages of medicines listed in the Drug Department of the catalog. Bronchial Troches promised "relief for coughs, colds and sore throat," and Slippery Elm Lozenges were "a demulcent for roughness in the throat and irritating cough."

Katrin listened dazedly, blinking and nodding, until Birdie, sensing that her words were as chaff flying in the wind, finally concluded helplessly, "Well, just try and make sure he has a handkerchief with him wherever he goes." To Katrin's blank look she repeated *handkerchief* and *hankie* until, in desperation, she snatched her own small scrap of cambric from the cuff of her sleeve where it was kept and demonstrated.

Understanding flooded Katrin Nikolai's face, and she nodded agreeably. With considerable relief Birdie turned to the distributing of the cards, turned to find herself face-to-button with a masculine chest.

Birdie raised her vision from the shirt button to find the broad, beaming face of Wilhelm "Big Tiny" Kruger several inches above her own. She retained her dignity and her place, and it was Big Tiny who stepped back with an apologetic murmur. If he studied her face searchingly for a moment before breaking into a full smile and speaking, it was not obvious, and certainly Birdie didn't notice. For, truth be told, though she maintained her poise as a teacher ought, she was somewhat flustered.

"Please don't ask if I always creep up on people," Big Tiny said lightly.

With a lift of her chin, Birdie answered pleasantly, "How nice to see you again, Mr. Kruger."

And truly she had reason to be grateful to him for the timely lift home that day of her misery and mortification, and reason to appreciate the sensitivity he had shown in not indulging in meaningless conversation, giving her time to recover herself to some degree.

"You have Nelman's report card, ya?" Big Tiny asked, bridging the small silence that fell as both of them, perhaps, remembered that other time and the wordless sense of camaraderie that had existed, if only for the moment.

"Yes, of course," Birdie responded, and she began riffling through the cards still in her hand. "You'll be glad to know that Nelman did very well academically. As for deportment—well, we need a little work there." But Birdie smiled slightly as she said it; one might almost have said she dimpled.

"No more clock-winding escapades?" Big Tiny asked.

"You know about that?" Now Birdie was uncomfortable, remembering the chastisement she had meted out—and her subsequent regret.

"Of course," the big man said. "We—Little Tiny and I—have no one else to talk to, nights when we're alone. We like good company," he twinkled, "and good conversation. And so we tell each other everything we can think of. I tell him about his mother and his grandparents back home; he tells me what's happened at school and what he's learned that day. That's how I learned about the Cree."

Big Tiny was referring, Birdie knew, to their conversation the day he had dropped by after school and they had looked at the map of Saskatchewan together. Looked at the map and talked animatedly about history—with the letter lying like a live thing between them on the desk. Two weeks and a lifetime ago, it seemed to her now.

When Birdie stepped aside and walked toward another group of families just arriving, Big Tiny matched his steps to hers for a time, then turned aside toward his son to share with him the good news from his report card. It seemed good to Birdie, somehow, to walk in his shadow. Comforting.

"Oh, Mrs. Buckley," she called, seeing that large, sober-faced woman unpacking her box of food. "I have Harold's report card. Is he here?" Birdie looked around.

"Buck's gone north to work with his brother in the woods," Mrs. Buckley said, setting out a plate of sandwiches and covering them with a tea towel. "Left as soon as school was out."

Birdie couldn't help the surge of relief this news gave her. She was able to say, generously, "Well, you'll be happy to know he finished his grade satisfactorily."

And as she handed over the report card, she mentally washed her hands and—hopefully—rid her mind of the entire miserable affair of the letters.

Her cards all handed out, Birdie's perambulations around the picnic spot and through the crowd had no further point to them. She faltered momentarily, unsure of herself and her welcome with any of the huddled groups—people seemed to have drifted into pairs, walking and talking together; middle-aged women sitting companionably in the shade; men deep in discussion here and there; young people engaged in games and competitions.

"Miss Wharton!" someone called, apparently noticing her solitary figure and her hesitant manner.

Birdie swung around to see several young women sitting in the grass on a slight rise, like Saskatchewan wild roses, blooming and sweet, watching the ball game and the display of manly ability being enacted before their interested eyes.

"Over here, Miss Wharton." Someone in the group raised a hand and beckoned.

Gladly Birdie made her way to the group, responded to the nodded and murmured greetings, and took a spot cleared for her between a couple of the girls. Both spoke at once, and Birdie swiveled her head to hear, to smile, to respond.

"I'm Molly Morrison. I've met you at church, of course—"

"Of course."

"And I'm Marfa Polchek, and heaven alone knows how I'm going to get myself up off this ground." Marfa patted the bulge that indicated she was very near full term with her pregnancy. "And that's my husband working himself into a lather over there with the children's three-legged race, not a job he asked for, that's for sure! Parker Jones has a persuasive way about him! Wouldn't you say so, Molly?" And Marfa looked teasingly at Molly, to all intents and purposes the choice of Pastor Parker Jones, though no definite announcement had been made.

"I've seen you both, of course," Birdie said, grateful for the friendly gestures, "at certain school gatherings, and at church. But only to say hello, I'm afraid. I guess I have to admit I'm a rather . . . solitary person. I haven't made the effort to get acquainted as I should have." Suddenly Birdie regretted the long, barren winter and the few contacts, mostly people who had dropped by the Bloom home.

"It's impossible in the winter, so think nothing of it. You've done a great job this year, everyone says," Molly said comfortingly. "And we're all glad you'll be staying on. Will you be leaving Bliss for the summer?"

Birdie was into an explanation regarding her lack of close family and, therefore, the need to stay in Bliss for the summer months,

141

when a couple wandered by, heads close together, faces rather flushed, deep in conversation. Birdie was aware she had lost the attention of her listeners.

"Excuse me," Marfa said, breaking into Birdie's explanation, and her face—even to the stranger who was Birdie—was surprised, perhaps shocked, "but that's . . . that's Vonnie." She spoke in a whisper, though she needn't have—the young man and woman were oblivious to anyone else. "Vonnie . . . and . . . Tom."

"Strange," murmured Molly Morrison. "By the way, where's Ellie today?"

"I haven't seen her," Marfa said with a small frown, following the couple with her eyes.

"Well! I can't let this pass!" she decided. "Two of my best friends, and I'm whispering?"

Marfa raised her voice and called, "Vonnie! Tom!"

With a start, Vonnie Whinnery, the young widow, turned toward the gaggle of girls perched on the grass nearby, paused, and turned her steps toward them. Tom Teasdale, her companion, followed, perhaps reluctantly.

"Hey, you two!" Marfa called out in her friendly fashion. "What're you so deep in conversation about? And where in the world is Ellie, Tom? I haven't seen her; didn't she come?"

Briefly, Tom answered, "Her father's not well today."

"Sit down, both of you, and join the conversation. Vonnie—have you met our schoolteacher? Birdie Wharton . . ."

The young man and woman looked at each other momentarily. Then Vonnie sank gracefully to the grass, while Tom stretched himself out at her feet, leaning on one elbow, plucking at the grass, putting a blade in his mouth and chewing it, occasionally pushing back a stubborn lock of hair that insisted on falling over his forehead, and listening, mainly, to the chatter of the girls.

But when the dinner bell sounded and boys and girls, men and women began converging on the long, loaded tables and Tom sprang to his feet, it was first to Vonnie—then the bulky Marfa—he extended his hand.

And when plates were filled and everyone sought a spot to settle and eat, Vonnie and Tom chose a grassy area separate from the others. And while Vonnie leaned back on her elbows, slim legs extended and ankles crossed in careless and pretty abandon, it was Tom who leaped to his feet, taking their plates to the tables for replenishing and, finally, ice cream and cake.

Birdie, ignorant of the situation, counted them a "couple." And then wondered why Marfa's glance was turned so often in their direction and why the sunshine seemed to have fled from her pleasant, sunny face.

Conversation on the way home helped clear up the matter a little.

"Did you see," Lydia said thoughtfully, jouncing along tiredly but happily, "Tom and Vonnie?"

"I saw," Herbert said laconically.

"Well, what do you think of it?"

Herbert "ahemmed" a few times, a great habit of his when words wouldn't come easily. "Ah . . . well, it's their business, I guess."

"But Ellie, Herbert! Ellie Bonney! What's one to think, anyway!"

Herbert ahemmed again, and the rest of the ride home was accomplished with little else to break the sleepy and satisfied mood of the picnickers.

Home again, Birdie, with a litheness long missing from the aging Herbert and Lydia, jumped from the wagon, turned to the house, and stepped up on the porch, more than ready to get to her room and put a refreshing washcloth to her dusty face. About to reach for the knob, she paused.

Something . . . something was stuck in the door. Slowly Birdie pulled it free and found herself staring at an envelope. A white envelope with her name on it. Another white envelope.

I've got to stop by and see Ellie on the way home," Marfa said thoughtfully as she walked with George toward the buggy. His arms were laden with a box of dishes—empty dishes, he noted with disappointment—and Marfa carried the ice-cream freezer, also empty. They, George and Marfa, were not empty; it had been a day of feasting for the people of Bliss.

Before George could answer, Marfa said, her mind obviously veering to the soon-coming event of the birth of their child, "Just think, George. This could be the last time we'll walk to the buggy . . . or anywhere . . . just the two of us."

Somewhat alarmed, George stopped in his tracks. "Is it the baby? Is it time for the baby?"

"No, silly!" Marfa trilled. "I just mean it'll be soon now, very soon."

George, relieved, gave the joyful thought sufficient consideration, then switched to his wife's earlier statement.

"Why do we haff to go by and see Ellie? Look at the time, sweetheart—chore time! This is not the time to go by and see anyone, as much as you may haff missed them at the picnic. Even Ellie."

"I've got to, George," Marfa said, seeing no reason to raise her voice to her beloved, sharpness being something she seldom found occasion to resort to. So much could be handled with patience, thoughtfulness, and kindness. So Marfa believed, and such she had practiced all her life.

George, not quite so placid, not quite so soft-spoken but adoring his dumpling of a wife, tried again, chiding just a little. "Cows need milking; pigs need swilling; chickens—"

"I know, George. But if I don't see her now, when will I? You'll be too busy to take me, and you won't let me drive myself." Marfa didn't really mind her husband's rules and regulations concerning her health at the present time; she thrived on his care and concern.

"But what for?" George asked, setting the box in the buggy and reaching for the freezer. "Are you worried about her dad?"

"Not her dad, no. It's *that!*" And Marfa's dark head nodded slightly in the direction of a neighboring buggy: Vonnie, though she had come to the picnic with her parents, was climbing into Tom Teasdale's buggy.

George whistled soundlessly but said cautiously, "Do you think you might be making a mountain out of a molehill? Aren't they old friends?"

"It isn't just the ride, George. Nor the fact that they spent the day together, ate together, seemed absorbed by each other. It's the . . . the look on her face! Oh!" she stopped, frustrated, "I can't put it into words. Unless you knew Vonnie and Tom too, you'd never understand what I mean. I know them both so well, George, and I see . . ."

Words failed. Marfa—what with weariness and worry—was near tears.

But Marfa was right. Vonnie's blue eyes, so prone to change— from sympathy to superciliousness and back again, from fun to freezing, from concern to disdain—had glowed and sparkled all day, speaking louder than words. Her slender form, curved in Tom's direction, swaying toward him, and the numerous light touches to his arm, his shoulder, his hand, had said volumes to the watching Marfa. Oh, yes, Vonnie's very artlessness spoke of cunning.

"Hey, hold on!" George said, hurrying to his wife's side, putting his arms around her no matter who was looking, hugging her close. "Whatever it is you see, or tink you see, it's not worth gedding upset about."

"Ellie and Tom," Marfa sniffed against George's plaid shirt, "have been special to one another ever since he and his family came to Bliss. Now—now something's not right. I know it! And why? Something must have happened—"

"But, sweetheart," George said kindly, the "sweet" coming out as "sveet" in his broken English but no less dear to Marfa for that, "is it any of our business?"

"Everything that matters to Ellie is my business, George Polchek!" Marfa, indignant, was as roused and ruffled as a mother hen. "And I can't risk anyone but me telling her about what's been going on today! How can I just go on home and say nothing? She'll hear it from somebody and wonder why I kept silent!"

With a small grin at her intensity, George loosed his wife and helped her up into the buggy.

"You vin," he said, climbing in beside her, picking up the reins and clucking to the horse. "But we bedder not waste any time."

<hr/>

Ellie had been restless all day. Unable to persuade her father to lie down or even stay in the house, she had watched him walk slowly to his workshop, had checked on him occasionally all day, had served the pseudo picnic at noon—a strangely dissatisfying meal, with neither of them having much to say—and turned from one task to another the rest of the time. Strangely, it felt like Sunday. Knowing it was a holiday for everyone else, Ellie felt a reluctance to dig in and do the day's usual chores. Consequently, she puttered.

Puttered and thought. Trudging dinner's leftovers to the well, putting them in a pail, and lowering it to the small shelf provided below, she thought of other things. Sweeping a clean floor, with little or nothing to show for her efforts, she pondered the situation. Shunning the ever-necessary weeding of the garden and settling down to the mending of socks, she thought some more.

Thundering through her head, tearing at her heart—her surprising pronouncement to Tom.

The morning's confrontation had surprised her as much as it had Tom, erupting without forethought or plan. The walk to her special place had been spontaneous; the words that had come tumbling from her mouth were startling. Had they been hidden in some inner place, fretting and troubling, gathering momentum over the days and years, and threatening explosion?

Whatever possessed me—to do such a thing, to say such things, to be so decisive! With a yank Ellie pulled the wool through a hole in the sock stretched over her mother's darning egg. And thought some more.

And yet—whatever the prompting, the decision had a feeling of rightness about it. Having prayed about the nagging situation where an urgent Tom was concerned and her own sad sense of inadequacy, wanting to do the right thing, could it have been a matter of "open thy mouth wide, and I will fill it" (Ps. 81:10b)?

Still, she couldn't blame the Lord for it! Why then the small but settled conviction that she had acted more rightly than she knew?

When her thoughts began to whirl—condemning, confirming; hurting, healing; regretful, relieved—Ellie cried out, "Oh, Lord! If there's peace for me in this confusion, please help me find it!"

A portion of that peace was immediately forthcoming, perhaps in fulfillment of the invitation and promise "Cast thy burden upon the LORD, and he shall sustain thee" (Ps. 55:22a). And though panic at her own actions and the imagined result of them threatened to overwhelm her from time to time, she fled to the prayer and the promise, and endured.

She endured when the memory of Tom—the puzzled question in his eyes turning to blazing realization—came to haunt her. She endured when a picture of the future—unknown and empty—rose to taunt her. She endured when Marfa and George stopped by on their way from the picnic.

She met them at the buggy. Looking up, her eyes sought Marfa's. "Is it the baby?" she asked. "Is it time?"

"It's not the baby," Marfa said, and there was no use trying to pretend; Ellie knew her too well. "I want to . . . need to talk to you, Ellie."

Silently now Ellie helped her friend from the buggy.

"Dad's in the shop, if you want to spend a few minutes with him," Ellie said to George. "Or come in, if you wish."

"I'll go talk with Bran," George said, suiting action to words, stepping down, securing the horse, and turning in the direction of the farm buildings.

"I have to watch the time," Marfa said. "George needs to get home."

Ellie nodded. Pointing to a padded rocking chair, she directed her waddling friend to a seat.

"What is it?" Ellie asked, attempting lightness but prepared for seriousness. Marfa never would have stopped by this late in the day if it weren't important.

"Have you and Tom had some sort of . . . falling out?" Marfa asked her bosom friend directly.

So that's it. Something had happened to spread the news. Possibly Tom himself, wrestling with anger as he had been when he left her, had shared with his good friends Marfa and Vonnie. Soon everyone would know; no doubt it was for the best.

There was no beating around the bush with her closest friend. "Tom stopped by this morning to pick me up," Ellie began. "And it all came rising up inside and came rolling out, almost in spite of me."

"All—?"

"All my hesitations. All my fears. The impossibilities. The nightmares—"

"The nightmares, Ellie?"

"I've never told you about the nightmares, Marfa, not really, except to treat them lightly. You see—ever since the fire, ever since Aunt Tilda died, I've blamed myself—"

"Oh, Ellie!" Marfa made a convulsive move toward her friend, as if to rise and rush to her, though she was just a couple of feet away.

Ellie shook her head and put up her hand, palm out, stopping her. "I'm all right. It's nothing new to me; twelve years is a long time. The thing is, Marfa, I feel so guilty, so responsible, that it seems to have, well, warped me in some way. Much as I think of Tom—and I do; I truly do!—I can't seem to feel the love for him that a woman needs to marry. I see you and George, and I know how Tom feels. But I'm like a person set aside, seeing, and not participating. There's no use pretending anymore. Tom is in his mid-twenties; he's waited for ten years or more. I can't, I simply can't let him go on hoping when I can see no end in sight, no change in me, no change in the situation.

"I had to," she explained, turning hurt-filled eyes on her friend, "let him go. I had to make him . . . mad, so that he'd believe me. I had to make it definite."

"Well," Marfa said with a very deep sigh, almost collapsing against the back of the chair, "that would explain it."

"Explain it? Did Tom see it, tell it, differently?" Ellie asked.

"Tom said nothing." Marfa found it hard going. It was all unbelievable; it was heart-wrenching; it needed to be talked about. But Marfa found it hard to do.

"Well then?" Ellie prompted.

"Tom spent the day with Vonnie." There! It was out. Marfa looked pleadingly at her friend, as though to ask forgiveness for the words she'd said.

"Tom and Vonnie are friends, Marfa, just as Tom and you are friends—"

"Listen to me, Ellie. Tom and Vonnie were . . . were *together* today. All day."

Marfa's simple words, along with the emphasis of her voice and the desperation of her eyes, told the story very clearly. Ellie drew a long breath.

"I see," she said. And she did. Tom, weary of waiting, hurt and now hopeless, had reacted, and acted.

150

But that he had turned so quickly, so readily, to someone else—Ellie hadn't been prepared for it. And to Vonnie! It seemed now, to Ellie, that Vonnie had ever and always been there on the outer edge of Ellie's and Tom's relationship, her narrow blue eyes speculative on Tom, patient on Tom.

"I can't blame him, Marfa," Ellie said, and she firmed her voice to reflect the firming of her spirit. "After all, I can't expect anything else. I've set him free; he's got to go on and live his own life. And I'll live with it; I'll just have to live with it. It's the closing of a door."

<hr />

That night the nightmare came again. Creeping upon her like fog, silent, insidious, it spread its evil tentacles around her sleeping mind and through her somnolent soul, smothering her with its smoke before ever it flickered into flame. Engulfing her in a fury of fire before she could fight free.

Gasping, fighting for her life, Ellie struggled into wakefulness. Fortunately, her father, still curiously "not himself," had not been roused.

This time, there wasn't even the glimmer of a moon through the window. All, all was darkness, inside and out.

It was all too much: the burden, the guilt; the meaningless life—behind and before; the loss of Tom, making her more truly alone than ever; the shattering report of his near-instant rapport with Vonnie.

Ellie stuffed the pillow into her mouth, stilling her chattering teeth, while the tears ran—tears of fright, tears of hopelessness, tears of desperation.

And once again—prayer, the lifeline that was a single fragile cobweb heavenward throughout the pointlessness of her days and the apprehensions of her nights:

Oh, God—help me! Hold on to me; never let me go! Bring me out of this living nightmare and set me free!

N umb with shock, Birdie stood at the door momentarily, the
envelope in her hand. Behind her, Lydia was stiffly maneuvering her cumbersome way out of the wagon, and Herbert was
helping.

"Hold on," he was saying, followed by "Let go," while Lydia
fussed and fiddled and made numerous abortive attempts to get
herself down from the high wagon bed and do it in a ladylike way.
Finally she did indeed "let go," falling into the arms of her portly
husband. Herbert, plucky to the end, staggered but kept upright.

"Either we'll have to be more agile," he grunted, "or they'll need
to redesign these modes of conveyance. Maybe some sort of an
automatic lift . . ."

Lydia, righting herself, patted him fondly. "Not in our time,
old dear. Maybe we should cart a ladder with us everywhere we
go; ever think of that? Now if you'll just reach for those boxes,
I'll help carry them inside."

With a start, Birdie snapped from her frozen stance at the door.
Quickly she turned the knob, anxious now to get inside and destroy

the envelope before Herbert and Lydia were there to observe the strange act of burning an unopened letter.

For open it she would not. She had had enough of this foolishness. Hurrying across the linoleum to the kitchen range and preparing to thrust the envelope inside, Birdie realized the fire was out, and the envelope would not burn as she longed to see it do. No, it would only lie glaringly apparent on the grate when Herbert, any moment now, made a fire for the evening needs. Birdie intended to make no explanations.

Hearing Lydia's footsteps on the porch, Birdie turned toward the stairs and her room, the letter clutched against her body, away from Lydia's vision should she be inclined to look her way.

Closing the door to her room behind her, Birdie slowly lifted the envelope until she could see it clearly. Since it had been hand delivered, there was no stamp. Like the others it was addressed to Miss Bernadine Wharton. But this time the troublesome *t* was in its proper place in Saskatchewan. This was no surprise; of course it would be; she herself had drawn the misspelled word to the attention of that big, bungling boy Harold Buckley, perhaps the last thing she had taught him.

But Buck, according to his mother, had been gone from Bliss for over a week. How then had he managed this? A terrible foreboding presented itself: Perhaps there was some sort of alliance of boys diabolically devoted to harassing her—but that was foolish speculation. She rejected the suspicious thought and, almost with loathing, threw the envelope from her. It would take some maneuvering, but she'd find a way and a time to burn it. Silently she vowed she would never give the writer the satisfaction of reading his wretched message.

Turning to the washstand, Birdie poured water from the pitcher into the bowl, wrung out a cloth, and dabbed at her forehead, her flushed cheeks, her wrists.

What a miserable end to a pleasant day! Well on the way to making a few associations that could spell the difference between just living in Bliss or becoming a part of Bliss . . . having taken a step in the direction of getting to know folks other than on a parent-teacher level . . . finding pleasure in small talk that had no connection whatsoever to school and children, *this* had happened.

It had been interesting, at the picnic, to observe the families whose children she had taught. At times she could clearly see a connection, a similarity in behavior, seeds in the parent that might bring forth certain growth in the child. She felt she would better understand her pupils, recognizing why they behaved as they did, why they were what they were.

The Nikolai children, for instance, so independent yet so clannish. They had little individual attention from their parents and must have learned early on to make their own decisions and to look after themselves. Yet at school they stood together as a unit, defending each other, the older ones looking after the younger ones.

Ernie Battlesea, an only child and continually under his mother's watchful eye and restrictive thumb. No wonder he relished his freedom at school until he could almost be said to be out of control. Now Birdie understood, and she knew she could have more patience with the explosive little boy next year.

Victoria Dinwoody—whose prim little mouth would never soil itself by uttering a gee or a golly and who reproached those who did (what a little prig she was!)—walked and talked decorously when in her mother's line of vision, only to pinch a bottom on the sly here and there, or "accidentally" trip a fellow competitor in a race.

And then there was Nelman—Little Tiny. Over-large, to be sure, but filled with boyish enthusiasm and an energy not suspected. Perhaps that bunglesome body was not so much fat as bone and muscle; certainly it appeared so in his father, whom he strongly resembled. Birdie had watched Little Tiny with interest in a setting other than the schoolroom. Somehow she was not surprised to see him wait patiently for little Ernie Battlesea when the boys all took off for the lake and Ernie lagged, almost weeping, in the rear. She saw him receive a bowl of ice cream, only to hand it over to bent and aging Grandma Jurgensen, who was having trouble standing in line. She saw him, time and again, run to his father's side, look up, smile, say something, and dash off again to play.

And again, as previously, Birdie's heart had panged for the sweetness and the sadness of certain memories.

Big Tiny—Wilhelm Kruger—now there was a surprise if ever she had encountered one. Seeming such an oversized mass of manhood, he was remarkably fine-tuned. For such a mountain of incipient energy and force, he was amazingly controlled, like a powerful engine throttled to a mild and manageable hum. For one so massive, his movements were precise, bordering on delicacy—a pussycat of a man parading as a tiger. The man who had expressed an interest in learning was certainly as given to mind as to muscle.

Birdie's evaluation of the day and its people ceased abruptly when her gaze fell again on the bed and the envelope, innocent enough in appearance but like a coiled rattlesnake ready to inject its venom.

Prompted by anger and pain, Birdie snatched it up. About to rip it in half and tear it to shreds, she paused: The end of the story was not yet written; the last word had not been spoken. There would come a day when its pages would shout, "Wicked tormenter!" There would come a day when the letter itself would unveil and disclose the evil behind the deed. She was so sure of it that she almost wished she had kept the first two, with their evidence of the mean heart of the writer. Anonymous letters— as low as a human being could sink.

Thoughtfully she turned once again to the chiffonier. Here, in one of its drawers, she laid the incriminating letter. Turning the key, she drew a deep breath, noting only then that she was trembling.

That's that! And just as certainly as she locked the chiffonier drawer, she put a lock on all thoughts of the envelope and its cruel intentions.

Now for a good summer! Buck was gone; there'd be no more foolishness.

19

W ork. Housework, yard work, farm work. Hard as it was and
unremitting, it could be a blessing as well as a burden,
a panacea as well as an endless pressure. Perhaps it was even a
godsend.

Blessing, panacea, godsend—work, for Ellie that summer, was
all of those.

As with all homestead children, Ellie had taken her place in the
family work pattern at an early age. Before school age, boys and
girls alike had the task of filling the wood box, hunting up broody
hens and getting them back into the hen house, going for the cows
at milking time. They learned to identify weeds in the garden and
to pull them carefully, already well aware of the necessity to pre-
serve the food supply for the dreaded winter months. At six or
seven they milked their first cow, carrying pails so large and full
they flopped painfully against their shins; equally large pails of
water were trudged into the house for the reservoir, and pails
of slop were lugged out of the house to the pigs.

By ten or eleven a boy was riding a rake, gathering together the hay from the meadows and from around the sloughs; cleaning the barn; hauling stone boats of manure to the fields and unloading them; handling a pitchfork taller than himself; handing his father tools when he repaired or oiled machinery; lending a hand at countless tasks, constantly working at the side of his father, learning the ways of the farm.

Mothers taught their daughters the rudiments of housekeeping; after all, they too would be wives and mothers someday; the well-being of their family would depend on them. Baking—first biscuits, and eventually, when their small muscles could manage it, bread. Washing clothes—sorting, scrubbing, bluing, starching. Ironing—beginning with handkerchiefs and serviettes, hefting the irons around while standing on a stool, suffering many a burn, many a weary arm. Every girl knew how to milk a cow as well as her brother did, how to harness a horse, how to light a fire.

The work was there to be done, and they did it; eventually it became automatic. They put their clothes on in the morning, and they went about their chores. When they had eaten breakfast, they walked to school. Sometimes they plowed their way to school, the drifts of snow being unbroken by previous walkers or riders. They walked home or struggled home, to work again.

But not a bush child grew up without fond memories of happy times, the comfort of a warm home, the association of good friends. Not a bush child but what blessed his parents for choosing the life of a homesteader; not a child but loved Bliss and counted as home every farm within its boundaries.

Children made their own fun. They fashioned rough bows and arrows; they made their own bats and balls; they made whistles. They played tag, hide-and-seek, run-sheep-run, pom-pom-pull-away, and mother-may-I; in winter they played crokinole and checkers. They built log forts in summer and snow forts in winter. They exchanged or bartered gooseberries in the spring and hazelnuts in the fall. They made heaps of snowballs in the winter and engaged in some of the greatest battles the world had ever seen. They slid down hills on whatever was available—sleds if they were so fortunate as to have them, boards, shovels, hides. They made snow angels; they built snowmen.

In winter, by the light of a coal oil lamp and huddled close to the side of a blazing heater, they read. Bliss children were good readers. Every magazine, every book that found its way into the district went the rounds from home to home, as prized as rare gems. Puzzles were made from magazine pictures pasted on cardboard and cut into pieces; checkerboards were handmade, the pieces sawed from a small, round limb. Button boxes offered endless fascination.

Especially favored was the child who had a parent with imagination, if not skill, who could contrive gifts for Christmas—something whittled by a father, something sewn by a mother: a tiny wagon, a toy rifle, a few building blocks; a rag doll, a ball, a pair of mittens, a scarf.

Across all the years, Ellie's vivid imagination, her lively interest, her ability to make something from nothing, had been responsible for a trail of fun, frolic, experiments, and accomplishments, touching and enriching not only her own household but those of her friends. One year she and Vonnie, Marfa, and Flossy had made a gift for each Nikolai child—and there were about seven of them at that time. With many meetings and plannings and scurryings to and fro, with materials gathered and lists written and rewritten, they sewed, for the small children, something that resembled an animal (no one knew quite what it was, though the mane of yarn hinted at a lion), soft and cuddly, cut from old scraps of flannel and stuffed with batting. For the older children, various puzzles and games with enough mazes and directions to keep them absorbed for hours. The awe of the Nikolai children on Christmas morning that year could only be imagined.

Children—hardworking, inventive, imaginative—were an important part of the community, keeping hope alive with their eager spirits and never-failing expectations, bringing cheer, music, and games into the most remote cabin, and making all the hard work and effort worthwhile for the overworked homesteader.

Children were the future; children were cherished; children were important.

With no children on the Bonney farm, Ellie had it all to do herself, the small chores as well as the big ones. Time and again all day long, every day, she made trips to the woodpile or to the well. There were the chickens and turkeys to feed, the eggs to gather. Although her father did the milking, there was the milk to care for, the butter to churn. There was bread to bake—six loaves at a time. Every Monday there was the washing to do, the ironing every Tuesday. In between times there was the canning of the vegetables as the garden flourished and produced; there was the making of jams and jellies, the storing of summer's bounty in the cellar. There was the mending, the darning.

Through all the long, hard summer, Ellie was rather desperately grateful for the unrelenting round of things to do. Rising early, she worked until late and went to bed exhausted, seeking the oblivion of sleep, dreading the intrusion of the nightmares.

Bliss's summer was notable for three things: a birth, a death, a wedding.

⸺

The first was natural enough. And expected. Marfa Polchek—to the interest of the community that had first hoped, then grieved, with her and with George through three previous pregnancies—had grown increasingly uncomfortable, alarmingly puffed, reduced to a waddle, but she had remained consistently cheerful.

"Everything will be all right; you'll see," she maintained in the face of her husband's anxiety, her friends' concern, her mother's hovering solicitude. It was a confidence born out of prayer.

Marfa had been through too many disappointments, shed too many tears, to trust in luck. A casual Christian most of her life, she had, early in this pregnancy, tied the frail craft of her faith to the Rock, and there she anchored, buffeted and storm-tossed but weathering every storm.

Marfa raised a tumult of protest from people and pastor alike when she dared quote, as her scriptural portion, "Unto us a child is born, unto us a son is given" (Isa. 9:6a).

"Marfa, Marfa," one and all admonished, "don't you know that's a prophecy, a promise of Christ's coming?"

Though at first Marfa had been tempted to bristle and become defensive, she had learned to smile and to stand firm against this assault on her anchor. "But I can appropriate it for myself, can't I?" she asked, and who among them, including the pastor who was always encouraging them to stand on the promises, could tell her otherwise, expounding that certain Scriptures were not for her?

"Doesn't the Bible say," Marfa asked reasonably, "that all Scripture is given by inspiration of God? So isn't all of it available to me?"

"Well, yes," they would respond guardedly, not knowing whether this might lead to some heretical doctrine. Bliss Christians were strong on the Word and in believing in "rightly dividing the word of truth."

"And doesn't it say it is 'profitable for doctrine, for reproof, for correction, for instruction in righteousness'?"

"But," someone pointed out triumphantly, "it also says that no prophecy of the Scripture is of any private interpretation!"

Driven by their superior knowledge back to her original stand, Marfa insisted, "It says *all* Scripture, and this one is mine." And who among them could take that refuge from her? So they held their peace, while fearing and trembling for her faith should there be another dead baby and another grave in Bliss's cemetery.

As with all of them, whether in childbirth, injury, agony, or even death, Marfa had received no medical consultation, examination, or advice. For years the only help available had been from the Mounted Police medical officer, but finally a doctor had settled in Prince Albert. Poor overworked man that he was and skimpily equipped to handle the traumas of these backwoods, he was apt to be gone when a sick person struggled to his office for help or a lone rider galloped up pleading with him to put bag in buggy and hasten to a bedside many miles away.

Grandma Jurgenson, Bliss's midwife, had little confidence in doctors. "Him and his pills!" she castigated. "Thinks they'll cure everything, and they cure nothing!"

Creaky and old as she was, Grandma Jurgenson never turned a deaf ear to a plea for help. Not only was she midwife and doctor to the area but undertaker as well. And for Marfa and George she had laid out and prepared three babies for burial.

Still, called a fourth time, and though it was in the middle of the night and though she was eighty years of age, Grandma Jurgenson rose from her bed, dressed herself, picked up her bag of potions and medicines, and climbed creakily into the buggy with George.

"We'll stop and tell Ellie," George said, chirruping to the horse, whirling the buggy out of the yard and down the road. "Marfa wants her there."

Grandma Jurgenson was agreeable. She knew her days were numbered and that someone in the community would need to take on the job, a job that had fallen to her because of desperate need. She had found no way to back out ever since she had sewed up the first bull-gored farmer.

And who better to take over for her than Ellie Bonney? Hadn't Ellie, since childhood, mended every broken bird, splinted every dog that limped, soothed every tearful child, fed every wayward cat, and rescued every baby bird that tumbled from its nest?

"I'll drive myself over," Ellie told George when he came to the door. "I'll need a few minutes to get myself together and hitch up the horse."

Before she left the house, she put her head into her father's room, making an explanation and reminding him that there was a pot of beans bubbling in the oven overnight.

"I don't know how long I'll be gone," she said. "After all, it's not a first baby. . . . It could come easily and quickly."

Not so. Marfa struggled the rest of the night, struggled all day, struggled until the dawning of a new morning.

Though Grandma tried to shoo the worried George out, as was right and proper, he never left his wife's side. Fortunately there were enough young Polcheks around to take care of the chores, for those were far from George's mind.

Grandma knew all the tricks of her trade—the breathing, the pulling, the pushing. And still they were not enough. That was when Ellie, new as she was to childbirth, stepped in with her bottle of laudanum. She would not, could not, bear to see her friend suffer.

"It isn't right!" she insisted. "And surely it isn't good for her. She's worn out. Why not let her get some rest between pains? Why not lessen the pain if we can?"

Grandma Jurgenson raised her eyebrows. "It's natural," she objected. "Pain's natural. Women understand that they bear their offspring with pain; it's supposed to be that way, has been ever since Eve ate the apple."

Having respect for her elders, if not Grandma Jurgenson herself in this particular matter, Ellie bit her lip and refrained from an impatient "Oh, bosh!"

Aware of her inexperience, Ellie was careful about overriding the older woman's hard-learned expertise. But in her heart of hearts she considered herself a modern woman, beyond the old wives' tales of former years, eager for any advances in medicine or health care.

Grandma, fond of both Ellie and Marfa and more than a little uneasy about another disastrous birthing experience for Marfa, shrugged and subsided.

And, the old lady had to admit, Marfa's thrashing and struggling calmed considerably after Ellie doled out the precious soother, a "stupefier," the tincture of opium available to one and all—without oversight or restraint, as often as wanted, as much as was wanted—by an obliging catalog.

Although it may have slowed the process, it certainly made it easier. Ellie soothed her friend's fears, smoothed her forehead, rubbed her limbs—anything and everything she thought might be encouraging or helpful. And eventually nature, though grudgingly, took care of the rest.

At dawn the miracle took place—a new life was thrust, screaming and kicking, into the world. A living, breathing human being—not here one moment, here the next moment. Irrevocably here, for sixty years, give or take a few, whether good or bad, whether happy or miserable, whether loved or despised; to count for something or to count for nothing; to live a life of service or selfishness. And eventually—to reproduce in the endless cycle that was called generations.

As for now, little George Bonney Polchek was greatly desired, greatly loved, greatly blessed. Whatever he would or would not become, he started well, not something everyone can count on.

Exhausted, wan, and weak, Marfa resisted the curtain of sleep and medication that lured her to rest and held her son, cradling him on her breast, baptizing him with her tears.

And thanking God. Thanking him for the fulfillment of her Scripture.

And Ellie, almost equally weary, turned homeward. But with empty arms, empty heart.

Rest was not to be hers. Not then nor for days to come. Tears were hers in abundance.

20

Birdie was astonished on the occasion of her first goose plucking.

Knowing only that her bed was wonderfully soft and comfortable, warm and cozy, she hardly understood the reason for it, and the procedure not at all. Feathers were feathers, weren't they?

It was to be her first summer in Bliss. Waking with no school duties to look forward to, no children awaiting her instruction, Birdie had sighed luxuriously, turned over, and gone back to sleep. Rising leisurely, she found Lydia hard at work, going from one task to another like a machine. And with no end in sight. Barely was one task completed when another called. Besides the regular tasks of the well-ordered week: washing, ironing, mending, churning, cleaning, baking; and the normal routine of the day: breakfast and dish-washing, dinner and dish-washing, supper and dish-washing, and the regular chores sandwiched in between, there were the extras that could be done only during good weather and "before the snow flies." Extras such as berry picking, canning, whitewashing, curtains taken down and washed, stretched,

165

and rehung, quilts washed and dried and put away for another cold season.

And bed ticks refreshed or replaced.

Ticking, a tightly woven material almost as heavy as canvas, and almost always striped, was purchased by the bolt. Cut to the size of the mattress, it was stitched to form a bag of sorts, ready to be filled and sewn shut. There was no mystery about the ticking.

It was the feather procedure that boggled the mind of Birdie Wharton. Never again would she snuggle into a feather bed without a keen awareness of the human-and-goose cooperation it took to assure comfort and warmth; never again would she complain of the odd feather or two that managed to protrude from the ticking, to prickle and annoy.

She had never given a thought as to where and how the tick got its contents. Perhaps she had supposed the feathers were garnered every time a bird was killed, collecting slowly until enough had been saved for a tick.

While Birdie watched, Lydia produced a strange contraption she called the "goose bonnet." It was a small wickerlike cage that fit over the head and bill of a goose, and its function was to keep the goose from pinching its handler while it was being plucked. Plucking—obviously a procedure a goose resented, though it was not injured. Or so Lydia maintained.

The feather-gleaning was done when the birds were molting, losing their feathers naturally. Plucking at this time was fairly easy and wouldn't harm the bird. Or so Lydia claimed.

Getting custody of the bird itself was the hardest part, and here Birdie, after watching Lydia's fruitless efforts, offered to help.

First the geese were herded into a pen; then, one by one, they were cornered and subdued though they put up a battle, honking madly, wings flapping, necks craning, bills slashing. One almost had to get astride the broad back, Birdie discovered grimly, and clasp the silly creature with one's knees in order to clap the bonnet on it. Finally, holding the resentful creature in a tight grip, it was hefted off the ground—no small task in itself—and presented to Lydia for the plucking.

"Don't worry about them," Lydia said, noting Birdie's strained face as the birds struggled in her clutch. "I think they must appreciate help in getting the feathers off. You'll notice I don't nearly take all of them, just the ones that come off readily."

But Birdie was not convinced, and she watched sympathetically during the picking and plucking and then as the outraged bird was released to waddle its bulky and somewhat denuded body away, hastening back to its cronies, complaining loudly of its treatment and perhaps apologizing for its disheveled appearance.

"This part," Lydia said, cradling a goose and pointing out a certain area, "is called the rump, and it's covered with the best of all—fluff. That's what it's called—fluff. This on the keel," she pointed out a portion of low breast, "is good, too."

"Fluff? Keel? I never knew geese had anything but a bill and a breast. Oh, and webbed feet, of course."

"This is the nostril . . . the bean . . . the dewlap . . . the shank . . . the pinion coverts and the wing coverts—"

"Coverts?" Birdie asked, transfixed by the anatomy lesson.

"Means hidden, or sheltered." Lydia didn't know much about book learning, but she certainly knew her geese. With her hands occupied as they were, she blew upward, dislodging a feather that had settled on her nose.

A windless day had been chosen for the job; even so, feathers spread everywhere, stubbornly resistant, it seemed, to going into the sack. The choice soft and downy feathers, for pillows, were kept separate.

"They still have to be washed and dried," Lydia explained, pink of face and rather tense of mouth from her exertions.

Washing feathers? The very thought was more than a bewildered Birdie could comprehend at the moment.

And so she was relieved when Lydia, weary and wearing a festoon of goose down on her shoulders and in her hair, suggested a cup of tea.

Brushing themselves off, scrubbing the grime and oil from their hands, the two women sought the kitchen gladly and the kettle simmering there.

167

"Sit down," Birdie said, aware that Lydia, older by far, had done most of the work. Lydia sank into a chair, flexing her fingers, painful and swollen but not allowed to interfere greatly with the tasks that had to be done.

"I declare," Birdie said, getting out the teapot and swishing warm water into it, "I'll never think of a goose as just a good meal again. And I suppose I'll never see it as fully feathered and decently covered again. Somewhere in the back of my mind will be the picture of it scuttling off in high dudgeon, its backside bared ignominiously of its fluff, barnyard dignity lost forever."

"That's life, I guess," Lydia said thoughtfully. "It starts out so beautifully. Babies, of all kinds, are so adorable, so full of promise, human babies the same as animal babies. Now take that new Polchek baby—Bonney, I think they call him—"

"For Ellie."

"Yes, for her friend Ellie Bonney. No baby could be more wanted, more prized. No child will be more loved, I suppose. And yet, with the best the parents can give, with the best the world—Bliss's world, at least—has to offer, it could turn out to be a rascal, a ne'er-do-well. On the other hand, the potential for good is there, too. Just think—one day Thomas Alva Edison was just a helpless baby. Who knew, just looking at him, that he would invent the marvelous talking machine—"

"Telephone. In Greek it means a voice from afar." Birdie didn't know much about geese, but she did know her Greek.

"—and people could throw their voices miles and miles." Lydia lived for the day when she could talk to her small grandson, her dead daughter's child, on the prairie three hundred miles to the south. Three hundred miles that might as well have been three thousand, so seldom did she see him and so few and far-between were letters, particularly in winter.

"Edison had no schooling, you know," Lydia continued, "and he became a trainboy—that's what the article said, trainboy—on the *Grand Trunk* when he was twelve. From there he went on to great things, and he's still turning out those inventions—a boon to mankind. On the other hand, there was Louis Riel."

Still fresh in the memories of Northwest homesteaders was the insurrection of the Saskatchewan half-breeds under Riel, the uprising of the Indians in their own area under Beardy and One-Arrow, the attack on Fort Carlton and the battle at Duck Lake, causing great excitement all across Canada . . . the massacre at Frog Lake, the looting, the burning. Remembering, Lydia shuddered, though she had been far away in the east at the time.

"The half-breeds were afraid, of course—and rightly so—that the surveying of the country by the Dominion government would dispossess them of their land—" Birdie the teacher explained.

"And little good it did them. They all gave up, finally and forever—"

The two women were silent, recalling the execution of Louis Riel and appreciating the comparative quiet that had prevailed in the territories ever since.

"Well, we certainly wish better for the Polchek child, I'm sure," Lydia said, concluding her brief philosophical discourse.

Lydia and Birdie turned their attention to cheerier subjects, like tea and leftover scones warmed and buttered and jammed. Their tired backs relaxed, their dull eyes brightened, their spirits lifted—and all through the magic of teatime.

Lydia struggled to her feet, her brief respite over. "I'll have to do something about those feathers," she said sturdily.

Feeling guilty, Birdie rose to her feet, prepared to help.

"No, my dear, sit still. Or go read your book. After all, you pay for your board. These are my things to do."

"But—"

"I'll call on you if I need you. How's that?"

"But—"

"And thank you so much for the help with the geese. It's a once-a-year job, thank goodness. People that don't have feather beds don't worry about it, of course, though everyone needs pillows, and no one has come up with anything to take the place of goose down. Tell you what—you might like to go with me when I pick berries—chokecherries are ripening, and then there'll be cranberries. Would you like to go with me to the river to pick cranberries?

It's a pleasant experience, I think I can say. Different. I look forward to it every year."

Lydia trudged off to the completion of one more task on her list of things-to-do-before-winter, and Birdie went to her room to remove her shoes, lie back on the goose-down pillow with new appreciation, and read.

Almost reverently she picked up the first of two volumes of *Les Miserables,* "library edition, complete and unabridged, 650 pages to the volume, 10 inserted illustrations printed on plate paper, durably bound in extra silk finish cloth, stamped in gold (neatly boxed)," priced at $2.50 but offered by the catalog "our price $0.95." A bargain!

When she was finished reading them, she thought, she would have to consider carefully who would benefit from them. For pass them on she surely would; such treasures were too good to keep to one's self.

She recalled her schoolhouse conversation with Wilhelm "Big Tiny" Kruger, his mention of the fact that he read what he could put his hands on. Perhaps he would enjoy Victor Hugo.

Big Tiny had mentioned the possibility of a class in the fall. Laying the book aside for the moment, Birdie let the idea take root in her mind. And grow.

She could use her summer to contact the community. She was accustomed to walking; she'd map out the district and the farms and begin a systematic survey, making a list of those who might be interested in such a venture . . . perhaps a reading circle. . . . It could be called the Penny Reading Society *because of the penny fee, which would go toward purchasing books . . .*

Birdie's head nodded, her eyelids drooped, and she drifted off to sleep full of vague plans for the dissemination of fine literature and the flourishing of adult education in Bliss. One last, rather uneasy possibility drifted into her fading consciousness: If the plan meant letting down barriers and opening herself to the scrutiny of . . . certain people . . .

Birdie was too nearly asleep to wonder why in the world she would care about what Big Tiny Kruger might think.

Long cold winters, short hot summers—the people of the park belt were accustomed to both and adjusted their lives to fit.

In the long cold winter, small cabins were like burrows, and their occupants, like beavers in a lodge and bears in a cave, holed up for the duration. If, like the squirrel, they had hoarded and stored enough food, and if they had hauled and chopped and stacked enough wood, they made it through, self-reliant in most respects. For emergencies, there were neighbors. For encouragement, there was the pastor. For strength, there was the Bible. Winters were times of hibernation for man and beast alike.

Summers, those short hot summers, were times of feverish activity. Driven by a need to garner and to store, every man, woman, and child bent their energies toward making it through another winter.

June, July, August—the growing time for cereal grain. The time allotted was short; everyone hoped and prayed for one hundred frost-free days. That meant ceaseless efforts during every hour of the day.

Nature—so often cruel and heartless—compensated for the short growing season by ordaining long days. The sun came early, poured out its light and its strength, often fiercely, and lingered late, as though loath to allow for any rest at all before it swung into place in the east again, calling slumberers to another sixteen-hour day. People in the park belt rose at four o'clock and accomplished a day's labor by noon. No wonder the midday meal was called dinner; it had to invigorate an already overworked body with enough strength for another eight hours' work.

The land's production, under these conditions and given proper rain, could be phenomenal. "Mary, Mary, quite contrary, how does your garden grow?" a weary parent would read, putting a drowsy child to bed, knowing the answer all too well: quickly, very quickly indeed. Weeds also.

Ellie was out in the garden early, picking green beans before the sun made the task unendurable. When finished, she would take the full pan of beans to the shade of the porch for snapping, then on into the house where the jars were washed and waiting. Beans took a long time in the hot water bath; more than one home had been stricken with poisoning from a batch of undercooked or improperly sealed beans. Ellie dreaded the thought of the kitchen's heat on bean-canning days.

Yesterday she had put down sauerkraut; her shoulders had ached fiercely before enough cabbage was shredded to fill the five-gallon crock. Her mother had sprinkled coriander seed along with salt over the layers of cabbage, and Ellie followed her mother's recipe. At the last, a plate wrapped in a clean towel was placed on top and pressed down with a heavy rock. Her father took the crock to the cellar, and there, in quiet and in the dark, it would "work" until it was ready for consumption.

Tomorrow she would do pickles. As she picked the beans, her eyes wandered to the cucumbers and noted their size; she knew they were ready. "Never put pickles into vessels of brass, copper, or tin," Ellie remembered her mother warning. "Acid on metals can result in poisoning. Porcelain or granite-ware is the best." The voice of experience echoed in Ellie's memory, as it had echoed in her mother's, having heard it from her mother who heard it from her mother . . . and back and back, as long as pickles had been made, Ellie supposed.

"Make a brine that will bear up a fresh egg," her mother always advised. Heated to boiling and poured over the cucumbers, the mixture was allowed to "stand" for twenty-four hours. Then it was discarded and the whole business was to be done over again—change the vinegar, add one pint of white mustard seed, one quart of brown sugar, one half cup of white cloves . . . pickles were a hassle! "If one peck of cucumbers is more convenient to handle," her mother had jotted in the recipe, "use one-fourth the same ingredients."

A peck . . . one-fourth. Ellie sighed. Arithmetic never had been her best subject. Now she wished she had paid more attention, for truly—as her teachers had warned—there had come a time when she needed that skill.

But all that learning, all that studying—for canning? Something in Ellie rebelled; something in Ellie would far rather have been counting out pills, measuring doses of paregoric; something in her would feel more fulfilled if she were mixing powders for a headache—healing bodies, not feeding stomachs!

And yet the work, whether canning or baking or washing or weeding, had to be done. Her father counted on her. And even if she were free to do otherwise, what, where, how?

It was a dream without a chance of fulfillment; the nightmare was the reality. The work by day, the nightmare by night.

Ever since Ellie had released Tom, her nights—even when the nightmare didn't emerge full blown—were restless, as though she hovered on the verge of slipping into the torment of the nightmare itself; as if a shove, a hint, one more step, a single deep breath, would tumble her into its heat and flame. Consequently, she rose and faced her days without vigor, without her usual enthusiasm, without hope. Without a future.

Now, picking beans, filling her mind with what needed to be done rather than what had already transpired and what would never transpire, Ellie heard the sound of a passing rig—it was Tom.

173

Often and often across the years she had looked up at the sound of his passing, happy to see him, to wave, perhaps to run to intercept him, to warm herself for a few moments at his quick smile, his ready response. Now it was different, so different.

She paused, straightened her back, lifted her head and watched steadily as he came abreast of her . . . as he drove past. But she made no attempt to call, was not prepared to wave. Once and once only since their break had she done so. Driving past one day, Tom had glanced in her direction, and she had spontaneously and from old habit waved a greeting. Quickly, immediately, Tom had averted his gaze. Or so it seemed. But who was to say whether—under the brim of his old, crushed hat—he had really been looking her way? Wanting to believe the best but thinking the worst, Ellie had been forced to face the change in their relationship, to accept that it was final. As of course it was; it had only made sense to discontinue what was futile.

Tom obviously had taken her words to heart; his separation from her at church proved that—to her and to everyone else. Tom sat now with the other single men and boys of the community. Ellie could almost feel the eyes of the congregation fixed on the back of her head—partly sympathetic, mostly puzzled.

As for Tom, whether hurt or angry and certainly not understanding, he went grimly, even purposefully, through his days. He could do no less than get on with his life.

And he passed her by unseeing.

Having been her love, he would never be her friend. Sadly Ellie came to the conclusion: She had refused his love; she would have no friend in Tom Teasdale.

Still, she straightened her back and watched him as he passed. Perhaps she harbored a feeble wish that this one, having been a friend, and for so long a time, might continue in that relationship.

It seemed it was not to be so.

That afternoon, with the jars of beans finally cooling on a towel on the table and the fire allowed to die down until suppertime should demand its services again, Vonnie drove into the yard.

Though they had once been close, members of the same gang, the same Busy Bee Club, the years since school days had separated the two. Vonnie had married and moved away; letters had been infrequent. And since Vonnie returned to Bliss, a widow, to take up residence at the home farm again, their only contacts had been at church and the one reunion time at Marfa's. The busy summer had not allowed for social gatherings; perhaps in the fall . . .

All that tied Ellie and Vonnie now were memories.

And it was memories they discussed as they sat together over a pot of tea. Lemonade would have been wonderful, but alas—there were no lemons, there was no ice. But with the door open, the afternoon breeze brought a measure of comfort into the house, and tea it was.

And wasn't tea proper at any time? Certainly both Bliss-raised girls thought so. Each could recall earlier days, times of poor crops and seasons of poverty and deprivation, when tea leaves had been saved and reused until the resulting brew was scarcely tinted. But warmed milk, added bravely, gave a measure of taste, and a hint of tea and a hot cup held in a cold hand helped one cling to the idea that the finer things of life had not been forsaken and that they would, indeed, flourish again. So tea, summer or winter, was more than a gesture—it was a rite.

"This is a nice surprise," Ellie said, welcoming her friend, helping her from the buggy, handing the reins over to her father, and turning toward the house. In fact, so unusual was it that Ellie was instantly alert to its possibilities for further surprise. "We should have got together long before this. But I must admit, I'm swamped with all there is to do. Now you, Vonnie, were a housewife for several years. Did you take naturally to it?"

"Not really," Vonnie admitted, with a shrug of her slim shoulders as she took the proffered chair, sinking into it gracefully. "I could always think of so many other things that seemed more important. Mum spoiled me, I guess, growing up. I was accustomed to just slipping out from under responsibilities. And when I realized, for instance, that there wouldn't be any dinner, or supper, unless I personally got in and prepared it, and that if I wanted clean sheets on my bed I'd have to wash the dirty ones myself, well—"

Vonnie's smile was fleeting. Pretty when she was a child, Vonnie, as an adult, had a certain fey beauty about her. Always mercurial—smiling one moment, frowning the next; teasing one moment, pouting the next; kind one moment, cruel the next—her features had a way of reflecting that same fickleness. Her face could be serene and lovely, only to turn, with a change of mood, to unattractive angles, flaring nostrils, tight lips. And watching, one wondered why Vonnie had seemed anything but ugly.

"And now that you're home again," Ellie said, smiling, "I suppose it's easy to let your mum take care of you. I know I would give anything in the world to have my own mother back. I think we could visit on a different level; I'd talk about things that are important to me now but that I didn't give a moment of my time before—"

"It's good to be home," Vonnie agreed, "but after being independent, it's not the same. But believe it or not, I do try to help."

Vonnie's tanned arms attested to the fact that she wasn't being a sheltered houseplant but was indeed doing her share around the farm. Her fair hair, tied up in a becoming knot on the top of her head, the sun-touched tip of her dainty nose, were further proof of it.

"When the gardens are in and the threshing is over," Ellie offered, "we'll have some time when we can get together. Would you believe I haven't been back to see Marfa and the baby—"

"Bonney. Sounds rather feminine for a boy to me."

"If he's anything like his dad, it won't be a problem. I'm so happy for Marfa. Isn't it wonderful to see one of us happily married, with a family—"

Ellie, knowing Vonnie well, noted the change of expression, the almost unnoticeable tightening of the skin over the fine bones of her face, the flicker of her long lashes.

"I'm sorry," Ellie said quickly. "I've been thoughtless. What I mean, of course, is that—here I am, an old maid, and you . . . you have suffered the loss of your own happiness—"

With a sharp rattle Vonnie set her cup on the table. Startled momentarily, Ellie began again. "What I mean is—"

"Ellie," Vonnie said abruptly and stopped, her hands gripping the arms of the chair in which she sat, her slender body curved forward, her face set.

"Yes, Vonnie?" Ellie carefully set aside her cup and turned questioning, puzzled eyes on her childhood friend.

"Ellie . . ." With a swift motion Vonnie got to her feet, snatching the serviette from her lap and holding it tightly in one hand.

Slowly, Ellie got to her feet also, her eyes fixed on Vonnie with some apprehension. "Vonnie . . . what is it?"

After one brief, intense look into Ellie's face, Vonnie turned abruptly toward the window. There, her back turned, one hand gripping the lace curtain, the other still clutching the serviette, Vonnie spoke. Her voice high, firm, steady; without preamble or explanation, Vonnie spoke.

"Ellie, Tom has asked me to marry him."

Standing in the dust of the road, Birdie paused and studied the farmyard spread out before her. But not spread very widely, for it was a small, new homestead, recently cut out of the bush, still raw, exceedingly humble, redolent not only with the tang of fresh-cut trees but with a mysterious drift of hopes and dreams.

"Go by the Dunbars'," Lydia had suggested when Birdie started out on her mission of acquainting the district with her plan for a reading society. "Tierney Dunbar, the dear, was with us several months as a domestic, having come to Canada under the auspices of the British Emigration Society."

"I've seen her at church, I believe," Birdie said. "Scotch, aren't they—she and her husband?"

"Aye, that is, yes. See, I'm still influenced by her. The dear." Lydia spoke of her former help with fondness, and Birdie, knowing Lydia well, was certain this Tierney lass had stepped into a happy situation when she found herself settled in the Bloom household. An unbelievable story, Lydia was explaining, for Tierney and Robbie, her true love and long parted, had found each other here in the mostly vacant deep and distant depths of Canada's territories. Lydia couldn't help but dwell on it happily.

"It's what happens when your life is in the Lord's hands," she explained, concluding her account, "and when you pray about everything."

"Yes, yes," Birdie murmured rather impatiently, only to regret her abruptness when Lydia added gently, "As I do. I pray for you. Daily I pray for you."

Now, looking at the peace if not prosperity of the Dunbar farmyard, Birdie wondered if there wasn't something to this praying after all. But it was a fleeting thought, for a slim figure, appearing top heavy with a head of vibrant hair, stepped from the low doorway of the cabin, a basket in her hands, heading toward the clothesline.

Stepping briskly now, Birdie made her approach.

"Hello there!" she called.

The amazing head of auburn hair peered around the corner of a sheet, followed by a vivid face. "Oh, hello! I didn't see you . . ."

"I'm Bernadine Wharton—"

"I know who ye are. And it's most welcome y'are, too. Gi' me a moment tae get these things from the line."

Laying her things aside, Birdie began unpinning clothes, folding them, and dropping them in the basket. It was a strangely rewarding task, simple, homey, satisfying. It was a task reminiscent of other days . . . other clothes.

"There, that's it, then. Coom now, Miss Wharton—"

"Birdie, please."

"Birdie it is. An' I'm Tierney. Tierney Dunbar o' Bliss, as thought she would never be anythin' but Tierney Caulder o' Binkiebrae." Tierney sang out the name and the statement as though they were a rhapsody. Here, obviously, was a happy and fulfilled young woman. "So, coom now, Birdie Wharton, and we'll hae a cuppa together and ge' acquainted."

The cabin into which they stepped, though spotlessly clean, was barren of anything but the basic necessities of life. And some of those were in poor supply. The table and chairs were of the homemade variety, sturdy and plain; the wash basin was scarred, the bit of mirror above it chipped; the pans on the wall were somewhat battered; the range was obviously secondhand. The teapot, however, when it appeared, was porcelain graced with a spray of anemones and glowed in the rude cabin like a jewel in a coal mine.

Tierney caressed it for a moment before filling it. "'Twas a weddin' gift," she explained. "Anything here that's new or shiny was given to Robbie an' me when we got married. The district jist took me in, as they had taken Robbie in when he first came. Hae ye heard the story, Birdie? 'Twould amaze ye, that's for certain . . ."

About to promote the pending reading society and explain how it was to be funded by the pennies of the members, Birdie did some on-the-spot revising of the rules. How could she charge people like the Dunbars, for whom, she was quite sure, a penny was not easy to come by and for which so many uses could be found? Here, obviously, was a couple who would benefit from the fellowship of the society, if not the literature itself. Even while she was thinking through the adjustments, Tierney spoke, softly, jubilantly, wonderingly, telling her story, a story Birdie had largely heard from Lydia.

Having come to enlist and enroll the young Dunbars in her project, Birdie stayed to hear once again the miracle that had brought Tierney across an ocean and a continent "straight as a sparrow to its hoosie," to the one spot in the world where her heart, in dreams and prayers, had preceded her.

"'Twas the loving hand of the Father himsel' that brought it aboot," the Scotch lassie said, concluding the story but still wondering and marveling that it should all have come about.

"An' now, Birdie," she invited, "did ye have summat ye wanted to talk wi' me aboot?" Tierney, in spite of great effort, had yet to correct her accent.

Feeling that her business was humdrum and drab indeed, and entirely without any praises to the "Father himsel'," Birdie briefly explained the tentative plans for a reading society.

"Of course," she concluded, "I'll get back to you when final plans have been made. I have to see what the reaction of the community is, whether enough people will be interested, where we'll meet, and when, and all of that. I'm just doing a sort of preliminary survey at this time."

"It sounds wonderful to me," Tierney responded with some enthusiasm. "Winters here can be verra lonely; we're shut in for days at a time. Of course," she added with a glow in her eyes, "I hae Robbie."

Rather than a trial, it sounded as though winter or anytime in the small cabin was close to being heaven itself to Tierney, because Robbie was with her.

When it seemed that the young wife was about to go off into more raptures concerning her happiness and God's goodness—a happiness and a goodness about which Birdie knew nothing—Birdie began hastily collecting herself together for departure.

"Ye'll hae to coom back an' meet Robbie himsel'," Tierney invited, as though she were offering a rare treat.

Birdie stepped from the hand-sawed planks of the floor of a rustic cabin, through a handmade door, onto split-log steps, feeling as though she were leaving as warm, as blessed a nest as could be found in this great Northwest. She felt that, for a moment, she had warmed herself at another's fire.

That's the way it ought to be, her lonely heart cried out as she turned her feet toward the road and the next farm.

Very shortly she heard the clip-clop of a horse's hooves behind her and, stepping aside into the grass at the edge of the road, heard the cheerful voice of Big Tiny Kruger.

"Whoa! And is that you, Miss Wharton, out and about in the heat of the day?"

Birdie couldn't keep the pleasure from her voice (anyone would be glad for a ride, wouldn't they?), though her prim words revealed none of it.

"Why, it's Mr. Kruger, I believe. And what are you doing out like this on a busy day?"

"Just taking the week's cream to Bliss. It's carted to Prince Albert today and will spoil if I wait another week. Climb in, and I'll tell you about it."

With alacrity, Birdie stepped up into the buggy, her hat tipping a bit in the effort, a lock of hair coming loose and her cheeks pinking—surely from the small effort involved.

"I know about cream, Mr. Kruger," she said when she had seated herself, speaking rather severely, perhaps to compensate for the fact that she was a little breathless. Clutching her papers and her bag with one hand, she attempted to right her hat with the other. It didn't help her equilibrium any to look up at the big man at her side and catch—without any doubt—a keen, *noticing* look in his eye.

Startled, and not quite sure what this meant but knowing she must proceed with caution, still Birdie's heart lifted. Immediately she stifled unacceptable responses; quickly she took it for what it obviously was—a look of friendship. And yet—against her very will, in opposition to her good sense, without her permission, a frisson of pure pleasure ran through Birdie's rather gaunt frame.

"So you know about cream," Big Tiny said, a twinkle replacing the previous glint in his eyes, a glint of unknown meaning.

"I come from a small town, Mr. Kruger. A town where cows were kept behind many homes. My family had to buy its milk, but still, I knew where it came from." Birdie's tone was crisp, as though she couldn't believe she was engaged in a conversation concerning cows and their output.

"But did you know that we keep it from souring by hanging it down the well?"

"Of course," Birdie responded with some annoyance. "The Blooms, however, have an icehouse. A reasonable edifice to erect, I should think."

"To dig, you mean. It's mostly underground. And I'll have one, I suppose, in due time. When I've been here as long as, er, some people." Good, kind Big Tiny Kruger would not point out the obvious—that the Blooms had been here much longer than he and, moreover, were able to afford a hired man.

Realizing that Herbert and Lydia had arrived with money to invest and ease their way, while many homesteaders arrived with little but their bare hands for resources, gave Birdie a small sense of shame for her small dig concerning the icehouse. She thought back to the Dunbar farm and cabin—meagerly supplied, poorly furnished, hardly productive, struggling in all respects, yet bursting with everything that mattered, like hope and confidence, youth and resilience. Money wasn't everything; an icehouse wasn't the answer.

"And did you know that the selling of it supplies us with our living expense?" Big Tiny was saying, continuing their conversation. "Cream and eggs—the money they bring in is how we get by from harvest to harvest." His big fist indicated the box at his feet, a box he had removed from the seat at his side when he invited her to ride.

Big Tiny was returning from the store with a few items he couldn't raise for himself—sugar, tea, yeast, salt, baking powder. He would set these simple staples into his cupboard with a grateful heart, knowing that, once again, he had kept the shadow of starvation from his door by his own hard-won provision. What satisfaction these homesteaders must feel! Having left all things familiar and secure, striking out into the unknown to survive by the skill of one's own hands and wits—it was a moving thought to Birdie Wharton. It made her comfortable paid position seem most colorless in comparison.

"How did we get to discussing the price of cream and eggs," Big Tiny said, shaking his head, "when there's so much more to talk about? You, for instance—weren't you going to tell me why you are trudging these dusty roads when you don't need to, when school is out and you should be enjoying a well-deserved rest?"

Of course! The reading society! Birdie had found her thoughts straying far, far from the business at hand.

"You remember, Mr. Kruger, that you mentioned an interest in some kind of class, to begin in the fall, that adults might attend, learning, studying together?"

"Ya, I remember," Big Tiny said. "Have you been working on it?"

"Yes, indeed." And Birdie was off and running along lines that were familiar to her, once again the teacher, once again properly businesslike.

"My idea is to make it a reading society. We can go from book to book and subject to subject, fine literature, historical matters, even novels. That way it will be a pleasure as well as a learning tool."

"Sounds good to me," the good-natured man responded.

"But it will depend on how many people show an interest, as the Dunbars already have. I think I may count on your interest, Mr. Kruger, right?"

"Ya, of course. I'm very enthusiastic about it myself."

"It was your suggestion that put the entire thing in motion," Birdie said and wondered why it gave her such satisfaction to supply this large man with this bit of appreciation. Why did she feel such a glow about it all?

Riding along companionably, it occurred to Birdie that here, in this soft-spoken, bighearted man, she might have a friend. She—the friendless one—might have a friend. Along with the glow came a lump in her throat.

Life, indeed, seemed to be opening up for Birdie Wharton. Life in Bliss might yet be just that—blissful.

"By the way," Big Tiny said, reaching down into the box of supplies, "I picked up the Bloom mail."

Dropping the reins momentarily, which made no difference whatsoever to the plodding horse, he shuffled through the assortment of letters and papers headed for homes along his route.

"Here," he said, turning toward Birdie, a small sheaf of mail in his hand.

On top, staring her in the face—a plain, white envelope bearing her name. No stamp, obviously stuffed into the Bloom box by hand—a local epistle.

Birdie's eyes widened. For one long moment she looked at the envelope, then raised her eyes.

Big Tiny Kruger's expression seemed incongruous; holding toward her an envelope that was a cruel stab to her heart, his face was kindly, his smile open, his eyes interested.

No doubt he saw her expression; perhaps he sensed her turmoil of spirit. "It'll be good news, I'm sure," he said gently.

"We'll see about that," she said grimly. And taking it in her hand, she thrust a thumbnail under the flap and ripped the envelope open. No matter that Big Tiny was watching; no matter that she might unveil and reveal the whole miserable account of the previous letters. Birdie had had enough. Without care for the repercussions and with a certain fury, she dragged forth one white sheet, opened it, scanned it . . . and blinked.

Blinked several times, frowned, read more slowly:

> The spacious firmament on high,
> With all the blue ethereal sky,
> And spangled heavens, a shining frame,
> Their great Original proclaim.

> Joseph Addison, 1712

She read it once; she read it twice. Then, stupidly, she read it a third time. Expecting some tommyrot from Buck or perhaps one of his brothers, she couldn't immediately grasp the beauty of the scribbled quotation. Even the quick reading, with her mind half on the poem, half on her questions concerning it, the wonder of it gripped her; the meaning of it demanded earnest thought and study, perhaps memorization.

When, dazed, she looked up, it was to find Big Tiny's blue eyes—from underneath his black mop of hair and above his black mop of beard—twinkling down at her like two stars in a dark night.

Slowly she folded the paper; slowly she inserted it into the envelope.

"Well?" Big Tiny questioned.

"It's . . . it's nothing. That is . . ."

"It's not upsetting, then?" he probed, possibly worried on her behalf. "Not unwelcome——?"

"No. No . . . I think it may be . . . rather . . . good news."

"That's good, then." And Big Tiny turned his attention to his driving.

Staring off into Saskatchewan's "blue ethereal sky," her heart struck by the thought of the Originator of it and all the other beauty around her, and someone's——some unknown someone's—— concern to bring it to her attention, Birdie's hat slipped again, and the recalcitrant curl escaped and her color heightened, and she knew it not, nor cared.

23

If her cup had been full, Ellie would have scalded herself, so startled was she and so violent was her reaction upon hearing Vonnie's announcement: Tom had asked her to marry him.

But her teacup was almost empty. And, thankfully, Vonnie was not watching; her back was turned as she gazed, seemingly intently, out of the window at nothing any more fascinating than the familiar farmyard.

Carefully, as though in a dream (or was this another nightmare?), Ellie set her cup aside, dabbed automatically at her trembling lips with her serviette, and spoke. Spoke in as calm a tone as though Vonnie had announced that a chicken had escaped the hen house. And the words she spoke were casual, as though chickens escaped the hen house every day; the tone was conversational, as though a chicken's flight was an incident not unexpected, certainly not to be worried about.

"Well then, I wish Tom, and you . . ."—though Vonnie hadn't said, Ellie had no doubt that she had accepted the proposal—"much happiness."

Now Vonnie turned from her study of the farmyard—or the bush, or the sky, whatever she had fixed her attention upon while she had, simply and starkly, blown Ellie's world to smithereens.

"We're planning a quiet wedding," she said rapidly, fixing Ellie now with her light blue gaze. "After all, I haven't been a widow for very long, and Tom—well, Tom's been ready for marriage for a long time. That is, his place is ready . . . his house—"

Vonnie, for all her outward aplomb, was actually stumbling.

But was his heart ready? Ellie, though her lips spoke proper words, was having trouble with her thoughts, which were wildly scattered. Was Tom really and truly heart-free and ready to turn from one love to another? Or was he acting from hurt, rashly? And would he live to regret the day and the decision?

Caring for Tom as she did, as she always would, yet not enslaved by him or by the need to keep him tethered to her, Ellie may have been more troubled than torn, more filled with sympathy than sorrow.

And yet the haste with which he had made the transfer of his interest couldn't help but sting—one more wound that would need the Lord's healing. Along with the nightmares, Ellie laid the fresh hurt, almost a humiliation, at the Father's—her heavenly Father's—feet. If there was healing for the one wound, there was healing for the other. It was all that made the future—the long, chill winter, for body and soul—livable.

Still, when Vonnie left, with cheeks ablaze and a triumph in her eyes that she couldn't hide, perhaps didn't care to, there was for Ellie the refuge of her earthly father readily available to her.

She sat at his feet, her head on his knee as he rocked gently in his old chair at the side of a dead fire, his rough hand caressing her head, soothing her brow, and her choked voice poured out the story. Bran had known, of course, that Tom hadn't been coming around, that Ellie was ominously silent concerning him, and that things between them were not as they had been. Now Ellie explained, to some extent, and Bran listened gravely.

"I know," she said finally, "in my heart of hearts I know I made the right decision—for me, for Tom. And yet it hurts that he could turn so quickly to . . . someone else." Especially to Vonnie, was the unspoken accusation.

"If you're sure—" her father said hesitantly, wanting her happiness above all.

"You see, Dad, there was no future for us," she rather dully summed up. "I'd held on to an empty dream for too many years—"

"I don't understand, have never understood," her father said with a sigh, "why you can't just settle down and marry and be happy. But that there's some obstacle I understand, though you've never wanted to . . . or been able to . . . put it into words. That's all right," he insisted loyally as Ellie's eyes squinched shut in the secret pain she had harbored for years. "Your business is your business, and you don't need to make explanations to anyone if you don't want to. But where will it end, Elliegirl? How will it all end? I won't," he added gently, "always be here."

"Only God knows," Ellie said, her voice muffled against her father's overalled knee. "But I feel, in some ways I feel as though I've taken a step out of darkness. And yet I can't see ahead."

"One step at a time," Bran confirmed, "is all you need. It seems God is at work. We'll watch for the next step."

All too soon—the next step.

That night the nightmare returned in full force. And this time there was no silencing the struggle Ellie went through—experiencing the fire and the smoke and attempting to escape it—and she had desperate need of her fathers. Her earthly father, hearing her cries, hastened to her side to shake her awake, put his arms around her, and comfort her. Her heavenly Father, ever present, ever loving, also put His arms around her, to bring her to the dawning.

"I'm all right, Papa," she managed at last, the soother rather than the soothed. For Bran Bonney, on his knees at his daughter's bedside, was groaning in his helplessness, with unaccustomed tears wetting his cheeks.

"It's all right, Ellie," her heavenly Father murmured, as she moaned in her helplessness and fear and with accustomed tears dampening her cheeks.

Comforted by both fathers, earthly and heavenly, Ellie went back to sleep. Nothing could be so bad but what, with her fathers, she could make it.

Breakfast was ready; coffee was bubbling in the old granite pot; oatmeal was simmering; toast awaited, browned and buttered, in the warming oven. Bran, for some reason, was delayed at the barn.

Pouring herself a cup of coffee and adding cream—the only thing that made it palatable to Ellie, a true tea drinker—she sat down beside the window, opening her Bible, needing its solace, perhaps its confirmation regarding the direction her life was taking. Sometimes she felt so alone, walking, as it were, a strange path far removed from the accepted and recognized way, a path that led . . . she knew not where.

"Fear not: for I have redeemed thee, I have called thee by thy name; thou art mine" (Isa. 43:1b), she read.

How comforting! Indeed, God had seemed to call her by name in the night, assuring her He knew where she was. Perhaps, even, where she was going. Encouraged, she read the next verse: "When thou passest through the waters, I will be with thee; and through the rivers, they shall not overflow thee—"Yes! Yes! Yes! One could lie back in the Father's arms and rest, *float* through the deep waters of life. ". . . when thou walkest through the fire, thou shalt not be burned; neither shall the flame kindle upon thee"!

As lightning strikes a tender stalk of wheat, so God's Word—personal, pungent, apropos—pierced the trembling heart of the reader.

Unable to talk to any human being, and seldom to God, about the tragedy that had taken old Aunt Tilda's life and the burden of responsibility that had settled on her, hampering and hindering her life, she understood, at last, that the Lord had known, had cared, all the time. Into Ellie's mind sprang the chorus of a familiar hymn: "Some thru the waters, some thru the flood, some thru the fire, but all thru the blood . . ."

Having been through the blood, Ellie would trust her heavenly Father through the fire.

It was with a lighter heart than she had known for some time that she arose, ready to go about the day's duties.

But Papa—where was Papa?

When it seemed the porridge must simmer to a thick goo and the coffee to a black and bitter brew, Ellie went to the door, searching for some sign of her father's whereabouts. And saw nothing.

Stepping out, Ellie raised her voice and called, "Dad! Breakfast's ready!"

Nothing.

Quickly now, impatiently, Ellie stepped off the porch and headed in the direction of the cow barn; the cows had not been turned out, so she knew the milking was not completed.

Ellie paused in the doorway of the low building, taking in at a glance the six milk cows in the shadows of their stalls, three to a side. The sun streamed through the wide door and illuminated the walkway in the center. In that spot of sunshine, beside a tipped pail of milk and Wrinkles the cat daintily sipping—lay a darkly huddled and motionless figure. Papa!

With a cry, Ellie sped to his side. Kneeling in the noisome mix of the cow barn, she grasped her father's shoulder, tugged and turned him, while Wrinkles mewed and moved away, to sit and lift a milk-covered paw to his tongue for a fastidious cleansing.

The exposed face was flesh and bone only, all life having fled. And though the flesh and bone were dearly loved and cherished, Bran Bonney was gone. With his departure had gone the animation, the expression, the reason, the spark that made him unique. All, all had fled when the man Bran Bonney forsook his earthly tabernacle for his heavenly.

Having helped at deathbeds and burials, Ellie knew death when she saw it. Gently she laid this stranger's—this beloved stranger's—

head back, back onto the ragged bit of straw that was his temporary bier.

The cat ceased his ablutions, ambled over, tail aloft and waving, to rub against the bowed figure. Automatically a hand went to the silky head; piteously the broken voice cried:

"Oh, Wrinkles! Whatever shall we do now!"

24

Without an axe you were nothing. Homesteaders, heading into the bush, were advised to have two of them, perhaps three. For if one should break or be lost, and you had no replacement, life was at a standstill.

Clearing the bush was hard. And yet it had to be done to prove up the land. Every man jack of them—coming to farm, to grow grain, to make his livelihood—worked harder at it than he could have imagined. Swinging an axe from dawn till dark was hard, hard work and was only accomplished grimly. It was a hard land; it was a hard life.

On the prairie, if there was any chopping to be done, it was just willow roots, and then one could put in the plow, sow, and reap. In the park belt, called the parkland, there were trees to contend with, thick stands of trees: pine, cottonwood, poplar, birch, all intertwined with bush—hazel, pin cherry, chokecherry, willows—until you couldn't see fifteen feet. At the end of a day's work, you still faced the same near-impenetrable tangle of growth to be tackled on the morrow. Exhausted, the hewer and chopper and digger of stumps fell into bed.

Men gave up, succumbed, overcome by the harshness of the bush. The weak wilted, overwhelmed with the struggle against early frost, hail, drought, flies, climate extremes, and trees, trees, trees. For those men who endured, the hardships left their mark; slowly their bodies bent, their hands twisted, their skin darkened and hardened, their eyes lost their sparkle. And yet, if you looked closely, those eyes were filled with a quiet determination. Falter, maybe, but go on they would, revived again with the advent of spring and the possibility of a good crop.

Struggle—the name of the game. In early days it was between man and the elements as he came in pursuit of furs; then it was between the invading white man and the native; then between the immigrant and the soil. From it all was born a people of resilience, tough, resourceful.

And friendly. As Birdie walked the dusty roads and byways of Bliss, it was often to the ring of the axe as homesteader after homesteader spent his day and his strength in clearing his land. And yet he would pause to wave, to speak, to listen. A warm invitation would be given to stop in at the house and get acquainted with "the wife." Birdie encountered not one rude or impatient person along her route. Her admiration for the homesteader grew, as did her understanding of the unimaginable obstacles each had grappled with and was still grappling.

She spent an interesting thirty minutes with Marfa at the Polchek homestead. George, clearing land with a couple of younger brothers, had paused, wiped his brow, leaned on his axe, and waved as Birdie passed by, heading toward the cabin set back from the road, almost hidden in bush.

"Come in, come in," Marfa urged, holding open the screen door with one hand and cradling the baby with the other. Her gaping dress revealed her present occupation—nursing small Bonney. The young Polcheks had waited too long for his appearance to be anything but attentive to his every need.

"I'm so glad you've come," Marfa said, settling herself in a rocking chair after seating her guest and automatically pulling the teakettle from the back of the range to the hot front lids. "I'm glad we had a chance to get acquainted at the picnic, but there's so much more to talk about. I've been out of commission for a while due to the baby's birth and all. But I hear there's a possibility Bliss may have its own Penny Reading Society. Is that right?"

Thrust into it, Birdie had no trouble enlarging on the reason for her call. "I don't know whether or not we can call it a Penny Reading Society," she explained eventually, "because small though that cost is, it may make it difficult for some folks."

"You're right, of course. Sometimes we don't have two cents to rub together," Marfa admitted ruefully, herself appearing well-fed and contented, and small Bonney the picture of health and happiness.

"Do you have any preference concerning what we should read?" Birdie asked. "And do you have any books you'd care to submit to the group? For borrowing purposes, of course. I thought it would be a good idea to distribute what material we can, for additional reading at home."

Marfa looked doubtfully toward a small shelf of books. "Most of mine are already borrowed," she said, "and have been the rounds. But yes, they can be handed out again and yet again. Just step over there, if you wish, and take a look."

Birdie did as invited. "Shakespeare!" she said, eyebrows lifting as she noted *Macbeth.*

"Yes, and perhaps you can be the one to interpret him for us."

Birdie lifted the slim volume and opened it. Someone had underlined it in numerous places. She read:

> If you can look into the seeds of time,
> And say which grain will grow and which will not,
> Speak.

"It seems to me that some of it doesn't need interpreting," she said thoughtfully as she turned to the first page, which was inscribed "W. N. Kruger."

Birdie hadn't supposed Big Tiny, Wilhelm Nelman Kruger, to be a thoughtful man. But she had no time to wonder further, for with an exclamation Marfa was buttoning up the bodice of her gown.

"Someone's coming, and I think it may be Vonnie," she said. "Would you be kind enough to take wee Bonney for a moment? Just until he belches—"

Setting the book on the table, Birdie reached for the baby, somehow positioned him over her shoulder, and automatically, as though she'd done it all her life, began the timeworn practice of jiggling and patting. Marfa was hastily adding wood to the range, obviously with the intent to make tea.

"Yoo hoo, it's me!" Vonnie's light voice sang out as she put her face to the screen and peered inside.

"Come on in!" Marfa invited, hurrying toward the newcomer and ushering her in and to a seat.

"No tea, please," Vonnie said, noting Marfa's efforts and fanning herself.

"You remember Birdie Wharton? From the picnic? Bliss's teacher?" Marfa asked.

"Of course. Good afternoon, Miss Wharton. Do sit down, Marfa. It's too hot to flutter around so. I've come for a very particular reason." Vonnie's eyes sparkled, and she smiled delectably. "A very particular reason."

"Well, then . . ." Marfa responded and took a seat, looking doubtfully at Birdie and the baby.

Bonney chose just then to emit a fine and satisfactory belch. Marfa smiled fondly, and Birdie, pleased at the success of her ministrations, continued standing, rocking back and forth slightly, humming inaudibly in the soft ear pressed against her lips.

Vonnie paused, a bit impatient perhaps, allowing time for attention to turn from the baby to herself.

"Yes, Vonnie?" Marfa asked.

"*Tom and I are getting married!*" Vonnie had leaned forward in her chair and spoke in rapturous tones. If she had expected hand-clapping or huzzahs, she was disappointed, for her announcement was followed by silence. Even Birdie, sensing the dramatic, ceased her humming and turned toward the pair sitting at the side of the oaken table. Marfa was staring, wide-eyed and open-mouthed, at her guest.

Vonnie's laughter was a trill of triumph. "Don't look so astonished!" she said.

"You and . . . who?" Marfa asked.

"Tom! Tom Teasdale! Surely you guessed, the day of the picnic, that something was going on!"

"No, no, I didn't," Marfa said slowly. "After all, Tom's been our friend for a long—"

"Well, it's gone beyond friendship now, I can assure you," Vonnie said firmly. "And—"

Was Vonnie a little defensive? A bit too emphatic? Even Birdie, not knowing her well and all at sea concerning whatever currents were surging between the two young women, sensed it.

"And," Vonnie continued, "we're not waiting to get married. After all, it's the custom here—women don't wait long, don't have a chance to wait. There's always someone begging marriage. I've had several other opportunities. As for Tom, we all know he's long overdue to have a wife and a home of his own.

"Well, anyway," she said when the silence dragged on, "I've come to ask if you'll stand up with me."

Another silence. An uncomfortable silence.

Vonnie sighed and leaned back. "I know you very well, Marfa," she said. "Your first thought is for Ellie. I never could compete with your affection for Ellie, though I never understood why. Well, I've talked with Ellie—"

"And what did she have to say?"

"Not much. What can she say? She's freely given him up. I think, myself, he should have been freed a long time ago. Poor guy—tied as it were. Well, he's grasped the fact now that he's free. What did she say? Just wished us happiness. Can you do the same?"

"I, I'm not sure, Vonnie. I'll have to . . ." Marfa's voice faded away while she grappled with the news.

"You'll have to talk to Ellie. That's it, isn't it?"

"I suppose so. It's a . . . a very awkward place to be in. I'm not sure I can see happiness ahead for you and Tom. And feeling that way, it would spoil the day, not only for me but for you. For, as you say, you know me well."

"Oh, for heaven's sake!" Vonnie erupted, rising to her feet impatiently. "Just forget it, Marfa! I might have known! Marfa and Ellie—always sticking together! Well, never mind, if you're that reluctant. I'll try and see if Flossy can come home; she'll stand up with me, I'm sure. And if Flossy can't make it, then—how about you, Miss Wharton?"

Birdie, startled, looked up from her contemplation of baby Bonney's tiny fingers. "Oh, no, thank you. I . . . I don't think—"

"Never mind. It was just a thought. Someone'll do it—maybe Molly or one of the Nikolai girls; there are always several of them still around, though the ones I knew are all married and gone, I suppose. Maybe I'll ask my mother to do it. But it would have been *nice* if one of my friends—"

"I'm sorry, Vonnie," Marfa said miserably. "I'm sure, after I get used to the idea, I'll be able to wholeheartedly wish you and . . . and Tom every happiness."

"Thank you; I'm sure we'll be very happy."

"When is the wedding taking place?" *Gracious!* Though the exclamation never passed Marfa's lips, her face spoke for her. Speaking calmly, she looked dismayed.

"Sunday after next," Vonnie continued imperturbably. "We've talked with Parker Jones and have it all set up. It'll be at my parents' place, of course, with just a few friends and family members present. Do you think," Vonnie's blue eyes had a certain pleading in them, "you could at least come?"

"I'll come, Vonnie. Of course I'll come. It's just that—"

"Say no more." Vonnie, in her mercurial way already forgetting her chagrin, was all smiles and spoke lightly, "I understand."

Marfa saw Vonnie out the door and turned, speechless and shaking her head, to take wee Bonney from Birdie.

Just before Birdie put *Macbeth* back on the shelf, the book fell open, and she read, "So foul and so fair a day I have not seen."

25

In wagon after wagon, buggy after buggy, they came. No matter that the day had a hundred other things—important things, life-changing and life-preserving things—to do, they came.

One after another they pulled into the Bonney yard, eventually filling it and overflowing onto the road itself. From each rig sober, Sunday-dressed people climbed to make their way gravely toward the yard in back of the house, some of them with flowers from gardens or garnered by the roadside to set in Mason jars as humble love offerings to the departed man and his grieving daughter. Here, on sawhorses—not far from the house he had built on one side, the barns he had erected on the other—had been placed the handmade coffin containing the final remains of Brandon Bonney, neighbor and friend. A fitting epitaph, more than one person thought somberly, would have been, "Worked himself to death."

Around the makeshift bier had been placed the home's few chairs. Boards laid over kegs and crates made additional seats, and here the elderly and the ailing were placed. Behind them, standing and pressing close—the remainder of Bliss's people.

Sitting up front—the one and only remaining member of the Bonney family—daughter Ellie. If there were other relatives, they were too far away to have received word of Brandon's death, let alone make the trek west for the occasion of his burial. Funerals were conducted with dispatch in the summer. And still it was better, many vowed—having lived through a winter death—than placing your loved one in cold and lonely isolation in a barn or granary to await the spring thaw when the ground would yield reluctantly to the shovel. Better a hasty burial than the torment of long months of waiting.

At Ellie's side and, at times, gripping her hand, her friend Marfa. If there were those who wondered why Vonnie, another member of their well-remembered "gang," was not with them, they didn't wonder for long. In the back of the crowd, standing close together—Vonnie and Tom Teasdale. Tom's face, in the bright morning sun, showed white through the summer tan. Difficult as it may have been to come, there was no way to ignore the funeral of a man who had been close to him across the years, and Tom, grimly perhaps, came to show his respect. Why Vonnie, in this hour of her friend's grief, had not chosen to be by her side was a troubling question in the minds of some, plainly understood by others. Vonnie, everyone knew, could be dependable and sympathetic at one time, coldly uncaring at another.

Parker Jones, pastor to this group of people who were isolated by their own choice, dying far, far from home and family, drew the little band together for one more farewell.

But Brandon Bonney—overworked, under-paid, worn out too young—was not to go in defeat. Rather, triumphantly, the overcomer rather than the overcome, the victor rather than the victim. "I have fought a good fight, I have finished my course, I have kept the faith" (2 Tim. 4:7), the pastor read.

"And that," Parker Jones said sincerely, "says it all."

Still, he enlarged on the good fight that Brandon Bonney, and all of them, had been and were still engaged in. He confirmed the way in which the departed one had been committed to his faith. He rejoiced in the comfort of "Henceforth there is laid up for me a crown of righteousness, which the Lord, the righteous judge, shall give me at that day" (v. 8).

"'. . . and not to me only,'" the minister concluded with such confidence that those listening—the bent, the broken, the struggling, the deprived of this world's goods—felt a surge of gladness as an amen rose in their spirits, "'but unto all them also that love his appearing.'" Such comfort! And how good to be reminded of it. There would be a day when the final harvest would be in. And God, being faithful, as He always has been and always will be, would gather the precious sheaves to Himself. It was their confidence and their hope.

There was the long and cheerless ride to the cemetery, the dusty line extending half a mile as, one after the other, worn and weary rigs followed the wagon, a rude catafalque bearing the coffin and the final remains of Bran Bonney.

There was the committal as the coffin was lowered into place; Brandon and Serena would lie side by side once more.

There was the ride, less dismal this time, back to the Bonney home where kind neighbors had a generous repast ready for the mourners. There were the final hugs and assurances of prayer—"Just let me know how I can help." There were the final tears.

And then Ellie was alone.

Before the silence in the house became unbearable, Ellie grimly and steadfastly changed her clothes, donning work gear. The silence in the barn was no better. Desperately Ellie set about the chores.

When at last, weary to the bone and emotionally exhausted, she pulled the covers over her head and went to sleep, it was only to plunge into the nightmare. As often as she had experienced it, the fear and horror hadn't abated over the years; the sound of the fire and the sight of the flames were as vivid as the first time it happened, the struggle to waken just as convulsive. But this time, there were no loving arms to go around her, no soothing voice calling her from the nightmare's chilling grip to blessed release.

203

Papa! . . . Papa! . . . Father! . . . Heavenly Father.

Though the arms of the one were denied her, the everlasting arms were faithful. In them she sobbed out her fear, her heartbreak, her anguish, her loneliness, and found herself not alone after all, not helpless, and not hopeless.

⸎

The wedding of Tom Teasdale and Vonnie Whinnery took place as scheduled. Because of the haste, and because Vonnie was such a recent widow, it was done privately, with only family members and a few invited friends present. Ellie's bereavement had neatly settled, for Vonnie, the problem of whether her childhood friend should be invited, and, for Ellie, the problem of how to refuse such an invitation.

Having been urged to come and having said she would, Marfa attended with George and baby Bonney. Throughout the entire ceremony Marfa was sadly torn, even feeling a certain anxious disloyalty to her dear friend Ellie. Consequently, when next they met, Marfa could only ignore the subject of the wedding with guilt, and this she could not abide.

"Shall I tell you about it, or not?" Marfa asked, not knowing what Ellie would prefer or expect and wanting to do the right thing.

"Yes, tell me," Ellie said quietly. "I might as well know as wonder, conjuring up all sorts of scenes. Though I try not to."

"Well, Flossy came, after all, and stood up with her. Yanni Nikolai stood up with Tom."

"It's been so long since I've seen Flossy. I wish she might have stayed over."

"She brought her baby with her. There are three more at home, she said. She looked a little worn, I thought. She said to give you her love."

"Dear Flossy. She meant so much to the three of us, in her quiet way, and I do miss her."

"There's really not much else to tell," Marfa said. "They stood up in the front room and Parker Jones married them. Vonnie was, I suppose you'd say she glowed. And Tom . . ."

"And Tom, Marfa?"

"Tom was Tom. Rather more quiet than might have been expected, I thought, but with no halting or stumbling, either. Vonnie was vivacious enough for both of them."

"I can picture her quite clearly. Vonnie glows magnificently. Not only her eyes but her skin, though that's hard to imagine. Looking back, Marfa, I think Vonnie has had special feelings for Tom for years. Those looks she gave him from time to time, even as a child, were very . . . well, telling, is the word. They said a lot."

"Tom always took it casually, just sort of basked in the interest and adoration of all four of us. We all felt he was the most special boy on earth. But we knew, right from the beginning, who his favorite was."

Ellie, remembering, drew a deep breath. "The good old days, I suppose."

"When Parker Jones asked if there was anyone who knew any reason why Vonnie and Tom should not be joined in marriage, I . . ."

"You what, Marfa?"

Marfa looked uncomfortable. "I wanted to speak up. I wanted to say, 'Yes, there's plenty of reason!' I wanted to say, 'Tom loves someone else!'"

"I'm glad you kept quiet. I believe—if Tom did love me—it's faded, or at least fading. And that's good, Marfa. I don't want him going through life grieving over a lost love. Neither would I want to cast any kind of a shadow on his marriage or stand in the way of his happiness. When I made my decision, it was the right one. And if it's right for me, it's got to be right for Tom."

Marfa sighed. "I suppose so. Well, he's got a lot of years to be happy about his decision, or regret it. But what about you, Ellie? I worry so—"

"Well, don't. The future looks pretty blank right now, of course, but just before Dad died he said something that has stayed with me—he said, 'God is working.' He said, 'Watch for the next step.' And right away there were two steps—his death and this marriage.

I'm holding on to the fact that the steps will come in the right order and at the right time."

It seemed frail hope to Marfa, whose practical side wanted something more substantial.

"It keeps me wondering—what next." Ellie managed to sound cheerful.

Marfa sighed. "And in the meantime, you'll try and hang on here, Ellie? Doing the chores and all? It seems too much to ask of a woman. You've never done much outside work."

"Other women have done it, Marfa. I'll keep up with the day-by-day chores—the milking, the hens, the pigs, the garden. I'll have to see about someone to help with the harder things, like getting up the hay, the wood, and so on. Especially the threshing. I admit the thought of threshing gives me the chills." Ellie's voice trailed off. In spite of her insistence that she could carry on, what she was contemplating seemed insurmountable, impossible.

God would, indeed, need to come through with a next step.

26

The summer fled by, for Birdie as well as for all those more passionately involved in preparing for the coming winter. Her preparations for the opening of school seemed simple compared to the efforts being expended by the rest of Bliss's people and by all homesteaders across the vast expanse of the Canadian Territories—physical efforts, exhausting, dawn-to-dark physical efforts.

Sporadically, she helped Lydia with the workload that had that good lady overwhelmed. How she kept working, Birdie sometimes wondered, for her hands were twisted with rheumatism, and her slow gait indicated, at times, that her feet fared just as poorly.

The trip to the river had been a special day; Tierney Dunbar, whom Lydia loved as a daughter, went with them. The wagon, rattling across Bliss and filled with happy conversation, finally came to rest at a spot Lydia—who knew the area—deemed best for their purpose of locating and picking the highbush cranberries.

Here they clambered down, tied the team to a nearby bush, and prepared to invade the rampant growth that bordered the river.

Lydia was distracted momentarily when she spotted a few berries she identified as bearberry. "Or kinnikinnick," she said.

"I've heard of it. The Indians smoke it, don't they?" Birdie asked.

"They do, drying it and mixing it with sumac and willow leaves and, I believe, the inner bark of the dogwood. I guess it's no stranger than the white man and his tobacco!

"It has the most unusual tiny pink and white urn-shaped flowers that grow in clusters among the leathery leaves. The Indians boil the plant for tea. But," Lydia said skeptically, devoted to her aromatic beverage, "I can't say it would be a good substitute."

"Why," Tierney asked suddenly, suspiciously, "is it called bearberry?"

"Just as you'd suppose," Lydia said, looking around carefully. "Because bears like to feast on them."

Although bears largely had retreated northward with the invasion of the homesteader, encounters with them were not unheard of. Sobered by the possibility, Lydia, Tierney, and Birdie proceeded with caution.

With syrup pails cinched around their waists by a piece of twine and wide-brimmed hats securely fastened on their heads, protection from the thrusting bush they would encounter, the three made their way toward the river and were not long in locating a flourishing cranberry thicket. The girls, never having encountered highbush cranberries before, were delighted to find them hanging in clusters, able to be stripped off readily, a handful at a time. Pails filled rapidly; again and again Birdie and Tierney trudged back to the wagon to empty them into the boxes they had brought with them, saving Lydia the extra effort.

"It's a blessing we're in the bush," Birdie remarked, pausing to wipe her forehead. "Fancy what it would be like without the shade while we do this."

"We can dabble our feet in the river, if we wish," Lydia said, "but one has to be careful. It's a river to be wary of. Besides, here it runs between such deep escarpments it makes dabbling a risky business."

Dabbling, consequently, was rejected in favor of a rest in the shade while they ate the sandwiches they had brought with them, the bright, flavorful tomatoes, and the crisp cucumber slices.

It was then Tierney, flushing prettily and stumbling somewhat in her speech, shared her news.

"Ye'll be the first to know," she said, "other than Robbie, of course . . ."

"Yes? Yes?" Lydia, an incorrigible lover of news, asked urgently.

"Weel, I'm goin' to . . . that is, Robbie and me, we're havin' a babby."

Lydia's and Birdie's responses were wonderfully gratifying. Their oohs and ahs and other exclamations of approval and delight would have impressed any skeptic of the blissfulness of things maternal.

"And to think," Lydia said reproachfully, "we let you carry those pails of berries."

"I'm pairfectly healthy an' strong," Tierney assured her.

"Still, you should be more careful . . ." and Lydia delivered a small sermon on prenatal care, a topic largely ignored by reason of the heavy cares and responsibilities of life in the bush. No one in the bush had time nor inclination to pamper herself, and women carried on as usual whether sick or, in this case, pregnant, often working themselves into the grave. That it should not happen to "her" Tierney, Lydia was adamantly insistent.

"We'll hae to build on to our hoosie," Tierney said practically, changing the subject wisely, "but thass a guid thing; we need more room."

The remainder of day—picking until their boxes were full and then driving home—was filled with excited talk concerning the arrival of the newcomer.

"I'd like to think I'm about to be a grandmother again," Lydia said wistfully, her only grandchild far away on the distant prairie, and Tierney promptly confirmed it.

"With me own mither dead and me da too, this puir bairn'll need a grandmither." With that spate of Scots rolling forth, Tierney subsided and made an effort to speak more plainly again.

Tierney was dropped off at home, with the assurance of jars from the Bloom supply, and reluctantly giving over to Birdie the task of lugging a box of cranberries into the cabin. Birdie and Lydia made their weary way homeward, a little sunburnt, greatly mussed, somewhat dusty, and fully satisfied with their day away from humdrum tasks. It was too late, of course, to start the canning, so the cranberries were taken to the cellar to await the morrow and renewed strength and dedication to the task.

Though Herbert was absent from the house, obviously busy elsewhere on the Bloom homestead, someone had been to the post office and dropped off the mail. Spread out on the kitchen table were several papers, a letter from Buster, Lydia's and Herb's grandson, and—Birdie's heart quickened—a plain, white, unstamped envelope for her. Picking it up quickly, she slipped it into her pocket.

Soon she said casually, "I'll go on up and clean up," and she disappeared up the stairs to her room. Lydia, sharp-eyed and sharp-witted, noted the letter, observed the shifty hiding of it, understood the seemingly leisurely escape. With a shake of her gray head she went about her own wash-up and change of clothes.

Kicking off her shoes, Birdie dropped on the side of the bed and—it must be confessed—with a certain flutter to her pulses and a spark of interest she couldn't quell, opened the envelope.

As with the last one, it contained a few lines that, at first glance, revealed it to be another quotation. A closer look seemed to confirm that it was done by the same hand that had printed the other a few weeks previously.

With a strange mix of curiosity and dread—curiosity about the contents, dread that it might be a disappointment, she read:

> Through the dark and stormy night
> Faith holds a feeble light
> Up the blackness streaking;
> Knowing God's own time is best,
> In patient hope I rest
> For the full day-breaking.
>
> —John Greenleaf Whittier

Her breath caught in her throat. How beautiful! How expressive! How . . . pertinent. As though chosen for her. Was there someone—some sensitive someone—out there, watching, caring, tuned to her private, inner person? And comprehending enough to offer the encouragement of sentiments such as these? And such beautifully expressed sentiments! What a choice person this must be.

Wanting desperately to know who it was, it was wonderful *not* knowing. To know would spoil it; to know would put the burden of response on her.

Birdie clasped the page to her breast and felt her eyes sting with tears. That *someone* would share with her something so meaningful, knowing her that intimately, understanding the heart of her that personally, was deeply moving, even thrilling.

If Birdie had had any lingering doubts about whether or not the gangling young man Buck was responsible for the new rash of correspondence, she wondered no longer. Not only was he long gone from Bliss, and his brother, who might have been his co-conspirator, with him, but the thoughtfulness, the beauty, the meaning of the quotations proved otherwise. No, it was not Buck; it was someone mature, well-read, passionate of heart, fine of spirit.

And so, in her thinking, Birdie began to picture, to see with her mind's eye, perhaps with her heart, the refined man of the world, removed from civilization and secluded in the wilds, a man who spent his lonely hours and long winter evenings garnering literary treasures. And *sharing them with her!*

With a long, indrawn, quivering breath, Birdie arose from the bed and went to the chiffonier to locate the previous communication she had received, glad now that she hadn't carelessly discarded it as meaningless.

Now, in the light of the new letter and the insights she was gathering concerning the writer, the other was opened and reread, more appreciated than before, and finally also laid out on the bed. The scholar in her thrilled to the quality of the material; the woman in her was intensely curious about who it was from, and why; the hungry heart in her noted that each had a spiritual application, a pointing toward God. Thoughtfully Birdie read each quotation again.

They were not hard to commit to memory, so that when they were folded and put away, the beautiful phrases rose and rang like a sweetly tolling bell in her heart. Particularly—*In patient hope I rest for the full day-breaking!*

Was it possible? Could there yet be a daybreak for her? Almost . . . almost she found herself not quoting but praying. Was that, after all, the intent of the mysterious writer?

27

The first flakes of winter were drifting down, as gentle as a baby's breath, as deceitful as a faithless lover's kiss. Promising beauty, promising quiet and peace, by the flakes' rapid profusion the weather quickly turned threatening. Single flakes, airy and lovely, soon became a thick blanket, a shroud through which it was difficult to see clearly. The whiffle of snow on a horse's back and swirling around the buggy became a thick coating and a trackless wasteland.

As sight blurred, sound faded. Falling with no sound whatsoever, which could, of itself, be terrifying in its remorselessness, the snow deadened all of life's normal activities. No bird sang; the dog's bark was indistinct, issuing as it were from behind a curtain. Voices drifted as from an empty void, ghostly rather than human.

Ellie had been uneasy that morning as she climbed into the buggy and headed for a home clear across Bliss and well into the neighboring district of Fairway. One of the Monck boys had arrived, galloping up to the house furiously, announcing in a high, thin voice that his mum was in a bad way and needed Ellie to come.

It was Greta Monck's thirteenth child, and with every one after the third she had been certain she would not pull through. People suspected that, weary of bearing and raising babies, she had a secret, spiteful desire to go to her eternal rest and leave her husband with the gargantuan task of raising them all by himself. But, strong as a horse and more prolific, Greta always managed to pull through in fine fettle. The latest addition always blended into its host of siblings and was simply called "Baby" until the next Baby arrived, when it was granted its own name. All the family joined in the naming and scoured the pages of the Bible for their choices. Beginning with Asher, they had proceeded methodically through the alphabet.

It was Nimrod who came, pell-mell at his mother's urging, to engage Ellie's services for the birth of the thirteenth child. The three girls in the family, weary of the work and bombarded day and night by boys, gave two-year-old Baby the name of Uriah and declared that the newborn should be named immediately. Letters V, W, X and Y would be bypassed, and the newborn would bear the name Zebulun. There was no alphabet remaining; there would be no more babies!

Greta had borne Zebulun with the dispatch that had marked all her other births. By this time, the oldest daughter was practiced in the art of midwifery and had things well under control by the time Ellie arrived. Other than a few futile gestures, Ellie had nothing to do, and Zebulun arrived as easily and as casually as all the others. With a few encouraging words to the new mother, partaking of a cup of tea and a piece of bread and butter prepared by Jezreel, the middle girl, Ellie put on her coat, hat, and gloves and bade the boisterous family good-bye one more time. It was almost a relief to shut the door on the teeming horde of humanity—cooped up in their log house like baby chicks in a box, crowded and trampling over each other with happy carelessness—and breathe fresh air again.

When Ellie stepped outside, ready to mount the buggy and begin the return trip, she first congratulated the sheepish father who, as always, had escaped to the barn for the birthing ordeal, and then turned her thoughts to the weather, looking up with anxiety. Her earlier fears were confirmed: It was a snow sky.

Sullen in appearance, the heavens hung heavy and full; the buggy and its occupant seemed bug-size under the menace of the big Saskatchewan sky, and like bugs crawling through the bush, Ellie and the rig crept homeward to shelter.

And didn't make it.

The first few flakes of winter would have charmed her if she had been inside her own home, watching through a window, with the stove blazing at her back, the wood box and the water pail full, and a line stretched from house to barn. As it was, it was with mounting dread she noted the thick coat accumulating on the horse's back and, in spite of its body heat, staying. She had covered her knees with the old quilt kept under the buggy seat for such purposes but found herself shivering in spite of it, her hands becoming numb in their tight grip on the reins.

"Giddup, Ned!" she urged time and again, and Old Ned would quicken his pace, bobbing his head in rhythm, plowing through the unbroken blanket of snow that very soon covered the road before him, the grass at the side of the road, and the bush beyond that. It was, shortly, a white, white world.

In such a blizzard, it was easy to lose one's bearings. Bush people had reason to be grateful for the growth that crowded most roads, making turns improbable if not impossible; they could follow the road home whether they could see it or not. There were, however, numerous logging roads taking off here and there, entrances to homesteads, and, every mile, an intersection with its four roads.

Finally, the buggy looked like nothing so much as a snowdrift on the move. Ellie's shoulders were white, her head snow-capped, her lashes snow-laden.

Old Ned plowed on, slowly now, blindly, by instinct. The reins, Ellie finally realized, were useless, and she dropped them to pull the quilt up around her and huddle on the buggy seat, her inadequately gloved hands growing colder and stiffer by the moment, her feet becoming blocks of ice.

Where are we! Trees were no landmark, for they were everywhere. Now ghostly in appearance, they faded into the gray sky behind them. A sky that was lowering even more as the afternoon waned and the early dark came on, earlier and darker than usual.

We should be in Bliss by now! We must have taken a wrong turn! Ellie's eyes had been shut while she prayed. It was all she knew to do. But opening her eyes, it was to find herself completely disoriented. *It's up to you, Ned!*

Many were the accounts of horses making it through when driver or rider knew not where he was. Ellie was confident that Ned would make it home, make it *somewhere,* if she gave him his head. But would the buggy? Already it was dragging, bogging down. And the dark settled rapidly, making sight impossible.

The problem was the drifts that began to pile up. The wind, absent at first, now seemed determined to get in on the act. Hampered and bounded by the phalanx of trees and brush, it swept down the open area of road as though it were a tunnel, driving the loose snow before it, piling it in great heaps here and there.

As dark as it was, lamps would be going on in homes along the way, homes until now hidden in the shroud of snow. But Ellie saw nothing, peer as she might. Not all of Bliss, Fairway, and the other surrounding districts had been settled; there was still land to be homesteaded, land on which no tree had been removed, no home built. Ellie, certain now that she had taken a wrong turn, realizing the seriousness of her predicament and feeling as isolated as though she were on the moon, shivered with something other than the cold and redoubled her praying.

It was the cessation of movement that jolted her from a half-somnolent state. *What now?*

Pulling aside the quilt that half covered her face, Ellie peered out. Ned had stopped, his breath curling in white swirls around his drooped head.

Beyond Ned's snowy ears—a lamp-lit window.

Knowing that any tears of joy would freeze almost immediately into icicles on her lashes, Ellie allowed herself a few relieved whimpers as she swept aside the quilt and slowly, stiffly, rose to her feet. Reaching a hand to the armrest to steady herself, she lowered herself toward the ground. Her foot slipped on the buggy's small iron step, and she fell . . . *plunged* to the ground. No matter! The same snow that got her in this fix cushioned her fall, and Ellie—none the worse except that the snow managed, finally, to invade her person, sifting down her neck, coating her clothes, sticking to her flailing limbs—struggled to her feet and headed for the door of the dimly outlined house.

It was a snow-covered figure that stood in the shaft of light when the door opened in response to her repeated hammering. From beneath a snow-tilted hat and above a turned-up collar, Ellie's face, if she had but known it, peeped almost drolly out, her eyes wide and green in the light of the lamp in the hand of the man, the tip of her nose red, her lashes fringed with snow.

No wonder the man's expression was one of surprise, almost astonishment. Here was this snow-lady appearing, as in some fairy tale, out of the dark and the storm, to open her mouth and chatter, "May I come in?"

Quickly the man handed the lamp to the boy who pressed close to his side, curious about their mysterious visitor. About to draw Ellie in, practicality took over, and he paused.

"Here, wait a moment," he said, and he stepped out onto the small porch to brush a veritable storm of snow from his unknown guest's shoulders and coat, even raking off the snow that had settled on her head. Ellie, dazed but understanding, dutifully stamped her feet a few times until her feet were comparatively free of snow. Then, assisted by her unknown host, Ellie stepped into his house—log like her own, simple and snug—and felt herself to have arrived at a sanctuary.

Standing in the patch of lamplight, she said, "I'm lost," and she never knew why the man's mouth twitched as though he struggled with a smile.

"Well," he said gently, "thank God you're safe and sound."

With that simple statement Sam Dickson expressed his faith; with his gentleness he revealed his nature, while his square-jawed face spoke of the strength that gave him balance; his strong, well-shaped body revealed his maleness. His twinkle told of his humor. His glance—direct, steady.

Ellie, in that moment, felt a warmth—not of the heater—flood through her trembling body. Only then did she crumple, overcome by the ride, the fear, the cold, the rescue. The revelation. And as yet, she didn't even know his name. All she had time to comprehend, beyond the startling connection with those eyes, was that there was no woman hovering in the background.

Strong arms caught her, eased her to a chair at the side of the stove. Compassionate hands removed her wraps, her shoes. Gentle hands massaged her hands, her feet, until they began to burn and sting, and she flinched with a small cry.

Recovered enough by this time to be aware of her surroundings, Ellie noted not only the boy who had held the lamp and who now stood uncertainly alongside his father, but a girl, younger, smaller; they were probably about eight and ten years of age.

Ellie's hands and feet were pulsating with the blood that flowed through them. She could feel her cheeks blazing as they thawed out and was certain she looked like Mrs. Santa herself come to visit. What a way to make an acquaintance—first freezing, then flaming; first white with snow, then red as a beet.

The man slowed his ministrations to her extremities, sat back on his heels, smiled, and introduced himself at last. "I'm Sam Dickson," he said, and Ellie would have extended a hand, but it felt the size of a ham on the end of her arm.

"And I'm Ellie, that is, Elizabeth Bonney."

"From Bliss. I know your place. In fact, I met your father at a homesteaders' meeting once. Fine man."

"He's . . . my father is dead, did you know?"

"Yes, I'd heard. I'm sorry about that. I know how painful it is for you; my wife passed away several months ago. Childbirth," he said, and it was explanation enough—there was no woman in the household; there was no baby.

"I'm sorry," Ellie murmured, noting the wistfulness that came into the eyes of the children. Blue eyes and blond hair, clear, fair skin, and pink cheeks—the picture of what ideal children should be.

"These are my kids, Hans and Gretchen," Sam Dickson said, adding, "Their mother was Dutch."

The children nodded and murmured a few words, Gretchen turning a rosy pink, and Hans scuffing a boot on the linoleum.

The place was scrupulously neat, Ellie noted and appreciated.

"Gretchen," her father said, rising to his feet, "pull that soup pot to the front of the stove. Now, Miss Bonney—"

"Ellie, please." It seemed slightly ridiculous to answer to a formal title to someone who had been performing the intimate task of rubbing your feet.

"Now, Ellie, either you came walking or you have some mode of transportation just outside the door."

"Oh," she said, startled, "of course. My horse and buggy are out there. Poor Old Ned must be freezing to death! I guess I owe my life to him in a way. For I certainly was lost."

"What were you doing out in a snowstorm in a buggy?" Sam Dickson asked as he turned to the rack at the side of the door and lifted from it a heavy mackinaw.

"It does seem the height of foolishness. Believe me, I know better! But when I left home this morning, there was no snow. I hesitated but felt I had to go. I was called, you see, to the Monck place—"

"Know them well," he said, buttoning the coat and reaching for a flap-eared cap. "Another baby?"

"Right. The snow began about the time I started home. I truly think I might have frozen out there in a snowbank, except for two things."

"Old Ned," Sam said, and the children listened with interest.

"And prayer."

And thus Ellie confirmed, with a couple of simple words, her faith in the heavenly Father.

"Of course," Sam Dickson affirmed, with a nod of the head. "Now, I'll go out and take care of that faithful horse of yours. You relax, get acquainted with the kids, and I'll be back soon, and we'll have some supper. You'll have to be content to stay, you know. When the storm is over, perhaps by morning, I'll get the cutter out and take you home. I think the snow has come to stay. It'll be months before it's buggy weather again."

With a swirl of snow and a blast of wind, Sam Dickson opened the door, slipped out, and shut it snugly behind him.

Leaning her head back against the chair and closing her eyes briefly, Ellie found the tears, quenched earlier, now smarting her lids. *Thank You, heavenly Father. Oh, thank You!*

What she was thanking Him for was unclear; she didn't specify. She only knew that her heart was full and running over. Fancy losing one's way, putting one's life, as it were, into the keeping of a dumb animal, and ending up . . . ending up meeting *Sam Dickson*.

Lilting into Ellie's mind came a portion of an old hymn:

> God moves in a mysterious way
> His wonders to perform.

28

Birdie glanced at the Drop Octagonal ticking peacefully into a room charged with uneasiness. The school day had barely begun.

Even the children, young as they were, could feel the menace of the gray and lowering sky that shuttered the windows to all but its grim threat. Heads studiously bent over a desk would lift, would cock as though listening, tuned to catch a change in the wind, perhaps; eyes would shift from the distraction of a book to the reality of the viewless void that existed beyond the windows. And then those eyes would swivel, questioning, to Birdie, searching for any indication of nervousness on her part. Noting her calm demeanor and relieved for the moment, heads would bend again, eyes would center on book or paper, and for a few minutes, anxiety would be stifled.

But not for long; they were too well taught, too wise to the ways of the weather, too aware of the danger to be unconcerned. Again and again heads would bob up, seek the outline of a window and study the teacher's face, and the tension, though unspoken, mounted.

They had hardly been called in from early-morning play, removing their wraps and hanging them up, taking their seats and opening their books, before the first flake drifted down, unseen, but presaging the arrival of an untold multitude just like it.

It might have been exciting, fulfilling—winter was finally fully upon them—had it not been for the sky—weighty, pressing, portending doom in some mysterious way. The feeling grew as the snow settled silently, persistently, on the world and everything in it that was careless enough to be exposed. From their seats the children could see inch after inch of snow pile on the window ledges; Birdie almost expected an explosion of hysteria, so real was the sensation of being slowly, inexorably, suffocatingly enveloped in the cloying grip of the snow.

She glanced at the clock again, and this time, every head in the schoolroom lifted, and every eye checked the time: 10:45. All eyes turned, again, to Birdie's face.

"I think, children," she said, calmly for their sakes, "we shall discontinue school for the day. I think it would be well for each of you to leave your books and lunch pails here, and get home as quickly as you can."

Even as she spoke books were being shut, shoved into desks, and a great flurry of activity ensued as though the pent-up tension had burst its bonds, relieved to be doing something at last.

They were still going about the business of donning their wraps when the first rig arrived. Birdie noted it with relief. Obviously parents would concur with her decision; some already had hitched horses to cutters or sleighs for the first time that season and made their way through the curtain of snow to pick up their children and see they got home safely. There were those who lived farther out; if those parents were coming, it would take a while to arrive, and children decided to start out to meet them.

With considerable concern Birdie bade good-bye to those who trudged off on foot, to be swallowed up quickly by the snow and dimness of the day, disappearing into its gloom as totally as though they had stepped off the face of the earth. Hopefully, somewhere along the route, they would meet the family rig or perhaps a neighbor's—a small island of safety in a world in which they could lose their bearings.

With some reluctance she saw Little Tiny and the Nikolai children on their way, urging them to stay together, wishing she were free to accompany them; they lived in her direction. But she glanced down at the small face and big eyes looking up at her so trustingly and knew she couldn't send little Ernie Battlesea, the only child remaining, out into the storm alone. "Come, Ernie," she said briskly, "let's play a game of tic-tac-toe."

Ernie's face lit up. "Yeaaah," he said happily, forgetting the storm, unconcerned about their isolation, untouched by their aloneness.

Birdie chunked another piece of wood into the heater, regretting the voracious appetite of the metal monster and noting with concern the half-empty wood box. But for the moment they were warm and safe.

The next hour dragged by, with many glances at the Drop Octagonal, which, as always, ticked steadily and inexorably toward whatever the next minute had in store.

Birdie was about to suggest they eat their lunches when the door opened and a snow-covered figure—with a drift of snow and a blast of wind—stepped inside and slammed the door shut behind him. Big Tiny Kruger. Not the child's parents, not Herbert Bloom (whom Birdie knew to be sick with a bad cold), but Big Tiny Kruger.

Such a feeling of relief and gratitude swept over Birdie that, for the moment, she was speechless. Heart full, eyes blinking back silly tears, it was all Birdie could do to keep from rushing into those snow-covered arms. Big arms. Big enough for her problems. Big *snowy* arms. Snowy enough so that Birdie hesitated and the moment passed, and the mad impulse.

"Oh, Wil!" she found herself half crying, half laughing. For he was peering through snow-covered lashes from below a cap peaked with snow; ear flaps encased the broad face; whiskers and mustache were split by a wide and merry grin.

Whether it was the "Oh, Wil," the look on her face, or the absurdity of the moment, the man, so accustomed to being called Big Tiny and perhaps weary of it, had no concern about the snow on his person or the restraint she might feel and swept Birdie up in his arms. And they were, indeed, big enough for her.

Set back on her feet and never feeling the cold, Birdie listened to Big Tiny as he explained that he had met his son and the Nikolai children and, having learned that Birdie had no ride, had delivered them all to the Nikolai house and turned around to come for her.

"Get the boy ready," he commanded, while he warmed himself briefly at the side of the heater. "We'll have to take him home. It wouldn't do to take him to your place or mine. His folks might come looking for him."

As they did. No more than a mile from the schoolhouse, a horse and cutter drifted toward them like apparitions out of the ghostly shroud—Luella Battlesea herself. Her husband, she explained, had fallen and twisted a leg badly, delaying her trip to rescue Ernie. Somehow the transfer of the child from one rig to the other was accomplished; somehow both rigs got themselves turned around.

Birdie watched the Battlesea cutter disappear as totally and silently as it had come. Shivering, she found herself moving close to the large form at her side; she was quite sure it would be radiating warmth.

And so, companionably, Birdie and Big Tiny made their way homeward toward the fires awaiting, with fires of another sort kindling in the Kruger sleigh.

⌐───────⌐

To Birdie's intense satisfaction, the Reading Society had gotten off to a fine start. Meeting in various homes, it had a feeling of fellowship about it, as a dozen people and more read a chosen piece of literature and, later, shared tea and coffee and discussed their reactions, gave their opinions, voiced any criticisms. It had been food for the starving soul of Birdie Wharton.

Several times, as summer faded and fall with its threshing and the opening of school brought great activity to Birdie and all the people of Bliss, she had received the by-now-familiar white envelope. Each time it had spoken not to her ears only but to her heart. Along the way she had ceased searching the faces of the people she met for some clue as to the writer, content to relish the unusual messages without having to know who sent them.

The beauty, the sheer beauty of still another, charmed her thoroughly so that she went about half dreamy that full day, repeating the words over and over until she, too, should have them memorized. Her heart, she felt, was beating in cadence with that of the writer. A writer unseen, unknown, who spoke silently but powerfully to her innermost being; a writer who *knew* her; a writer she knew, in the ways that mattered most.

> Night's candles are burnt out, and jocund day
> Stands tiptoe on the misty mountaintops.
>
> —Shakespeare

"Jocund," she murmured to herself, savoring the new word, wishing for opportunities to use it and wondering if her Silent Speaker, as she called him, was using it also.

Another quotation, arriving in the midst of harvest, was tremendously moving for that reason if for no other: The man's thoughts were loftier than the mundane duties of threshing. Even in the midst of stress and toil, the writer's thoughts soared to the reflective, the meditative.

These lines, though not entirely new to Birdie, spoke to her as they never had upon previous readings. They pointed, as others had, to God:

> He prayeth best who loveth best
> All things both great and small;
> For the dear God who loveth us,
> He made and loveth all.
>
> —Coleridge

This man, this thoughtful man—why did his thoughts turn often to God? Because she had such confidence in the unknown writer and admired his mind so thoroughly, she had to consider this aspect. Was she, after all, missing out on the sweetest and best in life by ignoring God and the Bible? Sliding, gliding along in the sleigh in the overwhelming silence, Big Tiny at her side, Birdie had time to reflect on this.

This very morning Birdie had opened a desk drawer and found an envelope containing Bible quotations so beautiful in expression, so poetic in quality, that she was quite captured. Was her mysterious writer in tune with nature and its designs? As the day progressed, the words seemed prophetic.

Sitting quietly at the side of her good friend Wil Kruger, Birdie let the Bible's expressive words fill her mind, rolling the timely phrases over in her thoughts. If they were true—and her Silent Speaker seemed to think so—there was no reason to dread the day and fear the storm; in fact, there was great reason to rest and trust:

> Praise ye the Lord . . .
> He giveth snow like wool:
> he scattereth the hoarfrost like ashes.
> He casteth forth his ice like morsels. . . .
> He sendeth out his word, and melteth them:
> he causeth his wind to blow, and the waters flow. . . .
> Praise ye the Lord.
>
> —Psalm 147:1a, 16–17a, 18, 20c

"Wil," she said rather dreamily, and she never knew his breath caught in a special way at her use for the second time that day of his given name, "do you suppose . . . is it possible . . . that God sends the snow? Makes it and sends it? That it isn't just a whim of nature?"

"The Bible says," Big Tiny answered thoughtfully, "'he stretches out the heavens like a curtain . . . he waters the hills from his chambers . . . he sends the springs into the valleys . . .'"

"And 'casteth forth his ice like morsels.' That's what the snow is like—morsels. Isn't that a . . . a delectable way to say it?"

"Delectable?" Big Tiny said, and she could sense a smile in his words. "I guess I'd use another word. Descriptive, maybe. Yes, the Bible is wonderfully descriptive."

"Hmmmm. I'll have to look into it a little more."

Big Tiny was silent. But then, that wasn't unusual for Wilhelm Kruger, Birdie was beginning to know. How comfortable he was to be with. What a fine friend.

And then, all that was shattered.

"The Bible also says," Big Tiny said quietly into the face of the storm but not so quietly but what Birdie, at his side, heard clearly, "'Whoso findeth a wife findeth a good thing.' I think I've found that good thing. In you, Birdie. I think I've found that good thing in you."

Birdie was stricken dumb. All her dreams of friendship with this good man went crashing to the ground, tumbled by his words. Things could never be the same between them again. If he insisted, and she told him what she would have to tell him . . .

"Do you hear me, Birdie? In the middle of a snowstorm, cold as we are in body, can you feel the warmth of my heart in what I'm saying?"

If she hadn't been so dashed, she might have recognized the poetry in his remarks, might have thrilled to the originality of his words. As it was, her whirling thoughts were to stop this before it went any further, before a perfectly good friendship was spoiled, before things had changed between them irrevocably.

"Oh, Wil," she said, perhaps a trifle too shrilly, "don't. I can't . . . can't be anything but a friend to you—"

"I'll always be your friend, Birdie," Big Tiny said quietly, "but I am wanting . . . asking, for more." And he turned and looked down into her eyes with a look so tender, so deep, so meaningful, that her heart could only lurch, and she could only blurt, "Wil. Wil—listen to me, Wil. I'm not free to fall in love; not free . . ."

"Not free?" No wind was colder than the one that swirled around them now.

"I'm . . . I'm married. Wil—I'm married."

29

Morning brought with it a magical sight: The entire world was crisply, glowingly, scintillatingly white. The sky, having dumped its load as a pillow might expel its feathers, was unendingly blue, and the sun—muffled in darkness yesterday—sparkled so brilliantly from a trillion and more reflected points that the watcher's eyes were dazzled.

The turnaround—from dark to dawn—was typical of the bush and the lives of its people. Much of the time for them, it was feast or famine, pain or pleasure, glory or gloom. The sweet and the bittersweet kept close company. Those who had not learned along with the apostle Paul, "in whatsoever state I am, therewith to be content" (Phil. 4:11), were sorry people indeed.

Having made her way from the small bedroom she shared with the girl Gretchen for the night, Ellie found the house warm, the kettle steaming, and signs that Sam Dickson had opened the door, shoveled away a heap of snow, and made tracks for the barn. Literally made tracks; Ellie could see through the frost-encrusted window where he had plowed his way through knee-deep snow—

to the well, to the chicken house, to the barn. Here the door was open to the light, and a drift of steam emanated, lifting to the sky.

In the snowy yard, fluttering around the exposed tops of bushes and hopping over the drifts, chickadees sought seeds and rose hips—anything—for breakfast. Where had they been during the storm? Farm animals were safely harbored and sheltered, chickens snugly cooped; but the wild birds—where had they huddled, heads under wings, dumbly and numbly waiting out the storm and the arrival of a new day? As always, it was a puzzle to Ellie, and she greeted their cheerful presence with a rush of pleasure.

Turning toward the kitchen end of the long room, Ellie contemplated breakfast for herself, the man, and his children. There was no sign of oatmeal simmering on the range, and there wasn't time to cook it; it was a job that took hours, even overnight.

Pancakes! Pancakes would be perfect. Even now she heard thumps from the bedrooms that indicated the children were getting up; soon they would be out, hungry and, for once—if she hurried—finding breakfast ready.

Accustomed to making pancakes for two, Ellie quickly doubled the recipe. Locating the necessary ingredients in the kitchen cabinet, she set about the familiar task:

Beat 2 eggs until fluffy
Add ½ t salt and 1 T sugar
3 T bacon grease [easily located in a can next to the stove]
1½ c buttermilk

Finding no buttermilk, resourceful Ellie switched to sweet milk, omitting soda and adding 3 teaspoons of baking powder, then beating in 2 scant cups of flour or enough to make the batter—as her mother had taught her—the consistency of thick syrup.

By this time blond-braided Gretchen was at her elbow, her eyes sleep-filled but sparkling with the anticipation of breakfast fixed by someone other than herself.

When Sam stamped in to hand the pail of milk to Ellie and divest himself of his wraps, the children, seated at the table, had been fed; their plates, clean of pancakes, showed traces of the deep purple-blue of the chokecherry syrup they had doused them with. They greeted their father with a grin, obviously enjoying the rare treat of a good, warm breakfast served without a lifting of their own fingers.

"Well, what have we here?" Sam, cold-faced and cold-handed, rumpled the boy's fair head and laid his cheek alongside that of his daughter, who squealed and turned her face away—a frosty beard was no fun!

"Sit down and eat," Ellie—her face rosy from the range's heat—suggested, and Sam dipped warm water from the reservoir and washed his hands while Ellie watched several pancakes bubble, then turned them and poured a cup of coffee and set it beside the plate on the table.

"Hey, pancakes!" the man said, looking down at his breakfast and then at the cook. "But don't make me eat alone! Sit down with me."

Ellie filled her own plate and joined the little family, though the children soon excused themselves and left the table.

"Does it look like I can get the buggy out of here this morning?" Ellie asked.

"No, not the buggy. I'm afraid it's out of commission for the winter. It's cold out there! Probably twenty below. This isn't going to melt. It'll settle a bit, though, and then the roads will open as people plow through, crossing the district for one reason or another. There's no school, though, I'm sure of that, for Bliss or for Fairway.

"I should think that before the day is over I can get you home in the sleigh; luckily it's ready and waiting. I got the box put on the runners a few days ago, anticipating this. But perhaps you can stay over another day?"

Sam's uncertainty showed in his tone of voice; he well knew the problems of a farm left untended.

And he was right; chores called at home. There would be animals to feed, a trough to chop free of ice, longsuffering cows to milk, fires to build, a freezing house to thaw.

"I need to get home, of course," Ellie said and wondered if she sounded regretful. It had been a while since she sat at a table with anyone present but herself. She didn't relish the long winter just begun, shut in, isolated, cooking for herself, voiceless and alone, with only an occasional meow from Wrinkles to break the silence.

By early afternoon the snow—four feet deep in places—had settled under the bright but cold sun, and a rig or two had passed by on the road, breaking a trail and making it possible for Sam to take Ellie home.

With Hans and Gretchen bundled into the back of the sleigh, excited over the snow and the first sleigh ride of the year, Ellie sat on the spring seat beside Sam, covered with a blanket. The magnificence of the snow-wrapped world was breathtaking.

"And to think," Sam said vibrantly, "our sins, scarlet though they may have been, are made as white as snow. Now, that's some miracle."

Why, Ellie thought, did her heart rejoice to hear this small testimony? Surely it made a bond—each of them knew Christ as Savior.

At any rate, it led to a sharing of faith, a witness of the grace of God during the recent bereavements each had suffered, a voicing of faith concerning the future and the good things in store from the Father's hand.

Sam's faith had overcome the dread of raising his children without a mother; Ellie's faith reached out to embrace the help and grace she would need from the Father as she carried on alone, attempting to run a farm that was too much for her in all ways.

Did she secretly wonder if she might, in some way, be a help to Sam? Did he privately consider whether he might take on some of her workload? The vast silence of the land, if it knew or suspected, echoed only with possibilities, not prophecies.

Upon reaching the Bonney homestead, Sam insisted on staying long enough to get the fires lit in the range and heater, while

Hans and Gretchen filled the wood box, stacking extra on the porch. Sam chopped the ice from the trough, refilling it and bringing the animals to drink, one by one, and returning them to the barn. Hans and Gretchen fed and watered the chickens.

Finally, with the kettle boiling, Ellie was able to make a cup of tea. Removing their coats, the four sat around the heater, holding warm cups in their cold hands—the children's tea liberally laced with milk—and carefully nibbling frozen cookies.

With an expansive sigh, Sam set his cup aside and turned toward the hooks at the side of the door. "Sorry, but all good things must come to an end," he said, shrugging into his coat. Then, with a smile, he added, "It's an ill wind, they say, that blows no one some good. That one yesterday—it blew good to the Dickson family, I'd say."

"And a lot of trouble it caused you!" Ellie replied, feeling wonderfully happy at his comment.

"A good breakfast, a pleasant drive," he said.

"And now the drive home, with all your chores to do."

Putting his cap on his head and rescuing his gloves from the range's warming oven where they had been drying, the children fastening their overshoes and playing a final moment with Wrinkles, Sam said, "I hope our acquaintance won't just fade away, Miss Bonney... Ellie. Having begun so amazingly, so surprisingly, perhaps it's intended that we... that we... that is, that we get to know each other better. Would you mind terribly if the children and I drop in once in a while?"

"Please do," Ellie responded, so earnestly that it brought a light to the questioning eyes of Sam Dickson and the hint of a smile to the square-jawed face.

"And," he offered, "if I should be the one to help with your crop next season, well—we'll talk about that, all right? As for your buggy, it'll remain right where it is for now."

Ellie, a peculiar lightness in her heart, stood on the porch and watched Sam and his children as the sleigh headed down the lane, to the road, and out of sight.

Only then, as she turned to the house, shutting the door against the winter and its threat, leaning against it momentarily, did the thought—as cold as the north wind—strike a chill to her heart:

The nightmare! There was still the nightmare. . . . There was still the guilt.

W inter had dragged by for Birdie, day after similar day. Only the variation in the weather distinguished one day from another. For the most part it was snow on snow. But interspersed were days of brilliant sunshine and sparkling beauty, enough to enrapture any heart but the sourest.

If it had not been for the occasional contact from her unknown correspondent, Birdie would have found the days bleak indeed. Walk to school, walk home a few hours later; wind the Drop Octagonal every Friday, signifying another week had slipped away.

Her revelation to Big Tiny, made that day in the heart of the snowstorm, had in some subtle way made a difference in their relationship. True to his word, he remained her friend, picking her up often in his cutter and giving her a ride home from school; his smile was just as ready, his words as warm. But his eyes—something in his eyes had changed. Something she had not known existed but missed. Something had taken its place; something that Birdie sorrowfully identified as pain.

The revealing of her marital status—that day of the first snow—had undoubtedly been a severe shock to the big-bodied, bighearted man. After a silence, a silence compounded by the heavy snowfall that seemed to wrap them in a small and private isolation, Big Tiny had asked, rather heavily, staring straight ahead, jaw clenched in spite of his gentle tone: "Do you want to tell me about it?"

Not really. She hadn't wanted to mention it at all, ever, to anyone. She had wanted life to go on, barren in some ways as it was, with this great man as her friend and her Silent Speaker as a soul mate—for that's how she was beginning to think of the unknown sharer of words and thoughts.

Still, Big Tiny deserved an explanation, even an explanation of sorts.

"It was seven . . . eight years ago," she said haltingly. "Far from here. And it didn't work out. I had to get away, escape, I suppose you'd call it. And I've just sort of hidden myself ever since."

"I see," Big Tiny said quietly, clenching and unclenching his jaw.

But apparently he didn't see at all. How could he? There was no way she could tell—in a few sentences on a lonely strip of road whipped by snow and storm—of the bitter realization that happiness had, after all, eluded her, and dreams of love had been imagination and far from reality. Maurice—that was his name, Maurice Gann—had quickly changed from a mild, rather colorless man to a vicious monster. It was the drink, the liquor that she hadn't known about, that changed him so that at times he came home small and slender physically but ten feet tall potentially, and powerfully mean. In stumbling words Birdie shared this much.

It had been the boy. . . . Here—in her short explanation—Birdie's grief surfaced and her throat thickened, and the name Davey never passed her lips.

"Anyway," she finished, her thin tones barely reaching the ears of the man who listened, silent for the most part, his usually merry face strangely still, "I stood it until the school year was over, then packed up and slipped away, bruises and all, going as far as I could as quickly as I could, and started over. Eventually I came . . . to . . . to . . . Bliss."

The name had a hollow sound. Saying it, her voice faltered. A hamlet, a district, though called Bliss, made no promises, offered no assurances. Still, saying it now, it seemed strangely empty of anything at all.

Perhaps it was the sad disclosure made to Big Tiny and bringing into focus the hopelessness of her future, perhaps it was her own heart-need, but from then on Birdie's grip on her unknown correspondent tightened, perhaps a bit feverishly; she almost lived, it seemed, for the sweet, the meaningful, the beautiful, the satisfying phrases that flowed from his pen. Here was someone who thought the things, wrote the things, perhaps lived the things that she believed in. Oh, that she might converse with him! Might talk, hungrily and needfully, face-to-face! Though she felt she knew him intimately, he remained faceless, detached, a dream man if ever there was one.

While the relationship with Big Tiny changed in some subtle manner, Birdie was almost passionately grateful that her soul mate remained faithful, unchanged. From time to time, treasured portions of beautiful literature continued to reach her. Occasionally, at the Reading Society gatherings, she came across a book, perhaps by Shakespeare, that was in circulation among the group and around the district and wondered who had held it, had memorized, had copied, had shared with her its expressive words.

But occasionally a suggestion, uncomfortable and quickly stifled, presented itself to her: Had she fastened on to the unknown correspondent because it was safe to do so? Not free to relate to a flesh-and-blood man, had she substituted an insubstantial creature, one who made no demands on her, who called for no response? Not able to deal with fact, had she settled for flummery? And would it satisfy for long?

Birdie hugged to herself the small scraps of happiness that came her way and dared not wonder where they could possibly lead.

Transportation, though often difficult, was seldom impossible. And winter, with the ground covered, fields frozen, and seeds dormant, allowed time for fellowship, for socializing.

For Ellie, the time was spent far more happily than she ever could have imagined. Though missing her father and at times recognizing the barren place that once Tom had occupied, still, something stirred into hope, some tendril of new life put forth a shoot in her heart and struggled toward spring and resurrection. And those days that Sam and the children came over were times of deep and deepening pleasure.

There had been the usual Christmas festivities centered in the school and church. Miss Birdie Wharton had worked hard and long for the evening of the so-called "School Concert." Mainly a time of recitations and songs and a short play, it was the highlight of the year, and well attended. After the performance, gifts were distributed to each child—some small item ordered through the catalog and paid for by the school board and perhaps the only Christmas present some children received.

A Sunday morning had been given over to a similar performance by the Sunday school children, with a short sermon by Parker Jones following and bags of treats handed out to each child.

Ellie invited Sam Dickson and his children to attend the Christmas Concert; they, in turn, invited her to attend the Fairway school's program. Those times, and the occasions when the Dickson sleigh jingled its way to the Bonney place, usually on a Saturday or Sunday when the children were free, were high points.

More than once, Sam and the children stayed for dinner, the noon meal, leaving for home in time for the evening chores. Hans and Gretchen loved playing with Ellie's childhood toys; Sam was not content unless he made himself useful by mending and fixing, checking stock and equipment, and before he left, splitting a large pile of wood.

Ellie never asked them to attend the Bliss church with her, knowing for one thing that they had services in the Fairway schoolhouse on an intermittent basis, and also reluctant to stir up the curiosity their presence in Bliss would be certain to arouse.

Even to Marfa, her dear friend and confidant, Ellie had not mentioned the name of Sam Dickson nor the astonishing account of how Old Ned had taken her, straight as an arrow, to his door. Rather, she hugged the experience to her, a treasure not to be shared. At least not yet. Perhaps not ever.

Eventually, as the weather shifted and there was an occasional soft wind to hint of winter's demise and spring's birth, there came a day when Ellie and Sam touched on, just touched on, a subject that was warming each heart, calling for attention but until now only wondered at, dreamed of, prayed about.

Sitting comfortably beside the fire with a cup of tea, with Hans and Gretchen absorbed at the table in a game of checkers, Sam and Ellie, albeit hesitantly, guardedly, talked about the affairs of life that had brought them to this hour: he having lost his wife, she having broken off what was intended to result in a partnership for life, and the strange twist of fate that had caused them to meet so surprisingly, so summarily, almost abruptly.

Sam stretched out his long legs, leaned back, his cup raised and his eyes staring into it, and said the very thing Ellie had been daring to entertain: "Doesn't it seem almost unbelievable? I mean, how many times have you been lost in a storm? Doesn't it seem, Ellie, as if a hand greater than our own arranged our meeting?"

Ellie's eyes, though she never knew it, shone like stars and filled with an unspeakable sort of hope as she lifted them to his, now searching her own. "Oh, Sam, I'd like to think so! But . . . but I have to remember—the reason I broke off with Tom is . . . is still very much a hindrance in my planning a future with . . . with anyone."

"So," Sam said gently, "we'll just leave it there. I'm sure you, as I, pray about such matters—"

"All the time!" Her voice was earnest, almost desperate.

Looking at him sitting there, natural, relaxed, the picture of strength at rest, Ellie could think of no fine masculine trait that was not present in the form and face and character of Sam Dickson.

And she simply hadn't the courage to tell him of the death—*murder*—of old Aunt Tilda all those years ago and the conviction that she was responsible.

Arguments presented themselves to her now as before: She had only been a child—yes; doing a good Samaritan deed—yes; in the eyes of the world she was unaccused . . . yes.

But still, a woman, a helpless old woman, had died because of someone's carelessness. And try as she might, Ellie could not rid herself of the suspicion, perhaps the conviction, that it was she.

Though Sam waited for her to say more, Ellie could not bring herself to spread out before him and between them the miserable tale, pour out her abject fears, tell of her frightening nightmares. The moment passed; Sam took a sip of tea, and the subject was changed.

Often and often, as winter slipped away, Ellie was on the verge of confiding her problem to him. But fearing it might make a difference—if not with him then with her—she bit it back. She looked at the children and loved them. She looked at Sam—and loved him.

When Sam said he would be responsible for her fieldwork, Ellie's heart leaped. To see him often! To fix dinner for him! To have the dear children underfoot during the summer days!

It was because of the fieldwork that Marfa eventually learned about Sam. With a blessed chinook and the rapid melting of the snow, with black fields lying rich and ready, with hens becoming broody, with cows calving, with garden spots calling for attention, Marfa could be excused for her concerned probing.

"Can George be a help?" she asked one day, having stopped by Ellie's on her way to the store. "Ellie," she urged, when Ellie hesitated, "have you made any arrangements for the work?"

"Actually, Marfa," Ellie said in an offhand fashion, thereby exciting her friend's suspicions immediately, "I have. There's a Sam Dickson . . . from Fairway. Have you heard of him?"

Marfa had. Districts were small, clustered close around their individual schools so that no child had too far to go, and Fairway was dependent on the Bliss store for supplies. And though they were isolated, they were not ignorant. News in the backwoods traveled as quickly as a passing rig.

"I know *of* him," Marfa said, eyes thoughtful. "Didn't his wife die last year?"

Ellie nodded, playing casually with small Bonney's plump hand. "He's going to do the fieldwork for me. I'll manage the rest somehow—"

"Wait a minute, Ellie Bonney! How did this come about? Where did you meet him to talk to him that personally? What's going on here?"

"Oh, Marfa!" Ellie laughed lightly. "He's just a neighbor taking on some extra work. He'll share in the harvest proceeds, of course—"

"Ellie Bonney!" Marfa said again, crossly this time. "You can't fool me! What's going on here?"

With a sigh, knowing she couldn't mislead her friend and trusting her completely, Ellie gave in and confided the account— the rather romantic account—of her immurement at the Dickson home . . . overnight . . . in the snowstorm and the subsequent meetings with Sam Dickson.

When Marfa finally rose to go, it was to give Ellie a warm hug and say, almost tearfully, "Oh, Ellie! It's time something good happened for you! I hope—I do hope—"

"Don't say it!" Ellie interrupted with a shaky laugh. "Although . . . if you're like me . . . you may imagine it.

"But oh, Marfa—if you ever prayed, pray with me about this!"

31

When the last worn boot had scuffed its way through the door, when the final shriek of childish voices had ceased and the last hoofbeat faded away, Birdie sat alone at her desk, with only the sound of the Drop Octagonal breaking the silence. For some reason the usually unobtrusive tick seemed to swell in sound until it reverberated through the room, calling for her attention, calling insistently.

In obedience, Birdie's mind groped back a year ago, almost to the day, and the moment she had taken a scrap of paper and a pencil and deliberately and cheerlessly totted up the clock's unrelenting counting of the passage of her life.

Now, on an impulse, she opened a drawer of miscellaneous items and scrabbled around until she found it—the crumpled piece of paper she had recovered from the kindling box and hidden away: Sixty ticks per minute . . . 3,600 ticks for every hour . . . 86,400 ticks per day. Birdie's eyes slid away from the scribbling that so baldly pointed out the vast number of seconds that had ticked emptily away. It was too sickening to contemplate.

But her head knew what her heart refused to hear: A few million ticks had tolled away the sum total of her life, bringing her to this hour as lonely, as unfulfilled as ever.

A year, twelve months, 365 days, thousands of hours, millions of minutes—gone, all gone; it didn't bear thinking about!

And still the clock ticked on.

In cadence with the relentless ticking, certain words began rolling over and over in Birdie's mind until, listening, giving heed, she focused on the words of the last letter she had received from her silent correspondent. Ever since first reading them, she had been aware that they had dropped, willy-nilly, into her heart, surfacing from time to time in a gentle, persistent way. Suddenly it seemed important to read them again, to understand them, to get to the bottom of them, to make them her own.

With hands that shook now—so great was her dismay over her meaningless days and the urgency of the impression—Birdie turned to the desk drawer and withdrew the last quotation she had received. Though not from the Bible, it was spiritual in content and, like the Bible quotations, struck and quivered in her heart like an arrow to its mark. This unknown, unseen person, through his beautiful, meaningful, and persistent words, had witnessed to her as no preacher had ever done. And not seeing him, she could not refute what was said, could offer no argument, could only feel this growing sense of his confidence in Christ and her own emptiness.

Once again she read:

> Speak to Him thou for He hears, and Spirit with
>   spirit can meet—
> Closer is He than breathing, and nearer than
>   hands and feet.
>
> —Tennyson

It mattered not who wrote it, who copied it, who quoted it; it was the Holy Spirit Himself who spoke it now, piercingly and sweetly, into the hollow that was the heart of Birdie Wharton. It was as though He said, "I'm the one your heart is yearning for. Speak to me, for I'm listening. Come to me, for I'm here."

With a cry that was half anguish, half yearning, Birdie dropped her head onto the old scarred Bliss desk and there laid her burdens, her loneliness, her emptiness. There her wanderings ceased. There she cried out her repentance; there she received the acceptance she had been seeking; there she found the happiness that had eluded her. There she found God.

Finally, raising her head, it was to hear the Drop Octagonal chime out the hour: four o'clock, and Birdie marked it down as the happiest hour of them all, and blessed the clock that indicated, by its faithful reminder, that there was time enough to know life as it ought to be. There was time to do the things she ought to do.

First of all, with steady hands she searched through the desk, searching out any vagrant quotations that might be there, bringing them to the light of day; slowly, methodically, with a lifted heart, she tore them into shreds.

What they said was good and true; some would linger in her heart, used of the Lord to point the way, to encourage her walk, to bring beauty and blessing. But the slavish attention she had given them was broken; her reliance on them and on the one who sent them was finished. Birdie's world, rather than crashing like the biblical house built on the sand, was rising strong and sturdy on the solid rock.

Watching the little pile grow in front of her, Birdie felt like putting a match to it, so free was she. She would always be grateful for the part the quotations had played in bringing her to this moment; someday, perhaps, she would have occasion to meet and thank her human ministering angel. But there would be no more unhealthy attention given him.

Birdie would henceforth search out her own Scriptures, led by Another, who cared for her and knew her needs specifically, One upon whom she could call at any time. There would be no waiting for surreptitious messages through the mail; her daily bread would be supplied as she read and absorbed God's Word for herself.

Without hesitation Birdie forsook the unknown for the known. Her reliance, henceforth, would be on God's Word. And she would come to know the writer intimately.

The last shred had barely dropped from her hand to the wastebasket when there was the sound of a rig outside, then voices. Turning, she was facing the door when Big Tiny stepped inside, followed by an elderly man and . . . and a young man.

Though Big Tiny spoke, Birdie's eyes were fixed on the youngest member of the trio, her eyes puzzled.

"Miss Wharton, I met these folks in the Bliss store. They were inquiring about you . . ."

Big Tiny's words, only half heard, continued. "This is Mr. Abner Jacoby, and his grandson . . ."

"Davey. Davey Gann. *Davey!*"

With a cry Birdie was around the desk, across the floor, her arms reaching for and clasping the young man, who—unashamed—was spouting tears. He was taller than Birdie; his head dropped to her shoulder, and his thin, young body shook with the feelings that could not be contained. Nor did he try.

Birdie, no less moved, cradled the young body, rocking gently, crooning the precious name over and over: "Davey . . . Davey . . . Davey . . ." It was a lullaby of pure love.

Eventually the boy—young man—lifted his head, stared into Birdie's face as though not believing what he was seeing, only to drop his head again, be rocked again, lulled again.

Finally Big Tiny led them to a seat. Birdie lifted her eyes, comprehending the presence of the stranger. "Mr. Jacoby," she said, and the older gentleman took the hand she extended, cleared his throat of what might be suspected as some strong emotion, and smiled.

Never having met, she knew his name. Was he not, after all, the grandfather of Davey Gann, and had she not brought his letters, time and again, from the post office, to read them to the small boy who capered, excited and impatient to hear what the beloved father of his dead mother had to say?

While Davey searched out and used a handkerchief, sniffling and gaining control of his feelings, Big Tiny, standing by wide-eyed, dumbfounded, and startled into silence, had his explanation.

"Wil," Birdie said—and, one would suppose, sent another frisson of joy through his being at this new use of his name—"this is . . . oh, you've already met, of course. Can you sit down? And you, too, Mr. Jacoby."

"I told you, Wil," she said softly, her eyes alight and her hand holding the hand of Davey, "about my marriage, about my husband. But I didn't . . . I couldn't tell you about his son, Davey."

Birdie's eyes threatened to spill over again. Gulping, swallowing, she continued. "I couldn't begin to tell you about Davey. For one thing, it hurt too much. For another thing—he just defied description. Davey was . . . Davey is . . . the best thing that ever happened to me."

Suddenly remembering her so-recent moment of commitment, release, and victory, Birdie added joyfully—and Big Tiny's eyes widened—"Except for when I received Jesus as my Savior."

And though the conversation swirled back to Davey's and Mr. Jacoby's story, it was plain that Big Tiny put the salvation account aside for the moment only.

"Can you forgive me, Davey, for the way I left? For not telling you I was going, for not writing? I felt that I dare not—"

"I know, Mama Bird—" Davey, the child, spoke the loving title spontaneously. Still, it called forth another sob from Birdie and another round of hugs and pats and croons.

"I knew more than you thought I knew." It was Davey, the young man, speaking now. "I heard the beatings in the night; I heard your weeping. I've always been ashamed that I didn't do *something*—"

"Davey, no! You were just a little boy of ten! And it would have meant a beating for you, too. No, no! You are in no way to blame, not for any of it! It's I . . . I who left—"

"I was glad," Davey said. "Knowing you were safely away, I had a kind of fierce gladness. I was so glad you escaped. Things went from bad to worse after that, Birdie. Dad drank more, worked less, moved around more."

"How did you find me?" Birdie asked, fixing her eyes on Mr. Jacoby.

"We followed the trail of teaching positions you had held," the white-haired man said. "One led to another, finally bringing us to Bliss. An apt name, Bliss. Now we are on our way to my home in Glenfield—"

"I know where it is; it's not too far—"

"We can keep in touch, Birdie," Davey said. "I'll be with Grandpa and Grandma from now on."

"Your father?" The question came haltingly.

Davey blinked, as though surprised.

"She doesn't know, Davey," Mr. Jacoby said and continued, "Maurice is dead, Miss Wharton. Drank himself to death, in a way, though it actually happened in a fight. He started a drunken brawl, or so we've been told, and someone bigger, stronger, angrier, was more than he could handle. As soon as I got word, I came for Davey, and we've spent some time on our way home tracing your moves, locating you. Davey insisted on it."

"Oh, Davey!" Birdie's tears flowed freely now, and Big Tiny, sympathetic, handed her a large and colorful bandanna. But hers were tears of release, healing tears.

The afternoon waned as conversation flowed. Questions and answers, explanations, revelations, tears. And at last, smiles and hugs. Finally, Big Tiny, an enthralled listener to all, felt the pressure to get home and to work. "Tell you what," he suggested, "you can adjourn to my place, if you wish—"

"Oh, no," Birdie said firmly. "Though we thank you. Lydia will surely want to meet them, to hear the story. To find out where I've been all this time!" She glanced at the clock with an exclamation of dismay and jumped up, straightening her clothes, brushing back her tumbled hair.

Big Tiny, watching, saw a woman of action, of sparkle and vigor, a woman he had never seen before. It only enhanced the woman he already knew and loved.

Big Tiny made his reluctant way homeward. Climbing into Mr. Jacoby's rig, the others made their way to the Bloom homestead. Here the astonishing story was repeated, accompanied by fresh tears, fresh hugs, fresh smiles. Lydia capably stretched supper to include the newcomers, and the same account was told again to Herbert.

Eventually Mr. Jacoby pulled out a massive watch, consulted it, and with a sigh announced their departure. "We've been gone too long now," he said. "Minnie will be worried at the delay. But we just had to try this one more place on our way home. We'll always bless the decision. Now, Davey, it's time to say our good-byes. But we can promise you, Miss Wharton, that we'll keep in touch. We're less than a day's trip by buggy, and we'll see that Davey makes it every once in a while. In fact, he can ride over, which will be faster. And you, of course, will be most welcome to visit us. In fact, I urge you to plan on doing so."

"School will be out soon," Davey reminded Birdie, "and you can get away. Won't you plan on coming to Glenfield? Please, Mama Bird!"

Birdie agreed wholeheartedly. Having found her Davey again, she was not about to let him go permanently.

Lydia promised them a bed if they would stay the night; Mr. Jacoby said they would spend the night at the Stopping Place in Bliss and be on their way early in the morning.

It was a dazed Birdie who made her way upstairs and prepared for bed. To have found a son *and* a Father in one day!

Laying her head on the pillow, Birdie thanked her heavenly Father for the gift of His Son and for the restoration of the little stepson who had been lost to her for so many years.

My cup runneth over, Birdie murmured, reveling in a quotation of her own choosing.

The smells of spring were pungent, all the more so because they followed the olfactory vacuum of the long winter: fresh turned soil, damp leaf mold, manure piles steaming in the sun, sap oozing on tree trunks in golden globules, thick quilts redolent from months of human contact, winter woolens long unwashed.

Through it all the breezes of spring wafted with fresh fragrances: the purple violet, so elusive, so dainty, shouting "spring" in its quiet way; tender grasses and greening bush spreading rare perfume far and wide; pails splashing full of new, rich, sweet milk; Fels Naptha, that brown bar, a washday standby, sometimes replaced by the vaunted "Old Glory Mottled German Laundry Soap—thick, fancy-shaped, hard-pressed, and wrapped," changing the effluvia of every home as it was turned inside out—bedding, rugs, curtains, kitchen linens, clothing, all brought out to the relentless glare of the sun and the ministrations of the scrub board and the stomper, to be rubbed and stomped, boiled and blued, and finally spread out in the sun to bleach.

Sounds changed. No longer hampered in movement or shrouded in silence, dogs cavorted and barked with abandon, children jumped and shouted for the sheer fun of it, passing neighbors called cheerful greetings. The pail splashed into the well and was pulled, dripping, to be dumped into the trough to the noisy gulps and slurps of cattle now free of dim and silent stalls. Birds beyond counting filled the sky, flickered through the bush, perched on fence posts and barbed wire, warbling out their joy and staking out their territory; new calves bawled, baby chicks peeped; screen doors slammed with the going to and fro of people with a purpose. And overhead—a sight never accustomed to and stirring every winter-logged heart—a phalanx of honking Canada geese, their long blackks u necndulating with the sweep of their wings, circling and settling down to the sloughs and lakes of home.

Along with the sap rising in the trees, a certain vigor and *aliveness* flowed through the slender body of Ellie Bonney. As she shed the winter woolens, she seemed to shed winter's stagnation and inactivity and felt infused with an energy that could not be contained.

Spring housecleaning was a breeze; Ellie scoured and scrubbed, chinked and whitewashed, revived old and faded curtains and furniture, and freshened all of it.

Then, offering to do the same for Sam Dickson, she moved her operations to the Fairway home, much like her own and much like many another in the territories—built of sturdy logs, with a roomy half of it serving as kitchen, dining room, and living quarters in general, the remainder divided into bedrooms. It was compact for easy heating, rather sparsely furnished, and readily turned out to clean. Folderols were in short supply in the bush; gewgaws and gimcracks were as superfluous in bush homes as frills and furbelows on clothes. For the most part it was a simple life. And, for the most part, satisfying.

Laboring in the Dickson yard over the washboard, laundering the family's heavy wool quilts, Ellie was not surprised when she paused, straightening her back a moment, to find Sam not ten feet away. With one foot hoisted onto a block of firewood, one arm on the raised knee, and with his hat in his hand, his eyes were fixed on her.

It was no surprise, because as the winter slipped away, Sam's admiration had been expressed in more ways than one. By look, certainly. But also by word.

"Beautiful," he had murmured, reaching a hand to help her from the buggy, seemingly transfixed by her rosy cheeks and her eyes sparkling with good health and good humor, ". . . so beautiful."

Once, slipping up behind her as she stirred something on the stove, he had lightly placed his hands on her hips and, when she turned her head, laid his cheek against hers momentarily and whispered, "Desirable . . . so desirable."

Ellie, across the months, had learned the language of love, sometimes by words but more often by the expression in Sam's eyes. Biding his time, perhaps, there was a point beyond which his lips did not go; but his eyes, his telltale eyes, spoke eloquently. Spoke not only of love and longing but admiration, appreciation, satisfacation.

Now, looking up and recognizing a strong man's healthy regard for the woman he thinks of as the mate of his choice, Ellie's heart leaped. Color surged into her cheeks.

"What . . ." she attempted, flustered.

"You know what!" Swiftly Sam crossed the distance between them, took the tumbled, aproned figure into his arms, and kissed the astonished face thoroughly, very thoroughly indeed. Kissed the ready lips.

"I've been wanting to do that for a long time," he murmured when speaking became possible, and he dipped into the sweet honey again, and yet again.

Finally, knees wobbly, more flushed than ever, more starry-eyed, Ellie had opportunity to speak.

But could find nothing to say. Wrapping her arms around his neck, she leaned in for more of what her heart hungered for, and said, with her responsive lips, all that Sam needed to hear.

How the suds flew after that; how the windows shone, the furniture gleamed.

How the children hugged her and pranced about when, having sensed something in the air, they pestered and pried until they had been told: Daddy was going to marry Ellie.

How, later on, the old fears surfaced, the hesitations, the despair. Sam sensed it and was quiet, waiting. Ellie, restless, fought her old battle.

The evenings were lengthening, and it was during that quiet, tranquil time with the children abed that Sam and Ellie walked together, and Ellie, taking a deep breath, told Sam the story of old Aunt Tilda, her fiery death, the investigation that decided nothing, her conviction of herself. Her nightmares.

"It sounds like an unfortunate set of circumstances," Sam said. "But you say you are tormented by this?"

"Ever since it happened . . . well, ever since the Mounties failed to come up with a solution, didn't out-and-out clear my name. Though I was just a child, it seemed that a dark cloud of guilt dumped on me at that moment. And yes, it torments me, torments me to this day. Especially in the night. Out of the dark it comes, placing *me* in that fire, with *me* doing the calling for help as Aunt Tilda must have, *me* catching fire . . . burning . . ."

Ellie shivered, and her voice—high and thin and anguished—broke.

"Hey," Sam said, and pulled her into his arms. "You're safe, Ellie. Safe with me."

And so it seemed, for the moment. But standing in the circle of his arms, the thought of her wedding night rose in her imagination—the moment when she jerked and thrashed in her sleep, perhaps in her husband's arms, struggling and attempting to cry out, to finally come awake, shaking and jibbering, with the face of her husband frightened and dismayed. What would a bridegroom think? What sort of a blight would such a dreadful occurrence place on a marriage?

Ellie dropped her face into her hands, the prospect too grim and depressing to be accepted.

Sam led her aside to a felled log and sat beside her.

"It seems to me," he said thoughtfully, "that this is something unnatural, out of the range of the normal reaction of a child . . . a girl . . . a woman. Something that you've not been able to control, to handle, to change, try as you will. Right?"

Ellie nodded miserably. "I've tried. God knows I've tried. And prayed!"

"I know a little about such things," Sam confided. "When I was little, some boys locked me in a closet for hours. I was mortally terrified, of course, and ever after tormented by a spirit of fear. I believe now that certain sad or terrible or frightening things, especially happening early in life when a child is innocent, without defense, may result in a lifetime of harassment from . . . well, from the enemy, the one the Bible calls a thief. We know his mission in life is to steal and to destroy. Certainly he stole my peace of mind."

"Satan," Ellie whispered, the idea not a new one, so tormented had she been, so helpless to rid herself of the torment. "It makes sense, Sam. You're saying it's an attack . . . not coming from within but without."

"I believe so. I myself didn't come free until I was an adult and a Christian. And then someone who understood, who had experience with such fears, ministered to me. And, Ellie, I learned that we don't have to take this oppression. Greater is He that is in us than he that is in the world, right? And doesn't the Bible say in John 8:36, 'If the Son therefore shall make you free, ye shall be free indeed'?"

Ellie agreed, agreed wholeheartedly. "You're right, so right!"

"You're a child of God, forgiven, born again, adopted, part of his family. Right, Ellie?" Sam was laying groundwork here, good groundwork based on God's Word.

Once more Ellie agreed.

"And according to 1 Corinthians 6:19, 'your body is the temple of the Holy Ghost which is in you.' Right, Ellie?"

Ellie nodded vigorous assent.

"Well, then," Sam said, moving ahead methodically, certainly. "We'll tell this interloper that he is no longer welcome, that he has no place in God's temple—are you game? That is, are we agreed on this, too? Remember," he said, searching diligently for additional support for what he was about to do, "it says in Deuteronomy 32:30 that one can 'chase a thousand, and two put ten thousand to flight.'"

Caught up in the drama of the moment and the victory about to be claimed, still, Ellie had time to marvel at the spiritual insights of this man and to thank God that he had come into her life.

Taking her hand in his and turning to face her, Sam spoke the words, in the mighty name of Jesus, that commanded the release and freedom of this child of God, refusing any further harassment by the tormenting messenger of Satan.

Finally, putting in the last nail, he quoted 1 Corinthians 2:16, "'We have the mind of Christ'!" And Ellie, with a long and shuddering sigh, breathed an amen.

Through the lingering twilight, wrapped in unspeakable peace and in each other's arms, Sam and Ellie, murmuring into the fragrant night, lifted voices of praise and hearts of gratitude: "'Ye shall know the truth, and the truth shall make you free'" (John 8:32)!

━━━━━━

The sheer beauty of the awakened northland, the glory, the wonder of the possibilities, put a spring in Birdie's step, a light in her eyes, and a blush on her cheeks.

"I declare," Lydia said with awe to no one in particular, looking out the window, watching Birdie move down the lane, turning toward the schoolhouse and the last day of school.

Birdie's heart-change had changed her in all ways. Her outlook, her expectations, her values, her confidence, her demeanor— all reflected the abandonment of self and the embracing of the One who promised, "If any man be in Christ, he is a new creature: old things are passed away; behold, all things are become new" (2 Cor. 5:17).

"I declare," Lydia muttered again. "Even her clothes swish differently."

And no wonder. The figure inside them moved with a vigor, a purpose, a satisfaction never felt before. The heart, its cry satisfied at last, welled happily, and the mind, no longer putting self first, was at peace. It couldn't help but show; smiles seemed ready to break forth at any minute; Birdie came close to dimpling.

Part of it, of course, was the dreadful burden that had lifted when she had found Davey again, when Mr. Jacoby, reporting on Maurice Gann, said the words that set her free. Trying to grieve properly for someone once loved, Birdie found it difficult to do. It had been so long ago, and her memories were so miserable. So she laid this "unknown bundle," as the church folks termed it, on the Savior.

How ready she was to cast her burden on the Lord. She was, over and over again, coming up with an old habit, a dark way of thinking, a negative reaction, a doubt, things she had put up with previously, imagining they were part and parcel of her makeup or had been bequeathed her as an evil burden to be borne. Now she was learning to grow in grace. What a glorious growth it was, what an abandoned casting.

The day was useless as far as studying was concerned; the children were wild to be released. Birdie devoted much of it to reading and reporting, favorites with all of them.

Finally, glancing at the Drop Octagonal and finding that this day, as all days, had slipped away (but with what satisfaction!), Birdie announced, "Time to fold up for the year, children. Take all your papers with you, your scribblers, your pencils. Leave the books and texts; I'll lock them in the cupboard until school opens in the fall."

"Miss Wharton," it was Victoria Dinwoody, her face innocent but her eyes sly, "will you be coming back?"

"Why do you ask, Victoria?"

"Because my mama says . . ." Even Victoria, bold as she was, hesitated, wriggled, stuttered.

"Yes, Victoria? What does your mama say?"

"My mama says you'll be getting married."

Every activity stopped; every head lifted and poised. Every eye fixed on the teacher.

"It happens to most everybody sooner or later, doesn't it, Victoria?"

"Yes, but . . ."

"But what, Victoria?"

"Nothing; I just wondered, that's all," Victoria murmured, flustered, and disappointed that she had nothing to go home and report.

"Whether I will be teaching or someone else, the school board will see to it. The announcement will be made in due time.

"Now, children, that will be all for the year, except—"

All heads lifted in the teacher's direction; about to embark on their summer, they paused.

"Just one more thing," Birdie said. "We have one honor, one special honor, to award. Before the year is over, I want to recognize the child who has made the most progress. You have all done well in many ways, and I'm proud of each of you. However, there is one who has come along well not only in his studies but in his deportment. So well, in fact, that we'll bestow special recognition on him—Ernie Battlesea."

Ernie, caught totally by surprise, gasped, turned red, sank back into his seat in a rare moment of shyness. Near pandemonium broke out—whistling, the stamping of feet, clapping.

"And to recognize and reward his diligence, we're going to give Ernie the honor of *winding the clock*."

The noise faded; small bodies sat up straighter; childish breaths were indrawn; childish faces were filled with awe.

Miss Wharton took the key from the drawer and, amid the silence and the attention, encouraged Ernie to clamber up onto a chair, guided his small hand to the proper place, and then—all by himself—he inserted the key and commenced winding. "One, two, three, four"—twelve times the children chanted the number, the proper number of turns. Then, with a flourish, face shining with his matchless accomplishment, Ernie turned. Turned and, being Ernie, couldn't resist playing to the gallery (never had he had such an audience). Sweeping his hand in a wide arc, Ernie pressed it against his middle and bowed. Bowed gallantly and bowed deeply. So deeply, in fact, he lost his balance.

Ernie's great accomplishment and the favor of the winding of the Drop Octagonal was concluded to the screams of certain girls, the jeers of most boys, and the gasp of the teacher.

Setting Ernie on his feet, Miss Wharton used the opportunity to give the rascally boy a small hug. Flushed and proud, Ernie hugged her back.

The eager children were dismissed with the reminder that report cards would be forthcoming at the annual picnic.

If the Drop Octagonal was moved by the unusual experience, it gave no sign but ticked on as steady, as faithful, as reliable as ever.

One by one the children picked up their lunch pails for the last time, trooped through the door, casting smiles back and calling, "Good-bye, Miss Wharton. See you at the picnic."

Wandering around the empty room, picking up crumpled paper, straightening a desk kicked crooked by some child's impatient departure, moving to the window ledge to remove the pencil sharpener and empty it of shavings . . . Birdie stood transfixed for a moment, staring out at the birch ring and remembering.

What a distance she had come, and all due to the marvelous grace of God—

There was a sound at the door, and Birdie turned.

Silent, kindly, anticipating—Big Tiny. Slowly his arms opened, spread wide, waited.

Without a moment's hesitation, leaving the sharpener, dropping the crumpled paper, Birdie Wharton walked, straight and true, into the waiting arms. Arms that, she felt quite sure now, had been waiting all the winter long, perhaps all the year long. As they closed around her, she laid her cheek on the broad chest with a sigh that seemed to speak of rest, of complete contentment, of total fulfillment. Birdie—her flutterings past, her aimless flight abandoned—had found her nest.

The bliss of the moment only increased when Big Tiny, not as patient a lover as might have been supposed, tipped her head with his rough finger, bent his own, and kissed her. Kissed her tenderly . . . kissed her urgently . . . kissed her with enough passion to satisfy the tide of desire that surged warmly and generously through her starving heart and yearning body.

"Tell Victoria," he murmured, when speech was possible, revealing that he had been waiting outside, "that you'll be Mrs. Wilhelm Kruger before another school year rolls around."

"Oh, Wil . . ." Birdie offered no argument, thought of none.

Later, much later, in his buggy, her hand in his big paw, she made her one confession. A hesitant confession.

"Wil, there's been someone . . . someone I don't know, who's been sending me things in the mail. Rather intimate things."

"Oh, ya?" Big Tiny's head swiveled, and he cocked an eye at her. An eye in which curiosity gleamed, and speculation.

"But, Wil, it was all one-sided. I never once wrote to him—"

"No? And why not?"

"Why not? Well, I . . . I didn't know his name, you see. In all honesty, I might have responded, might have thanked him, at the last, for bringing me to Christ. But I didn't know his name—"

"Didn't know his name?" Big Tiny asked, his eyes going wide, his voice filled with astonishment.

"Why, no. They, the letters, were anonymous . . . unsigned."

Silence. Silence as though Big Tiny might be sorting through unusual areas of thought and finding it slow going.

The wheels creaked; the horse plodded.

A bluebird flashed past.

"'The bluebird carries the sky on his back,'" Big Tiny said thoughtfully, following the swift flight of the bird with his eyes.

The silence became deafening. Slowly Birdie turned her eyes on Big Tiny's face.

"Thoreau. Henry David Thoreau," Big Tiny added as an afterthought.

"Are you telling me . . . are you saying . . . what *are* you saying, Wil!"

"Are *you* telling *me*," Big Tiny said unbelievingly, "that you haven't known, haven't known all along, that I was the one sending those quotations?"

Birdie looked dazed.

"Wil, oh, Wil! Why didn't you tell me—"

"But I did." Now it was Big Tiny's turn to look puzzled. "First thing. I wrote you right after . . ."

"Right after?"

"Right after I put the fear of my good right arm into that . . . that Buckley kid."

Limply Birdie sank back. But her mind was working swiftly. Why should it surprise her that Big Tiny, with the sensitivity he had displayed, should discern what was going on with Buck? She recalled now that she had realized very quickly after she failed to meet him in the birch ring that the writer had changed. The messages had changed—

"My letter, Birdie. My first letter. Didn't you get it? In it I explained that certain callow youths wouldn't be bothering you anymore and that—if you didn't tell me not to—I'd like to share with you the things I was reading. From that time on I just kept leaving them here and there, at the post office, in your desk . . ."

Birdie had a clear picture of the small chiffonier drawer at home and the letter she had locked in it—unopened, unread.

And to think that here, at her side, holding her hand, offering love enough for a lifetime, sat not only kind, generous, sweet-natured Big Tiny Kruger, her friend, but her soul mate. One and the same.

It seemed fitting, riding along in the curve of Big Tiny's arm into the gentle spring evening, to find a quotation rising in her heart.

Softly she spoke it: "'O the depth of the riches both of the wisdom and knowledge of God! how unsearchable are his judgments, and his ways past finding out!'" (Rom. 11:33).

The "amen!" lifted from bush and tree, bird and beast, earth and sky and water, until Bliss echoed with praise.

With school out, Hans and Gretchen accompanied Sam each time he came to the Bonney place to work. Soon they felt quite at home, rousting out the toys of former years, becoming thoroughly acquainted with all the buildings, digging into the cookies when hungry or settling for a slice of bread and jam, haunting the bush for early berries, hunting crows' nests, trapping gophers.

Gopher tails, after all, brought a bounty of a copper a tail. And the array of candy choices at one cent apiece was exciting, even exhilarating, to a child of the bush: gumdrops, jawbreakers, hoarhound squares or twists, mints, lemon drops, strawberry drops, cream balls, lady kisses; the choices were endless. Why, a child could linger, enthralled, over the candy counter half a day, given a chance. Hans and Gretchen, clutching grisly gopher tails, accompanied Ellie to Bliss and to the store at times, to return sucking a favorite candy, and totally blissful.

After a winter of potatoes, beans, porridge, bread, and a few shriveled vegetables, young appetites craved something sweet, something store-bought, something *extravagant*. Older appetites were no different, and the first berries—wild strawberries, tiny, jeweled, luscious; or saskatoons, milder than blueberries, smaller than blueberries but blue in color—were gathered and relished with cream and sugar in a sauce dish or baked in a pie. As the sweetness exploded on the tongue, eyes closed in near ecstasy, and something long starved was satisfied.

Today, Ellie glanced with satisfaction at the bowl of ruby-red strawberries, freshly gathered as soon as Sam and the children had arrived, the children happily accompanying her to the meadow where the matchless berries spread like a carpet over the ground. On the table beside the strawberries sat a sponge cake, a delight in itself because the hens were laying once more and the twelve eggs necessary were available again. The kettle was boiling, and the best teapot was warming; Mum's good dishes were laid out on the table along with serviettes snowy and white enough to satisfy the severest critic.

The "girls" were coming for tea; the old gang would be together for the first time in years. Flossy had broken the ring of friendship and fun when she had married and moved away. Now, due to the illness of the grandmother who had raised her, she was back briefly. Marfa and Vonnie would take time off from their busy round of summer duties, escaping for this memorable occasion, this reunion. The four of them would, first, fall into each other's arms; then conversation would flow, as never-ending as it ever had been when they got together in years past.

They were no longer rambunctious children, however, but women having acquired the manners of the day and accustomed to certain amenities. And so Ellie would serve tea and refreshments. They could only enhance the occasion.

"You're welcome to come in and meet the girls," Ellie said to Sam before he left for the fields. "And you, too," she added, indicating the children.

"We'll see," Sam said, hedging. He would be in his dusty work clothes, and this was, after all, a ladies' tea. As for Hans and Gretchen, they were in their most faded, worn, shrunken clothes, and barefoot, ready for a day of exploring the meadows, the sloughs, the bush. Their last foray had yielded an elusive tiger lily, which they had borne proudly to Ellie, and which still graced the center of the round oak table.

Hans cast longing eyes toward the sponge cake, and Ellie had an idea he might not lead his sister too far astray today. How proudly she would introduce them, worn garments and all—and no doubt grimy—when they returned from climbing trees or any of the numerous activities that would fill their summer with memories never to be forgotten.

"I'll save cake for you," she promised, and she was rewarded by the boy's grin. A grin so like his father's that it twisted the heart of Ellie Bonney, and she flashed them all such a smile that Sam went to work with a song in his heart, and the children sped off to their particular pursuits with never a care in the world.

The arrival of Flossy, Vonnie, and Marfa was announced by chatter before ever the screen door slammed behind them. Bonds such as theirs would never be forgotten, never broken. The conversation was punctuated almost immediately by laughter and preceded almost entirely by "Remember when . . ."

There they sat, in a ring, just as they had so many times over the years. Now, however, they reclined gracefully in chairs, daintily handling china and refreshments, where before they had sat cross-legged on the leaf mold in some shady nook, nibbling wild gooseberries or hazel nuts or whatever the bush was yielding at the time.

Marfa, still chubby, still round of face, still cheerful, still pleasant. Flossy, more worn, slightly shabby, as quiet as ever, as gentle. Vonnie, best dressed, as vivacious as ever, more sophisticated, just as brittle. Ellie, less exuberant perhaps, less inclined to take charge, thoughtful, quick to speak but ready to listen, a woman of charm and grace.

When the "remembers" were exhausted and the reminiscences thoroughly discussed, the talk grew more personal.

How was Vonnie enjoying marriage? How was she adjusting to life in Bliss once again? "Fine," and "Fine, thank you."

How was small Bonney developing? Was there a brother or sister in the offing? "Growing like a weed," and a dimpling "Perhaps."

How was Flossy's grandmother doing? How many children were there now, and where were they? "Fairly well, thank you"; "five at last count," and "with their paternal grandparents."

And then all eyes turned with interest and curiosity on Ellie, long considered the "old maid" of the group.

"Is there somebody special?" Flossy, the absentee and largely ignorant of the happenings in Bliss, asked, while Vonnie seemed to listen tensely and Marfa, who knew all, sipped her tea complacently.

"I guess you could say so," Ellie admitted, having tried to prepare herself for the questions she knew would be forthcoming today.

"Sam Dickson, isn't it? Hasn't been a widower for long, has he?" Vonnie, widow of a few months when she married again, asked, and managed to sound as if the relationship might be a questionable one.

"Over a year," Ellie said patiently.

"How do you think you'll enjoy being an instant mother?" Again it was Vonnie; again there was a needling, very slight, carefully cloaked but there.

Why should Vonnie, married and presumably happy, need to insert unsettling remarks into the one brief visit the old gang would have together? Ellie, knowing Vonnie thoroughly, had expected no less; she took it in good grace.

"When you meet him," she said, speaking lightly but with a steady assurance to her voice, "you'll understand. And when you meet the children—"

The words were no sooner spoken than the door was thrust open and two bedraggled, sun-browned, bleach-haired, bright-eyed children stormed in. Stormed in, to immediately subside, abashed before the prestigious assemblage studying them over cups of tea.

Turning toward them, Ellie saw nothing any different than she had seen all across her growing years when she and her friends had played together—health, satisfaction, weariness. Happiness. All the things life in the bush did for a child.

"Come, Hans; come, Gretchen. I want you to meet my friends," she said.

The two, silent but curious, stepped forward. The introductions were made; the children squirmed, looked bashful, fiddled with whatever treasures they had accumulated and held in their hands.

"Gopher tails," Marfa said fondly. "Remember, girls?"

"Yes, I remember," Vonnie affirmed. "But I don't remember getting quite so dirty." And she looked critically at the small ragamuffins standing self-consciously before her.

"We were every bit as dirty! And happily so," Marfa supplied. "Oh," she squealed, and the others jumped. "What is that you have there, Hans? What is it? Could it be—?"

Startled, Hans looked down at the object in his hands, turned it over, rubbed it on his shirt. Held it out.

Marfa took it, blackened though it was. Marfa took it, turned it over in her hands, her mouth falling open in pure astonishment.

"Girls! Do you know what this is? You'll never guess!"

Round it was, with crimped edges. Once it had been shiny.

"Look," she said, squealing again. "Look!" And she took her handkerchief, spit on a corner of it, and rubbed the dark object. Some of the grime came off; some of it never would—it was permanently blackened. Blackened as though by fire.

"I think this belongs to you, Grand Panjandrum," Marfa twinkled. And she held out the insignia of the Busy Bees—the badge made from the end of a tin can.

A tin can lid that had been pounded and twisted into shape by Ellie herself, a tin can lid worn by each of them in turn.

Ellie took the object in her hand and stared at it blankly. Then, turning to Hans and Gretchen, she asked, her voice echoing oddly in her own head: "Where did you find this?"

"In that old burned-out cabin across the fields," Hans said proudly. "Me and Gretchen dug around in there all afternoon. We found some ol' bottles . . ."

"It has a hole so's we can wear it," Gretchen spoke up for the first time. "Hans is going to put some string through it so's I can wear it around my neck. What do you suppose it means—BB?"

"Busy Bees," Marfa said promptly. "It means Busy Bees. And I wore it when I wasn't a lot older than you. We all wore it. We never knew what happened to it. Say," she said in a puzzled tone, "how do you suppose it got into Aunt Tilda's cabin?"

The silence careened, screaming, around the room.

And three pairs of eyes swiveled slowly and looked at Vonnie. Vonnie's pert, usually fresh-colored face was pasty white.

◦━━━━━◦

Ellie called the meeting of the Busy Bees to order. She called for the reading of the minutes; no one, it seemed, had done anything to further the cause of the club, to carry out its purpose for existing.

"Hasn't anyone found something helpful to do?" Ellie, as president, asked.

No one had.

"Well, neither have you!" Vonnie pointed out triumphantly. "And if anyone should, you should. After all, you're the one wearing the badge most of the time."

"You've all had turns. And anyone can have a turn that wants it," Ellie defended, rubbing the shiny circle hanging from a string around her neck.

"It's my turn," Vonnie pouted. "Flossy had it, then Marfa, then you again. It's my turn."

Ellie removed the Busy Bee insignia; they were all fond of it, but she had special feelings for it, having designed it and pounded it out with her own hands. Still, Vonnie should have her turn.

"You can have it, oh," she offered generously, "for the rest of the month."

"That's better!" Mollified, Vonnie slipped the shining bit of tin around her girlish neck and fingered the crimped edges, preening a bit, an exercise that came naturally to her.

"We can't leave here," Ellie said, returning to the problem at hand, "until we come up with something to do to help someone. It's the purpose of the club, you know. What do you suggest?"

"Wash the heads of the Nikolai—"

"We did that already, silly!"

"But it should be done every week!"

Ellie interrupted the argument between Flossy and Vonnie, agreeing that something new, something challenging, was needed now.

"Knit winter socks—"

Flossy's tentative suggestion was silenced by the pained expression, the rolled eyes Vonnie turned her way.

After a moment's silence, Flossy, the compassionate one, tried again. "Help ol' Aunt Tilda?"

Voting it a good idea, plans were laid. Ellie and Vonnie would work as a team, Flossy and Marfa another.

"I'll start out," Ellie, the organizer, offered. "I'll explain to Aunt Tilda what we're doing and how I'll come each Saturday. After a couple of hours Vonnie can arrive, and on the following Saturday Flossy and Marfa can do the same. Right?"

Nods of agreement.

"Saturday, then," Vonnie said. "Fine with me. I'll be there with bells on."

⸻

But it had not been bells. Vonnie had arrived wearing the Busy Bee badge. The badge that disappeared and was never seen again, that never turned up, that was forgotten in the turmoil and trauma following the death of Aunt Tilda.

Now, years later, the girls recalled it; Vonnie's white, defiant face confirmed it.

The inquiry of the Mounties had not unearthed it; Vonnie had denied it. "I never went that day," she had reported.

"Vonnie," Marfa said now, slowly, "you were there that afternoon. You were there, after all."

Vonnie blinked rapidly, stammered an "Uh . . ."

Marfa continued, in a voice of absolute certainty, a condemning voice. "You . . . *you* were the last one to see Aunt Tilda alive."

Under the accusing eyes of the three people who knew her better than anyone else, Vonnie tossed her head, recovering herself.

"What of it?" she asked.

"It means that, that there was no fire when Ellie left."

"Who said there was? Not me, for heaven's sake! What other people thought—that's their own business!"

"The badge, Vonnie," Marfa pursued. "How did it get left in Aunt Tilda's cabin, to lie there in the ashes all these years?"

Panic rose in Vonnie's blue eyes. "The old lady grabbed it, all right?" she shrilled. "It was shiny, and she kept looking at it, and when I tried to fluff up her pillow, she grabbed it, wouldn't let go!"

"And when you jerked away, did you knock over the lamp?"

"It's not my fault the lamp was there! Ellie put it there, before she left—"

"It was dark in there; we all know that," Marfa, the reasonable one, said. "And it had to be close to Aunt Tilda so she could light it . . . blow it out—"

"What if the old lady shoved me into it! Whose fault is that, I'd like to know! Not mine!"

No one condemned her, but the eyes of Marfa and Flossy looked at her gravely, even sorrowfully. In Ellie's eyes the smallest flicker was lit, a flicker that presaged an eruption of gratitude to God so heartfelt it could never be adequately expressed. But she would try; her whole life long she would try.

"Anyway, it's all water under the bridge," Vonnie concluded belligerently. "The old woman was already on her deathbed, everyone knows that."

Silently, without further talk, the party broke up and the three visitors said their good-byes, Marfa and Flossy subdued, Ellie in a daze, Vonnie abrupt, her face no longer white, but as red as . . . fire.

Standing on the porch, as still as a statue, Ellie watched the rigs down the road and out of sight. At her side the children watched with her, their faces puzzled, their eyes wide and raised question-ingly to Ellie's face from time to time.

When the last buggy had disappeared into the bush, Ellie drew a deep breath as though coming awake, perhaps from a bad dream, and turned, looking down at Hans and Gretchen, reaching a hand to each, taking their hands in hers.

"Come, children," she said steadily. "We'll walk out to the field to meet your father."

Ruth Glover was born and raised in the Saskatchewan bush country of Canada. She has written many poems and books, including the Wildrose series for Beacon Hill. Ruth and her husband, Hal, live in The Dalles, Oregon.